Kokoro Press books from Sedonia Jacobs

In the Master's Eyes

I Was Hannah (Journey of Souls)
ISBN 978-1-937796-85-3
ALL RIGHTS RESERVED.
I Was Hannah (Journey of Souls) Copyright © 2015 Sedonia Jacobs

Edited by Jeff Erno
Cover art by Kim Jacobs
Interior design by Allison Jacobson

Trade paperback Publication April 2015

Kokoro Press is an imprint of Sedonia's Magic Words, Inc.

Published in 2015 by Kokoro Press, d/b/a Sedonia's Magic Words, Inc., 10435 Green Trail Dr. N., Boynton Beach, FL 33436.

Manufactured in the U.S.A.

I Was Hannah
Journey of Souls

Sedonia Jacobs

Author Note

The shtetl of Wolensk in which the story takes place is a fictional town, intended to resemble a shtetl that existed in that time period, with the vibrant and varied Jewish life and culture that once populated these places.

"Wisdom gives life to its owner ~ Rabbi Itzhak Luria in 'The Gate of Reincarnations'

Part One: Shabbos
Spring, 1938

Poor Solomon! He has such crazy ideas about life and love. He actually believes that real love between a man and woman is possible. But from what I have seen, people are too busy fighting and abandoning each other, and treating each other like *dreck* for real love to exist. And anyway, it's pretty ironic coming from Solomon who was abandoned as an infant by his own parents and was promised by his adoptive father at the age of fifteen to a girl he says he doesn't love and seems determined not to. He says that she is not his *besheret*, his destiny, and that he knows this deep in his heart. Which always makes my stomach flutter inside because I know by the *way* he says it what he's trying to tell me. But Solomon's father gave his word, and Solomon sees that as an obligation he must keep to honor the father who saved his life.

And so he's only proving my point, because the moment of his marriage marks the end of our friendship. Where's the love in that? You would think that at the age of twenty — twenty and a half to be exact — that Solomon would realize his idealism is going to be beaten out of him in the near future.

As for me, who just turned nineteen today, I once believed as he did. Even now, I feel the last hopeful bits of it creeping around inside me, but even those are being scraped away. I can't help it, because even though as I sit here on my bed, holding the beautiful prayer book Solomon just gave me for my birthday — he really is the most thoughtful person I've ever met — in my other hand is the latest letter from my father, Isidore Herzel, bearing his most recent explanation of why I will go yet another year without seeing him.

This year he and his friend David Rosen, with whom he immigrated to America, have parted ways and that he will have to look for a new place to live and, perhaps, a new job.

I had expected this. For two years now Papa's letters have been filled with complaints about Mr. Rosen, about how he drinks, how manipulative he is, how he spends too much money, on and on. I daresay Papa sounds like a husband complaining about a bad wife. Personally, I never found Mr. Rosen to be as unpleasant as Papa says. Just the contrary, really. Mr. Rosen always seemed concerned about me and how my parents' separation affected me. I always liked his ribald sense of humor, joking about people's funny habits and bodily functions, treating me like a grownup entitled to hear such jokes. He also taught me some useful things, such as how to iron my dresses properly and how to clean a floor. Sometimes I've even felt that he taught me more useful things than my own parents did.

If anything, it's Papa who does the very things he complains about and blames Mr. Rosen instead. But even so, it hurts that he doesn't give up and come back home. If he's going to be a failure, why can't he do it here in Poland with me rather than all the way on the other side of the world? I tell you, Papa's behavior gives me the chilling sense deep down that somehow all of his life has been an elaborate contrivance to avoid being with me.

I wish I could remember what I did to repulse him, but I can't. I guess I just made him unhappy somehow. And so did Mama. Her housekeeping was always terrible, and I used to watch him grumble to himself as he snatched her discarded stockings off their bedroom floor or sponged her talcum powder off the bathroom vanity. Maybe it was just that I remind him of her. Except for my blonde hair, which I inherited from him, I mostly resemble Mama, with her short rounded features and resistance to tidiness. But he says he loves me and I must take him at his word, grateful that he should say so, especially after what I said to him the day he left.

I try to explain all this to Solomon, but he insists that it is my father's faults which keep him away and not mine. He says if he had a daughter like me, he'd want to be with her all the time. But he doesn't know me as well as Papa did. Solomon and I have been friends for only a year and a half, not enough time for him to see how horrible I really can be. He wasn't there the day Papa left for America. He wasn't standing with us in the front hall of our apartment in Warsaw when Papa told us he was leaving for the Golden Land.

What a day that was! I can only call it "the day I screamed and screamed." It was the end of March 1934, a month before my fifteenth birthday. My parents had already been separated since I was nine, and Mama and I had moved in with my grandparents. When Bubby and Zayde passed away not long after, Mama and I were alone there. But at least Papa was still in the same city with me and I could take the bus to visit him every Shabbos. He shared an apartment with Mr. Rosen since he said to me, "Hannele, from now on, your mother and I won't be living together anymore." Those were his exact words. Burned into my memory for all time.

In the years since my parents' divorce, when I spent time with him, Papa would speak from time to time about going to the Golden Land to try and make his fortune there since he had failed to do it here in Poland. He blames his lack of success on the fact that he is an overly generous person who seems to have a tendency to get himself involved with, as he puts it, "lowlife *goniffs* who always end by screwing me over." The way he sees it, there are so many people in America that surely he would be able to find the right ones. During those talks, I never asked him if he would take me with him because I assumed he would even though he never actually said the words. Nor did he ever tell me he was actually in the process of getting his papers! He just came to the door that morning in a new crisp suit, his blond hair combed perfectly into place — ,Papa is quite handsome and always turns female heads when he walks down the streets of Warsaw — and told me and Mama he was leaving.

Mama's response had been simply to bury her face in her hands and turn away.

"Papa," I said, "You didn't give me time to pack. Give me a few minutes. I'll be ready to go with you." I started to turn when he stopped me.

"Hannah," he said, "You're not going with me."

"But why?"

"I need to…get settled there first. Then I can send for you."

Something in his tone of voice or in his eyes made me hysterical, as if deep inside I sensed I'd never see him again. I begged him to take me and he kept refusing, telling me he would be late if he didn't leave right this second. How could have do this? I, began to scream. I had never screamed like that before in my life, but once his words had entered my consciousness, the reality of his leaving rushed in on me like a butcher's knife to the neck of an unkosher chicken. I filled that apartment and the halls of the whole building with my bloodcurdling *geshrays*. I didn't care who heard me or who in the outside world knew our business. All I knew was that Papa was slipping away from me and the only chance I had to keep him from going was to release the depths of my distress on him, the way God released the plagues onto Pharaoh's people. I threw myself on him as if I could climb him, fistfuls of his nice woolen coat in my hands.

I must have been incredibly strong because Papa could not pry me off him and needed Mama to help. I felt her ineffectual tugs on my shoulders to get me off of him and utterly ignored her. I was half grabbing, half flailing at him and found myself screaming, "I hate you! I hate you! Don't, Papa!"

In a sudden gust of resolve, he grasped me hard and wrenched me off him, holding me at arm's length, staring at me like I was some kind of wild animal. His face looked painfully inflated, raw and red, a zigzag of veins in his temples. Strands of his blond hair hung in his eyes. His blue eyes flashed murderously. "How dare you, Hannah!" he said. "How dare you speak to me like that? Hate is the worst thing a person could feel!"

He released me like I was a poisonous creature and smoothed down his rumpled suit. I had knocked his hat to the floor in my outburst, and he bent to retrieve it, snapping it up like he did with Mama's stockings, only worse, showing me how deeply I had hurt him with my curses. I cringed in my shame, still ignoring Mama who continued to squeeze my shoulders while rubbing them at the same time. Silently, I rejected her feeble attempt at protective comfort, one I knew I certainly didn't deserve. She was sobbing quietly behind me, never saying a word. She never did know how to deal with life.

"I'm sorry, Papa," I whispered.

At my show of remorse, Papa relented and came forward, putting his arms around me. I squeezed him hard, fighting down the sickening combination of hatred and panic that was still there and which certainly had become his reason for leaving. I tried to show him only my desperation in my return embrace.

"I love you, Hannele," he said. "You know that. The distance means nothing. I really am doing this for us."

"I know that, Papa," I said, for I really so much wanted to believe it. He had, after all, always provided for Mama and me, hadn't he? We'd always had a beautiful apartment to live in, and he'd spoiled me with the finest dresses and books and piano lessons. All the necessary things for a good life. It wasn't his fault if bad people were always taking advantage of him, forcing him to go to America to get more money. Was it? Was it?

Papa released me and straightened. He smoothed back his hair, shiny and golden like the sun-drenched wheat of the peasants' fields outside the city, and replaced his hat. "I promise I'll send for you when I have enough money," he said.

"I know, Papa," I said again, really only wanting to grab him again and hang on. But I was probably already going to spend eternity burning in *Gehinnom* for what I'd just said. I could not risk anymore offensive behavior.

Papa brushed off his coat and looked at Mama. "You have my address where David and I will be staying?"

Mama only nodded. My back to her, I knew her plump cheeks had to be wet and shiny with tears. She still had not said a word, and I feared that she had lost all power of speech. I faced both the lonely prospect of my Papa's absence and cold silence from my mute mother.

I remember turning around and looking into her eyes, though, and seeing the same fear in them that I had. She, too, did not want to see Papa's eyes flash in anger that way or his face redden and swell as it had. Her own father had been angry and volatile. I had always hated being around my grandfather, and when Mama was my age, she had gone so far as to swear she would not marry a man like him. Well, she thought she had succeeded because Papa almost never got mad. Apparently, she had not noticed the signs of someone with suppressed anger, released in bursts when prodded enough.

Papa kissed us each on the cheek, in such a way that really, you'd have thought he was merely going on a short business trip rather than immigrating to America. He went to the door and turned to look at us one last time with an expression, I could have sworn, for one split moment, his pained expression conveyed doubt. But the softness that had come into his eyes, the trembling of his lips, had been just a flash, so quick, that I wonder to this day if I really saw it at all. And then he was gone.

When the door closed behind him, I surged forward, crying, "No!" Mama tightened her grip on my shoulders, halting me. "No, Hannah," she whispered. "Don't make it worse." I wanted to die when she said that. How could it have been worse? But she had surprised me with the sudden firmness in her hands, her fervent determination to spare me more pain. She can show that kind of strength sometimes in desperate moments, and it is this part of her that enables me to forgive her worst transgressions against me. The clarity of her intention in that moment compelled me to obey.

Papa's leaving changed our entire lives. Everything else we had left with him. Mama could not afford to stay in Warsaw without his help. But even if she could have, she wouldn't, for Warsaw was now the city of her complete undoing. So she sold the apartment and moved herself, me, and my cat Masha to Wolensk, the shtetl where she had grown up, 180 kilometers northeast of Warsaw, near the Ukrainian border, back to her old house where her brother, Leo Goldman, was living with his second wife, Sylvia.

Uncle Leo had not been thrilled about having us come to live with him. He never said this outright, but people's feelings often emanate from them in spite of what they say. The house had been a sort of honeymoon cottage for him and Auntie Sylvia since he had divorced his first wife and remarried. Well, I guess God decided that ten years for a honeymoon was long enough. But Mama softened the blow by giving Uncle Leo a sizeable share of the sale of our apartment toward expenses.

The only thing that made our move less drastic for me was that Wolensk is a good sized shtetl, not one of those one-horse-and-wagon shtetls made up of a small cluster of rickety, falling-down houses. The large Jewish Quarter has several synagogues, many blocks of houses, and a cemetery. The main street in Wolensk, Polaski Street, is wide and busy, full of shops owned and run by both Jews and Poles. That's where Uncle Leo's general store is. There's also a public library, a movie house and two market places, one for livestock and the other for fruits, vegetables and other wares. We have a volunteer fire department, manned by both Jews and Poles, plus several sports teams, social clubs and schools. I think that if it hadn't been this way, I should have been completely depressed. But as it is, there is almost always something going on to distract me from my troubles.

So contained in this personal history of mine lies the big truth that Solomon ignores in spite of all evidence. Simply stated, even if real love does exist, eventually it will be taken from you in some horribly cruel way, whether by death or betrayal or divorce, or by someone's fickle heart. Because that is the way God plays with His creation.

I suppose if I had grown up with Reb Weiss for a father, I, too, would see the world the way Solomon does. Reb Weiss is a pious and learned man, the beadle of our synagogue since the turn of the century. I reflect on this possibility every time Solomon's and my so drastically different views of life clash, and I can think only that maybe part of God's game is giving some people better parents than others, perhaps according to how much He either loves them or hates them. Certainly, Solomon would be among the loved ones, for he, though abandoned by his birth parents when he was only a few months old, had had the good fortune to be left on Reb Weiss's doorstep.

Really, the whole scenario could not have been more fortuitous for either of them. Reb Weiss was an aging widower whose wife had left him childless. His elder sister Zelda had come to take care of him years before while he was in mourning and never left. She *v'chodded* and *v'drayed* her brother for years to remarry, this time to a woman with a fertile womb. He always refused, insisting that he was not so anxious to replace his beloved Sarah, and that the Master of the Universe would give him a sign. Finally, after so many years, and neither of them really young enough to care for a child, Zelda gave up on him for a stubborn, foolish old man. These were Reb Weiss's exact words he used when telling me this story.

Well, apparently, the Master of the Universe did not consider Reb Weiss too old for the responsibility. On one chilly morning in late April, he stepped out from the caretaker's apartment just before dawn as he always did to light the synagogue and call the men to morning prayers. And there was Solomon in a basket, his little body wrapped in a tattered prayer shawl and a woman's woolen kerchief.

"That was my sign from the Master of the Universe," Reb Weiss said and pointed toward the ceiling. "He now saw I was no longer a foolish young man who didn't know love from an onion in the ground. Maybe now He was thinking I can be a father to this *pitzele*. It was finally His will that I have a son He reached out and gently ruffled the back of Solomon's dark hair, careful not to tip off his *yarmulke*. "I learned that day a most important lesson. We must be patient in this life," he said. "The Master of the Universe has His own time. And it is much longer than ours!"

So Solomon grew up in the glow of all that love, affection and romantic stuff. In the name of love, Reb Weiss even answered Solomon's mysterious origins. "Your mother and father were starving refugees of the Great War," Reb Weiss told him. "Many Jews were driven from their home by the Germans on one side and the Cossacks on the other. They could no longer feed you, and the Master of the Universe guided them here to me so I could care for you and raise you."

Reb Weiss is certain that this is what happened. His certainty is etched into the lines of his face, the wisdom of it woven into his beautiful sacred beard, a soft fan the colors of salt and pepper sifted together. He is a good man, Reb Weiss is, honored that Solomon came into his life, grateful to the Master of the Universe, and proud of the son who, by the age of ten, had distinguished himself as a scholar of Toyreh, and was constantly sought out by men many times his age for scriptural interpretations.

So the question is, how did Solomon and I end up as friends? How did a young religious man who, by the way, is next in line for the seat of spiritual leader of the Wolensk Hasidic dynasty, a Torah scholar who, aside from his virtuosic command of Scripture is also beset by mystical visions—which was what really brought the Wolensker rebbe's attention to him—who grew up poor and has never seen a moving picture, turn out to have as his best friend a young modern woman whose dresses do not completely cover her arms and legs, comes from a big city, is schooled in French, German and Polish, sees every moving picture possible and is someone he is not even supposed to look at or speak to, much less spend every possible opportunity with having tea in the kitchen? Ah, this is the story that stirs my heart because it is the first thing in my life I have ever really had to call my own, the only thing that cannot ever be taken from me ' under any circumstance — the way everything and everyone else will be, including Solomon. Or should I say, especially Solomon.

According to Solomon, our friendship did not begin the day that he and I actually spoke to each other for the first time, a winter morning in 1937 when he saved my life. Really, he says, it began the day Mama and I and Mashele moved in with Uncle Leo and Auntie Sylvia, which also happened to be the same day Reb Weiss told Solomon that he had been promised in marriage to Chava, the Wolensker Rebbe's daughter, securing his place as the Rebbe's successor.

You see, aside from Solomon's command of scripture, he was given from a very young age to flights of spiritual bliss, the kind of ecstasy that was known by the Baal Shem Tov, the father of Hasidic Judaism. The Baal Shem Tov, or Besht as he is affectionately referred to, was a poor man but overflowing with a wealth of God's love. He was known to hug trees and kiss flowers and weep tears of compassion for the suffering of every living creature. The Besht was scorned by the traditional Jews because he had no need of scripture and did not exhort Talmudic learning to his followers, whom he encouraged to find God's holiness everywhere and in everything, including blades of grass and in the most mundane tasks like sweeping a floor.

Well, after Solomon told me this story, he then described to me his own experiences. He says that sometimes he feels like his soul is floating out of his body and he can see everything in the world at once, including feelings and thoughts. At other times, he feels like his chest is on fire and his eyes fill with tears because in those moments he knows, without any doubt, that the Master of the Universe is everywhere, in everything, burning with His holy presence. And then, there are times when everything he looks at appears to have been poked full of holes and a very bright light, brighter than anything you could imagine, is pouring through the holes.

When Solomon was fourteen, he told his father about what was happening to him. Immediately Reb Weiss, a humble man who did not know what else to do when faced with his son's spiritual gifts, took him on a pilgrimage to the Rebbe's home on the outskirts of the Jewish Quarter. Rebbe Zalman took a long look at Solomon and asked him certain questions that he could only have answered correctly if his visions were authentic. Apparently they were, because when Solomon answered them, tears came to the old Rebbe's eyes and he thanked the Master of the Universe for not deserting them. You see, the Rebbe had no sons, only two daughters, and the Wolensker dynasty was to die with him unless a successor could be found. Suffice it to say that on that day, the successor was found.

So while Mama and I were on the train from Warsaw to Wolensk, with everything we owned in the world packed into the baggage compartment and Masha in a little cage on my lap, Solomon was sitting at the little wooden table across from Reb Weiss, in the caretaker's apartment where he had grown up, being told his destiny, signed and sealed into the Book of Life.

Solomon was fifteen then, and I was fourteen. That day held great sadness for both of us, because neither of us had chosen our circumstances. We were both faced with the gritty reality that our lives were not our own, and probably never would be. And Solomon was reflecting on this horrible truth while standing in front of the synagogue, haunted by the *dybbuks* of fate when Uncle Leo pulled up to the house in his motorcar, having just retrieved me and Mama from the train station.

I did not see Solomon that day. But I can imagine him standing outside on the street, a fifteen-year-old boy in the uniform all the *yeshiva-bochers* wore: black vest and trousers, white long-sleeved button-down shirt with religious fringes dangling, sacred earlocks growing from the temples, and yarmulke on his close-cropped dark hair. There he was, the next Wolensker Rebbe, watching me, my blonde hair spilling from its twist, dress and coat rumpled from the train ride, carrying Masha into the house. I was too busy taking Masha out of Uncle Leo's motorcar and retrieving my valise to notice him. But Solomon saw me. He saw my sadness, the end-of-life feeling I carried in with my arrival in Wolensk. He watched the whole time, distracted momentarily from his troubles, by the sight of us.

That moment, Solomon says, was the real beginning of our friendship.

I couldn't have known then that we would become friends, but that's when he began to appear. Everywhere I went, he was there too. As my awareness of Wolensk unfolded and I began to learn its quarters and distractions, the pulse of its life and ways, as it became my home rather than that faraway shtetl I had occasionally visited, of all this, Solomon was an intrinsic part.

The public library was the first place I found, and it quickly became a cherished haunt. Books had always been more reliable and kinder to me than people, and I liked to hide among the dusty stacks of them. Yet, I was almost never alone.

First, I'd feel a presence, a sense of being watched. When I looked up, he would be down on the other end of a stack, in the shadowy light, studying the titles on the shelf in front of him.

On Mondays, when I went to the marketplace to buy vegetables, I would feel that presence again, drawing my attention, an instinctive tug to look over my shoulder. And every time I did, there was a blur of black and white clothing as he ducked behind a wagon.

As time passed, he grew a bit bolder, bold enough to come into my uncle's store where I helped several days a week, except for Fridays when I cleaned the house and prepared Shabbos dinner while Auntie Sylvia and Mama worked. Solomon always bought the same thing, a Yiddish newspaper, plucking the *groschen* from the pocket of his black vest with trembling fingers, his face downcast. He put the coins on the counter for me to retrieve, so that our hands would not touch. He was, after all, a Hasid, at least in part. But when I think of that time, I remember that in spite of his boyish nervousness, there was a religiosity about him, religiosity being the only word I can think of to describe it. It was new to me and dispelled the weirdness his way of turning up everywhere I went evoked in me.

In fact, after months of being followed around, there came to be for me, a strange familiarity, a sense of comforting ritual in his presence that I came to rely on, almost to crave. Oddly enough, I had the feeling he was looking after me, wanting to protect me from life's ills. I also began to wonder about him. I knew he was Reb Weiss's son, and that he was to be the next Wolensker rebbe. (You can't live in the Jewish Quarter of a shtetl without knowing at least the basic facts of most of the people who live there.) But I knew nothing else of him. And so he crept into my imagination, making me wonder about his life when he wasn't peeking at me from around a library stack or ducking behind a wagon in the marketplace.

The only thing I didn't wonder about was why he did it. I had his reason all figured for myself. He was a boy, his passage to manhood visibly marked by the rapid filling-in of his beard. And I was a girl whose own development was obvious enough in the various swellings and curving of my body. I do not cover my legs and arms the way Hasidic women do. So what other reason would he have had to follow me around?

I, too, grew a bit bolder with him as time passed, and would actually say hello to him when he came in for his newspaper. To which he would nod politely then quickly look down. One time, when he put his coin on the counter, I did not pick it up right away, seized as I was by the most compelling—and I should say wicked—curiosity to see what he would do. He didn't turn and walk away as I thought he might, but stood there quietly, faced with my boldly questioning silence.

My stomach tightened, and I began to regret what I was doing, seeing in it some sort of cruelty. I found, too, I was frightened of scaring him away or making him think that I didn't want him to follow me anymore. I put my hand on the coin. "Thank you," I whispered. I expected him then to leave, but he didn't.

I looked up. Now he was staring at me, looking past that veil between him and the forbidden realm. I saw his eyes. Never had I seen them so close up. They were unusual and beautiful, their color reminding me of the jar of honey my grandmother used to leave on the kitchen windowsill to warm in the sun. I used to love its color when the light poured through, a deep warm gold. I knew then, with a most eerie shiver, that God wasn't always angry, not even with me, that He had moments of forgiveness and love, even if they were only moments.

For that fleeting gift, and for the distress I had probably caused to Solomon, I had to offer him something. Next to the cash register sat a box of sugar candies Uncle Leo kept to tempt customers to spend an extra groschen on impulse. I picked one out and put it on the counter, glancing over my shoulder. But Uncle Leo was cloistered in his back room over the books. "Take it," I whispered to Solomon.

Solomon's eyes widened and he almost smiled before looking away. He nodded thanks as he picked up the candy from the counter and stuffed it into the pocket of his trousers. He paused a moment then left with his newspaper. I watched him disappear into the bustle of Polaski Street. Sighing in relief, I remembered that Uncle Leo had asked me to dust the shelves, and I set to my task, muttering to myself about what a not-nice person I really was.

In the winter of 1937, almost two years after Solomon had begun his self-appointed vigil, the day came when he saved my life.

One freezing Monday morning, I went to the market as usual to buy winter vegetables. Until that day, I had always enjoyed the marketplace in the cold weather, when you can enjoy the activity, the sounds of haggling in Polish and Yiddish without the disgusting smells of the livestock and sweating people simmering in the heat of summer. That morning, however, as I stood at one peasant's cart, buying parsnips, someone began yelling, "Don't buy from the Jews!"

I froze in my spot. Fear prickled the skin of my whole body. The shouts continued, and a fight broke out several stalls down from where I was. The peasant who'd sold me the parsnips began yelling curses at the troublemakers, threatening to turn them over to the police. He ran out from behind his cart, accidentally jostling me aside. Still I could not move even though the brawl threatened to spill over onto me.

"Hannah, come away from here!" Solomon appeared in front of me. I stared at him, my senses glazed in fear. He reached for my basket, grabbing part of the handle. "Hold onto this," he said, as the shouts and grunts of fighting men and the screams of women grew louder. "Come." He tugged on the basket, pulling me out of my stupor. Obediently I followed him and we ducked behind some wagons, away from the confusion and violence, the sounds of shattering glass, and the nauseating thuds of fists on flesh.

With both our hands on the handle of my basket, we threaded our way through side streets where the Polish gentiles lived, streets lined with wooden bungalows, their tiny patches of naked winter yards, colored only by laundry lines. The clothing, frozen stiff in the unmoving air, looked so strange to me, glassy and surreal, as if the world were passing before me on a movie screen. I stumbled on a rock.

He stopped. "Are you all right?"

I nodded and we continued, only this time I kept my gaze fixed on the small black knitted yarmulke on his head, taking a strangely familiar comfort in the way his earlocks brushed his cheeks as we hurried along.

We did not slow down until we were back in the Jewish Quarter, with its simple wooden bungalows and synagogues, the slats economically nailed together. Except for the synagogue's ornately carved trimmings, our neighborhood looked as if it could be easily disassembled, moved, and put back together, the obvious legacy of a people forced to live as nomads for thousands of years.

At the door of my house we finally stopped, our breaths puffing heavily into the air. Solomon put his hand on the doorknob. "Is it locked?"

I shook my head and he pulled it open, ushering me in. Our hands both still grasped the basket, but once inside, Solomon took it and held it for me. I closed the door behind us, shutting out the cold and chaos, and the house enclosed us in its dark warmth. For the first time since I lived here, it felt like a sanctuary with its antique furniture, polished floors and nice oriental rugs, all meticulously cared for by Auntie Sylvia. She is quite the *balabosteh* who pays careful attention to details, down to the lace doilies put everywhere to protect the arms of the sofa and chairs as well as the dark smooth wood of table tops.

I leaned back against the door, waiting for the fear to pass, but the echoes of the hatred and fighting throbbed in my mind. I put my hands over my eyes, fighting back hysterical tears. "What's happening?" I whispered.

"It was the Endeks."

I had heard of the Endecja, a group of anti-Semites who wanted to gain political power by causing trouble in Wolensk and other places, trying to turn our gentile neighbors against us.

"They want to take over the government," he went on. "I read about them in the Yiddish paper."

The quiet house filled with the sounds of my ragged breathing as I sought to regain my poise.

"It's...it's all right," Solomon said, almost as if he were comforting a child. "You're safe now. They will be arrested."

The certainty in his voice calmed me a bit and I uncovered my eyes. Behind Solomon, Uncle Leo's grandfather clock ticked with gentle echoes, making us both aware we were alone in the quiet house. "Would...would you like some tea?" I asked.

In the shadowy light, I saw Solomon's Adam's apple slide up and down as he swallowed nervously. "Yes, please."

I hung up my coat and scarf and turned to him. He stood, watching me. I held out my hands. "I'll hang your coat for you."

He took off his coat and scarf and handed them to me as though he were afraid to touch me. I took his things and hung them up then led him into the kitchen. Warm and clean, it has always been my favorite room of this house. The small window above the sink shows almost the whole street in front of the house, including the synagogue where Solomon lives.

I gestured him to a seat, put up the kettle to boil and arranged a plate of almond cookies I had baked the day before. I set the cookies before him, remembering at the last second that he was much more religious than I and might not consider our kitchen kosher enough to eat in. I reached again for the plate, as if to take it away. "I'm sorry," I said, feeling sudden anxiousness that he might refuse the cookies, but also eagerness to please him. "Our kitchen is kosher. I...I made them myself."

Solomon smiled, perhaps the first time in all the times I ever had seen his face. "I did not give it a thought," he answered. "They look really good, actually."

I smiled and turned away, grimacing at my awkwardness. I busied myself with serving the tea before sitting down across from Solomon, my hands around my tea glass to warm the trembling out of them. I felt him studying me, and became self-conscious, especially of my hands with their thick twig-shaped fingers and bitten-down nails. "Do you take sugar?" I pushed the little sugar cube bowl with its delicate claw- shaped tongs in his direction. It had belonged to my grandmother. When I was little I loved to play with those tongs, going around and serving everyone their sugar cubes for tea after supper.

"Yes, thank you." Gingerly he picked up the tongs and dropped a cube of sugar into the palm of his other hand. Then he did the strangest thing. He put his sugar cube between his teeth the way the older people still do and grinned widely, making an exaggerated show of sipping his tea. This seemed so out of character for him that I began to giggle in spite of everything, and for a few moments, our mutual awkwardness disappeared. Solomon later told me that he did it to make me smile, that he couldn't stand how frightened and sad I looked sitting there, sipping my tea, traumatized by the fighting in the marketplace.

Masha came wandering into the kitchen. She approached Solomon and began weaving about his feet, rubbing her sides against his black trousers.

"Masha, don't bother Solomon," I told her.

"I don't mind." Solomon reached down to stroke her long soft hair. I felt a ripple of jealousy at how quickly Masha took to him, sitting quietly under his hand, blinking her green eyes in that manner of feline contentedness.

I watched them until my thoughts wandered back to what had happened. I had only experienced anti-Semitism one other time, but had never told anyone about it, not even Mama. Now, I found myself aching to spill my story to Solomon. "When I lived in Warsaw," I said, "I went into a store to buy some candy. While I was looking around, I heard the lady at the cash register mumbling to herself about the Jews, about how they want to get everything for half a groschen, and how 'that Hitler' in Germany will one day come and take care of the problem. I became so afraid I left. I guess she didn't think I was Jewish." I paused and took a sip of my tea.

Solomon had stopped petting Masha and now sat up straight in his chair.

"I never told anyone what happened," I went on. "Until…you. I thought if I didn't say anything, then it didn't really happen. But now…"

"It has always been that way," he answered with a tinge of pride in his voice. "They are jealous."

I looked at him, my brow furrowed. "Jealous? For what?"

"For our relationship with the Master of the Universe," he said, as if it were absolutely obvious.

I thought about his answer a moment then shrugged and reached for a cookie. "I don't know what we did to make them hate us so much."

Solomon also picked up a cookie and munched on it. He swallowed and washed it down with a sip of tea. "This is good," he said and set down his glass.

Nobody in my family had ever commented on my baking, and my cheeks burned. "Thank you."

Then we were quiet as we each ate a couple more cookies. I served more tea.

"Way back near the beginning," Solomon said, "Jacob smashed his wife's idols. The gentiles have idols. Ha Shem forbids idols, and our existence reminds them of their transgressions."

I stared at him and realized he had been reflecting this whole time on a response. Though drawn by the certainty in his expression, I didn't completely understand what he meant. But it felt true. Nevertheless, I didn't answer.

He seemed to have finished his commentary. The silence which followed brought back the earlier awkwardness, though not as strongly.

"I'm sorry if I've ever frightened you, Hannah," Solomon said. "It was not what I meant."

I smiled, but my stomach began to flutter madly. Any words I could say froze in my throat. How could I tell him all the ways I had felt every time I saw him following me? About the progression from wariness to comfort, to the sense of having something special no one else had? About what I had seen in his eyes that time in Uncle Leo's store? I did not trust myself to express any of it. "It's all right," I said. Meager words. "I haven't minded." More meager words.

I averted my eyes from his gaze. Strange, the way he was looking at me, as if I were completely alone with him in the whole world.

He then explained to me everything about his father's promise to the rebbe, and about seeing me that day, carrying Masha and my suitcase into the house. "I felt that somehow I already knew you," he said. "It is possible. It says so in *Sefer haGilgulim*."

I furrowed my brow. "In what?"

"*Sefer haGilgulim*, the ancient mystical text about the transmigration of souls. Of how they can travel together over many lifetimes as they move toward spiritual perfection." He paused and sighed. "Maybe it sounds terribly strange, Hannah. You probably think I'm crazy. But that's what it feels like to me." He looked down and his expression grew sad.

I had never thought about anything like what he was saying, but even so, something felt true. I thought then to myself that Solomon certainly wasn't crazy. A bit weird, maybe.

"Hannah? What are you thinking?"

An involuntary smile came to my face though I felt mercilessly shy. Yet, at the same time, I felt the oddest...ease, a comfort which enabled me to answer, to voice these intimate thoughts. "I...I was thinking that...you're not crazy."

He also smiled, once again dispelling the tension. I think we both knew at that moment we would be friends. And I had to admit, at least to myself, that it felt good to have a friend, even if he was going to leave and get married some day.

The only friend I'd made since moving to Wolensk was Marta Blumenthal. We mostly chattered about Aaron Levi, whose father owns the men's clothing store on Polaski Street, across from Uncle Leo's store, and on whom we both have a terrible crush. Aaron is athletic, with a broad chest and dresses smartly, in suits from his father's store. But he does not notice either of us at all. Why would he when he's dating Eva Schultz, the prettiest girl in Wolensk? I don't expect any man to notice me, anyway, especially when the only one who has seemed to notice me already has a bride. This is my luck, you see. Marta is more optimistic. She seems to know her destiny as a wife and mother. For her, it is just a matter of time. The world is that straightforward for her. I cannot relate to this simplicity, and so our friendship has already begun to wane.

Since the day Solomon rescued me from the Endeks, I have begun to experience some resentment of the fact that he will eventually have to end our friendship. Sometimes I feel like I hate him for that. But when that happens, I simply remind myself that I don't have anything to feel jealous about. I don't feel *that* way about him. We are simply friends. It's not that he isn't attractive. He kind of is. His face is gentle and scholarly, with a full sacred beard, dark and soft-looking, like my mother's mink coat. And he has a rosy tint in his cheeks, what you can see of them that isn't covered by beard. And, well, those eyes. I already said what they're like. Altogether, Solomon is very sensitive and intelligent, and I'm sure that Chava, the Rebbe's daughter, will be very happy with him as a husband. So really, there's no point in letting myself even think about him any other way.

Before he left my house that day, Solomon asked me to teach him Polish. You see, religious boys grow up only speaking Yiddish because they are not really exposed to the outside world. He already knew a little Polish, but he wanted to know more for when he served his term in the army. I agreed to help him, and he started coming over to my house each week after Shabbos was over and we'd sit in the kitchen for our lessons.

Can you believe, after Solomon left my house the first day, I realized I had forgotten to thank him for saving my life? Horrified at my rudeness, I baked him some almond cookies and took them to him the next day. When I told him why I had brought them, he smiled shyly. That awkwardness between us was still there and really has never completely gone away.

"It's all right, Hannah," he said. "I have gained something too."

Just because we became friends did not mean he stopped trailing me. He didn't. He still had a way of appearing in certain moments, especially whenever I emerged from the postal station with one of my father's invariably disappointing letters. Solomon believes firmly that no one should have to go through such things alone, and truthfully, I am glad when he is there.

This is where he found me today. Today, on my nineteenth birthday, just after I had picked up my letter and stood outside in the pre-Shabbos rushing world of Polaski Street, my shopping basket on the ground at my feet, staring at Papa's letter. I wondered how long God would punish me for having screamed at Papa that day.

I looked up when Solomon called my name. He had taken to appear with me in public on occasions that he felt called for defiance of the rules under which he lived. My distress was one of them. And I have to admit, the sight of him with his beard and earlocks, dressed in black and white like a religious man of centuries ago, always brought its odd comfort.

His gaze went from my face to the crumpled letter in my hand, then lowered, his face looking like a mourner at the side of a grave. "I'm sorry," he said.

I sighed and shoved the letter into the pocket of my skirt. "You have nothing to be sorry about. You're not the one who left for America without me."

"That may be true, but I know how it feels to be left behind."

I nodded. My throat had tightened painfully. I couldn't speak.

"I love my father very much," he continued. "But it still hurts."

I picked up my shopping basket with the Shabbos chicken in it. But Solomon took it from me. "Come," he said. "I'll walk you home."

"Thank you. I had better get back soon or my challah will have risen so high I won't be able to fit it in the oven!"

Solomon smiled. "You make the best challah," he said. "Papa agrees."

Cheeks burning, I looked down. "Thank you. Remember the first loaf I made?"

Solomon chuckled as we began to walk. "Yes. It was more like a tasty rock than a loaf of bread."

"Hey!" I laughed. Solomon's teasing never felt harmful, unlike that of my cousin Yoav, who used to tease me mercilessly until he lost interest in the activity and stopped.

Yoav — now there's a cause of *tsores* in my heart! Uncle Leo's son by his first wife who divorced him many years ago, my cousin is seven years older than I and has been a terrible tease since we were kids. I usually enjoyed his teasing except sometimes he'd go too far with pinching or name calling and make me cry. Still, I loved the attention and always came back for more teasing.

He grew to be a handsome young man with dark curly hair, brown eyes and a freckled complexion. He was my first crush, which has never really gone away. I had always hoped, like a silly girl, that one day he might feel the same about me, especially when I started to develop into a woman. But that's exactly when he started ignoring me.

It was the strangest thing. As instantly as one can switch a light bulb on or off, he began to ignore me. The first time, at a family dinner, he gave me the barest greeting. No teasing. No nothing. He spoke with Uncle Leo and Zayde about his studies at the University in Warsaw, about politics, his prospects for the future. He didn't even look at me or ask me anything. It was horrible.

But in spite of that, my heart has remained faithful and I always look forward to seeing him, however seldom he comes around. He has even begun to tease me a little again. But it's half-hearted and consists mostly of ugly pet-name calling. Even this little bit keeps me hoping and looking more forward to tonight's Shabbos dinner because he is coming.

Back at my house, Solomon followed me into the kitchen, setting down my basket on the table. The house was quiet, as it always was when no one else was home. Mama was still at the elementary school where she taught, Uncle Leo hadn't closed the store yet, and Auntie Sylvia was still at the bank.

Solomon sat, watching me brush the risen loaves of challah with a beaten egg and put them in the oven, politely remarking on how perfectly I could now braid the dough.

I had asked Auntie Sylvia to teach me how to make challah shortly after Solomon and I became friends. I really enjoy the whole process, kneading the dough, forming the loaves, watching them rise. And the smell of bread baking... Nothing smells better! And more than that, I feels good, giving Solomon and Reb Weiss bread each week. They enjoy and appreciate it, and Auntie Sylvia, who is busy enough, is glad for less to do.

"I see how hard you've worked on them, Hannele," he said.

I smiled, puffed up with my culinary pride like a real *balabosteh* and went to fill the tea kettle. Then I noticed that Solomon was still wearing his coat. "Don't you want to take your coat off?" I asked.

He shook his head, and I could see his Adam's apple slide in his throat, the way it always did when he swallowed nervously.

"Is something wrong?"

"Hannah, this is for you." He took a small package wrapped in tissue paper from the pocket of his coat and held it out to me. "For your birthday."

"Solomon…" I sat down at the table with him and accepted the gift, taking care not to touch his hand. "Thank you." My voice was but a whisper. Slowly I pulled open the paper. Inside was a beautiful prayer book, bound in leather with gold letters and decorated with more gold leaf. "It's beautiful!" I touched the cover delicately with a fingertip. Since I had started going back to the synagogue, I always used the common prayer books left on the seats in the women's section. They were worn and not so pretty. Many times I had wished for one of my own. Now, I not only had one, but it was exquisite! Better than a diamond! A sudden terrible guilt stabbed me. My family could easily afford such a book, but Solomon was poor. I looked at him. "I love it!" I told him. "Thank you so much! But—"

Solomon held up his hand to stop me. "Don't worry, Hannele," he said. "No one will starve."

My cheeks heated with shame, and I looked down. "I'm sorry," I muttered.

"It's all right. I wanted you to have your own prayer book."

I hugged the book to me and smiled. "I love it."

The pink in his cheeks deepened and he looked down. "I'm very glad."

That familiar tension rose in the quiet that followed. I still needed to dress the chicken and get it into the oven. "Are you still coming to dinner tonight?"

He looked up at me, surprised. "Of course I am. Why wouldn't I?"

I shrugged. "Well, maybe you would have to go to the Rebbe's like you do sometimes."

Solomon shook his head. "Not tonight, I wouldn't. This is important."

I looked down. "It's not that important."

"To me it is." Then he sighed and his expression sobered. "Papa may not come, though. He hasn't been feeling so well lately."

"Oh! What's wrong?"

"I think it's his heart. He doesn't say anything. He believes he's hiding it from me." Solomon shook his head.

"What can I do?"

"There's nothing, Hannele. He would feel terrible if he knew I said this much to you. We'll just let him rest and see him later on."

I nodded. I hate things like this. Old age. The prospect of a loved one's death makes me want to curl up into a ball and just give up completely. "I'll bring the challah and some food to him before shul then."

"Thank you. That will help."

"You're welcome."

We were quiet again. I took the chicken from the basket and put it into the roasting pan.

"I had better let you work," Solomon said after a few more minutes of watching me prepare the chicken.

"What about your tea?" I found that I really wanted him to keep me company while I worked. "The water's boiling. I can do my work at the same time."

He nodded. "I'd like that."

I made tea and went about shredding potatoes for kugel, glad not to be alone while doing such a boring task. "This always happens, doesn't it?" Solomon said.

I peered at him over my bowl of shredded potatoes. "You mean, you watching me shred potatoes?"

He grinned. "No. I mean, every time we have to part, we find a reason to stay longer."

My cheeks heated again and I looked back down at my work. What he said made me feel afraid, but I knew it was true. We always did that. Even at the door, he always had to say "You first," so I would go. Why did we linger like that? Why did we always need to know when we would see each other again? "Yes," I mumbled, pushing harder on the potato I was grating. "We do."

"You and me. We're like Shabbos and prayers. They must go together."

I sighed. Some truths were better left unvoiced, I thought. But when Solomon thinks or feels something it comes out of his mouth. Sometimes I envy him this freedom, and sometimes I find it very upsetting, like in this moment, but I smiled back. "Like *matzos* on Passover," I said.

He chuckled. "Well, yes. That too. But I hope I'm not that flat and tasteless."

I smiled. "I was just kidding. I knew what you meant."

"I knew that."

He stayed a little while longer while he finished his tea and then left with the promise to see me after shul. Then he bowed gallantly — to make me giggle, of course — and I saw him to the door. He stepped outside and stood there, facing me. As always, we both hesitated to say an actual good-bye. "You first, Hannele," he said in his customary way, indicating that I should be the first to close the door and finish our parting. As I did so, I felt that jealous resentment begin to well inside me when I thought of the impermanence of such times as this. Thank God I had so much to do in the next few hours. And Yoav would soon arrive as well.

I sighed and went back into the kitchen, thinking with a shrug, what is the point of torturing yourself over such things? This is the way things are. I was certain to have a dim future, one in which Solomon would be married and disappear into that ancient, black-garbed world. I certainly could not be welcome there, and I would have to get on with my life. That's just the way it was. That's the way God wants it. And how can you argue with God?

~~~~~

"What do you expect from your father, Hannele?" Mama said when she came home that afternoon and read Papa's letter. "He has his new life in the Golden Land. If he wanted you there, he would find a way to get the money. He doesn't sound like he's starving." She sighed as she pushed the crumpled paper across the kitchen table away from her, then put her hands together, digging the nails of one hand into the palm of the other.

I snatched the letter up and stuffed it back into my pocket. "You're wrong, Mama." How I hated when she said things like that. "It's not that way. He says that it will just take him longer to get money together now that he and Mr. Rosen have parted ways. It *will* happen."

Mama looked at me, the skin of her face chafed and red. There were lines around her eyes. "It's almost Shabbos," she said. "How is the chicken? Shabbos will not wait for it to finish roasting."

I glared at her, but went to the oven to baste the golden-brown skin of the chicken in its roasting pan. Before closing the oven door I deeply inhaled the aromas of the chicken, baked bread, and almond cookies. The potato kugel warmed in its pan on the stove next to the giant pot of hot water we kept over the Sabbath for tea. Not even during the week did the smells of food cooking fill my soul the way these did. On Shabbos, even the scent of food was holy.

I hung my apron on its hook and turned to Auntie Sylvia who was washing some things at the sink. "Where is Yoav?" I asked her. "Shouldn't he have been here by now?"

Auntie Sylvia shut off the water and spun around, her hand to her forehead. "Hannele! Oy! I'm so sorry! I forgot to tell you! He couldn't come. He's staying in Warsaw. He had an invitation to Ruth's house." She came and put her hands on my shoulders. "He did ask me to tell you happy birthday."

My shoulders sagged under her hands. "That was kind of him."

Auntie Sylvia missed my sarcasm and turned to Mama. "Finally! He's meeting her parents!" she said in a singsong. "You know what that could mean!"

"*Mazel tov*," Mama said, her voice dull and insincere.

"I'm going to change my dress for shul." I said, heading toward the door. "At least Shabbos always comes on time."

"Hannele," Auntie Sylvia said, "don't feel bad. There will be other birthdays."

"I look forward to each one!" I said as I left the kitchen and went down the hallway to my room.

I entered the small bedroom that had belonged to my other cousin, Devorah. Now it was Masha's and mine. There were two small beds in it, which was good, because Masha was always sleeping—and shedding—on one of them. I liked the room with its simple wooden furniture, even though I had never liked Devorah very much. She was always standoffish and quiet in a snooty kind of way. She was two years older than Yoav and had begun studies at the University until she met Isaac, fell in love, and married. Now she lived in Bialystock and had a little girl, Ruchel, who was almost three.

As usual, Masha was curled up on Devorah's bed. "Hello, Mashele," I said and sat next to her. She gazed at me with her green cat eyes and meowed, a plaintive cry for affection. I began to stroke her long, black, silky hair. "It is a good thing for us, Mashele, that Devorah is married now with her own home. She probably wouldn't like your using her bed."

Masha purred in response, vibrating under my fingertips. Seeing she was satisfied, I stopped petting her and pulled Papa's letter from my pocket though I couldn't bear to read it again. I looked instead at my new prayer book which lay on the other bed across from me. I leaned over and picked it up, sitting with the letter in one hand and the prayer book in the other.

Life gives such mixed messages! How can I know what to believe? How can I know what's really true? Solomon's friendship? I never let myself forget he is getting married. I harp on this point, but anyone would in my situation! Or Papa's not really wanting me? And, for that matter, Yoav's not really wanting me either. If your own blood doesn't think you're worth the trouble, how can you believe anyone?

A knock at my door interrupted my thoughts. It opened part way, and Mama poked her head in. "May I come in?"

When I nodded, she came and sat down on my bed, watching Masha and me. I saw her gaze fall on my new prayer book in my hand. She looked at me with raised eyebrows.

"It's from Solomon," I told her.

"May I?" She held out her hand.

I handed it to her and she examined it closely. "It's beautiful," she said. "Solomon is a very thoughtful young man."

"Yes," I said. "He is."

She pressed her lips together in a line as she handed it back to me.

"What is it, Mama?" I asked, knowing I would be sorry for my curiosity.

"Well, that is quite an intimate gift for him to have given you when he is betrothed to someone else."

I glared at her. "Solomon is my friend! My best friend! In case you haven't noticed, friends are difficult to find in this world!"

"You think I don't know that? Look at your own father, who takes off for America when God only knows what will happen to the Jews here!"

"Mama, don't! Papa would not have left us here if he thought Poland would be another Germany. You cannot possibly accuse him of that!"

Mama held up her hand. She sighed. "All right, Hannele." She rubbed her forehead. "I like Solomon. You know that. But I just don't understand."

"Understand what?"

"Understand why either of you give so much time to a friendship that…" She fell silent.

"That what?" I pushed stubbornly. I never learned.

She sighed again. "…that can have no future."

I threw up my hands. "Why do you do this? Why don't you want me to be happy about anything? I love that prayer book!"

"Judith." Auntie Sylvia said from the doorway. "Leo is home now." She eyed both of us. "I know it is a difficult day for both of you, but tonight is Shabbos. Tonight we put our troubles aside and rest." She turned and left.

Mama rolled her eyes and I smiled. She leaned over and kissed my forehead. "I must set the table now." At the doorway, she turned to me before going out. "It's a beautiful prayer book," she said softly. "Use it in good health."

I sighed. "Thank you, Mama."

After Mama had left my room, I sighed and rose from Masha's bed to change my dress then checked my hair in the dressing mirror, gently patting the blonde waves into place around my face.

I continued to stare at my reflection, which was framed by photographs of Papa and me and pinups of American movie stars that he'd sent me over the last few years. I certainly did not resemble women such as these, glamorous and sophisticated. Eva Schultz did, perhaps, but not me. I am a strange-looking girl with a small, rounded nose and chin. Grayish-blue eyes. I like my skin the best. It is pale, but very clear and smooth.

"You might as well go now," I said to the Hannah staring back at me. "This is as good as you will ever look."

I went to the kitchen and put together a package of food from each dish for Reb Weiss, knowing that I would annoy people for having destroyed the food's presentation. But what else could I do, let that nice old man go hungry? My best friend's father? I put the prepared meal and the challah into my basket then took my sweater from its hook by the front door. "I'm going to the synagogue," I said to Mama, who had just finished setting the table. She did not cook very much, but she set a beautiful Shabbos table, with her crisp white linens (gifts from her wedding) and Auntie Sylvia's best china and silverware.

"But Hannah, don't you want to light the candles with me? You love that!"

"Not tonight. I just want to leave now. I'm late as it is."

She sighed and I could almost hear her saying, "When did you get to be so stubborn?"

Uncle Leo had already left for the synagogue, so I walked the short distance by myself. It was just as well, for Uncle Leo and I really did not have much to say to each other. I mean, what is there to talk about with someone who really doesn't want you around but tries to act like he does and ends up lying to you all the time because of it?

Solomon and his father were already in the synagogue when I came to their apartment. They always left the door unlocked, so I went inside, put the basket on their table then set a place for Reb Weiss. When he came back after shul, everything would be ready for him.

Before going to the synagogue myself, I looked around the tiny apartment. Solomon had grown up here, and I always felt peaceful in this room although it was somewhat dark and spare. There was almost no furniture except for the table and chairs, a bookcase, and some small benches for the cheyder students. I could never look at those benches without trying to picture Solomon there as a little boy, sitting with other little boys, learning scripture. Reb Weiss had no photographs of Solomon, which is a terrible shame because I'm certain he was an adorable child.

I sighed. The peace I felt here made me want to stay and never leave. The burden of impossibility depresses me. No one can stay in the same place forever. Not even

Solomon would stay here. I turned. Reb Weiss's Shabbos candles flickered on the table. I gazed at the small flames for a few moments before going to the synagogue, hugging my new prayer book to me.

Solomon doesn't know this, but he inspired me to come back to the synagogue. Really, I'm not sure if I ever would have. I used to go when I was a little girl with my grandmother, Frumah Tzivele. Together we'd sit behind the heavy wooden screen which separated the men from the women. She never explained any of the prayers to me, but I used to watch her rock back and forth in her seat, her eyes closed, her lips moving quickly, murmuring the prayers to herself.

Since I didn't understand what was happening, I'd get bored and peek through the screen and watch the men pray. They, too, swayed side to side and stepped occasionally back and forth upon reaching certain points in their prayer books, while the wooden walls of the synagogue echoed with their dissonant murmurs and chants. I did not feel God there, so when I got older, I stopped going. No one cared because I was a girl and wouldn't have to prepare for a *bar mitzvah* anyway.

When Solomon and I first became friends, I expected him to urge me to go back to the synagogue. But he never did. Of course, I thought that he, too, didn't care because I was female. But one day, after a Shabbos evening I had sung *zmiros* after supper with him and Reb Weiss, he said to me, "Hannele, your voice is so pretty, the Master of the Universe delights in hearing it." That was the first nice thing anyone had ever said to me that I believed. And so I went back. It was enough for me that Solomon thought it mattered that I pray.

I still don't understand all the Hebrew, but thanks to his tutoring, I learned the prayers so well that I could feel them inside me. He was able to bring the words to life for me, and though I do not go to shul very often during the week, I never miss Shabbos.

Behind the screen, I become half like my grandmother, and half like the little girl I had been, spending part of the services swaying and murmuring to myself, my eyes closed the way hers had been, and then spending part of the time leaning forward in my chair, my prayer book open on my lap, ignored, watching the men at prayer. It's difficult to see them through the small holes carved into the divider, but I manage to catch glimpses. I like to watch Solomon, deep in prayer, the way his body sways back and forth, side to side, his eyes closed. He always sits near Rabbi Wolf, the rabbi of this synagogue. I couldn't help thinking how much Rabbi Wolf must wish Solomon would be staying here instead of one day leaving to become the Wolensker Rebbe.

Of course, I also spend an unholy amount of time staring at Aaron Levi, wondering about him, aching from my crush on him, until I feel so guilty for staring at him in a synagogue that I move on. One of the things I always wonder about Aaron is why he comes to shul since his family isn't particularly religious. Aaron is an ardent Zionist, with hopes of immigrating to Palestine. He even belongs to Hechalutz, which trains people to live on kibbutz there. Aaron's brother, Samuel, did emigrate several years back, and was tragically killed by an Arab bomb on a bus. So I think to myself that maybe Aaron was moved by his grief to come to shul.

Uncle Leo is there too, but I don't spend any time watching him. He isn't particularly interesting in his chalk-colored suit, swaying lightly around in the prayers, not seeming terribly interested in them. I've never asked him why he goes to shul if he doesn't really like praying. I can only suppose that it's either from old habit, or out of fear of my grandfather who, like Frumah Tzivele, was fiercely proud of being Jewish and kept a respectable degree of observance. Which is why our home is still kosher and we do not use the electric lights or cook on Shabbos. Uncle Leo was very afraid of his father and though he never says it, is terrified that Zayde will come back from the grave and punish him if he doesn't keep the Sabbath.

As the service ended and the men started shaking hands in Shabbos greetings, I slipped out of the synagogue and rushed home to help with the final dinner preparations. Solomon and Uncle Leo arrived soon after, and the two of them made the blessing over the wine and did the ritual washing of hands. They uncovered the loaves of challah of which I was so proud and blessed them. Thankfully, Mama and Auntie Sylvia had taken pains to present the chicken and kugel in such a way that no one could have guessed that I had carved into them earlier.

"So, Hannah," Uncle Leo began as Auntie Sylvia and Mama fixed our plates, "What's the news from the Golden Land? Did you receive your ticket of passage today?" His voice was full of the anticipation he struggled to hide, and I stared at my plate, dreading to tell him he was stuck with me for at least another year.

"Leo," Auntie Sylvia said in her usual conciliatory way, "Hannah is not going to see Isidore this year."

Uncle Leo cleared his throat, his reddish face pinched. "Oh, I'm sorry to hear that." He took a bite of chicken, but I could tell by his expression he hadn't finished speaking. He often spoke even while chewing. "You see, Hannele," he said, his voice breathy, the way it is when he's covering over how he feels, "you're at that age now when you'll want to consider your opportunities. Certainly you won't want to stay in Wolensk the rest of your life, an intelligent young woman like you."

"I don't know what I want to do yet," I said to him. "I love books. I've thought of working as a librarian, maybe in Warsaw."

"Hannele," Mama said, "Why would you want to go back there? It's so big! Where would you live? Only old maids work in libraries!"

"Mama!" I exchanged a glance with Solomon who sat across from me.

He smiled sympathetically. "Mr. Goldman, I have faith that when the time comes, Hannah will choose wisely."

Uncle Leo's lips tightened into a line and he patted his napkin primly across them. Knowing Uncle Leo, I realized that he was interpreting Solomon's simple remark as insolence. "I'm sure you're right," he answered.

"Well, I'm not worried about Hannele either," Auntie Sylvia said. "I know she will find her way. Let's stop fedraying her with such things." She looked round at all our faces, as if begging us just to be relaxed and happy. I felt sorry for her then, Auntie Sylvia whose role in life largely seemed to be peacemaker between Mama and me on one side and Uncle Leo on the other. She began to ask Solomon about his studies at the Yeshiva where he spent most of his time during the week.

After dinner, Solomon thanked Mama and Auntie Sylvia for having him to supper and shook hands with Uncle Leo whose face turned red. Then, to my relief, we were excused to go and see Reb Weiss.

We walked down the quiet street side by side. At this hour, we were not as concerned about being seen together, as most everyone was still inside having dinner. I guess even the yentas rest on Shabbos.

The spring air was sweet and cool, and I breathed it in the same appreciative way I did the aromas of the kitchen while Shabbos dinner was cooking. In the same spirit of welcoming spring after the long winter, some people had begun to open their windows again. The sounds of laughter and Shabbos songs and dishes being washed drifted in the air of the resting neighborhood.

"I'm sorry about my family," I said to Solomon as we walked the short distance to the synagogue. "My uncle is so annoying. He won't just come out and say he'd like me to leave. He's tired of taking care of my father's responsibilities." I sighed.

"Your uncle is a frightened man," Solomon said. He had a way of encapsulating a person's essence in a mere few words. "It's not your fault, Hannele."

"I feel like it is."

"I promise you, it's not."

We reached the little apartment behind the synagogue and he held the door open for me.

Reb Weiss was sitting at the table, his image outlined in the glow of the candles. In front of him were the remains of the meal I had left for him, and he rested his forehead on his folded hands, softly chanting the grace after meals.

Solomon and I waited for him to finish before approaching. When he looked up at us, the shadows and light played strangely on the deep lines of his face, making his expression appear both smiling and angry. "Solly, I didn't hear you come in." He tugged on his ear. "These ears don't work so good anymore." He chuckled then gestured us to the table. "Come, come. Sit."

"Good Shabbos, Reb Weiss," I said as I sat. I always felt a little nervous around him, knowing that he had never been happy about Solomon's friendship with me. "I hope you enjoyed your dinner."

"I did, Hannele," he said. "It is a mitzvah you do, feeding an old man like me."

I smiled and reached for his dirty plate, but he waved me away from it. "Leave it. Leave it. Just sit and keep me company."

Solomon brought us glasses of tea. Reb Weiss put a lump of sugar between his teeth. Slowly, deliberately, he sipped his tea, then set it down the same way. He studied my face, his eyes watery and sad.

After several moments, he said, "Solly told me about your papa. For this I am very sorry. The bond between parent and child is sacred. A girl should be able to see her papa."

I looked down, fighting back the sudden tears his sympathy evoked. "Thank you. But it will change some day."

"You are always welcome here, Hannele. You know that."

Silently I nodded, not trusting myself to speak without the tears spilling.

"You know that at first I did not think it was good that Solly befriended you. You understand why." Reb Weiss paused and waited for me to nod before continuing. "But I see how you are good for each other. Solly smiles a lot more. You should have seen him as a pitzele. So serious! But I always knew why. He has a great burden on him. Since his birth he has carried this burden. The great ones always do. How can you smile when the Master of the Universe wants so much? But now, burden or not, he smiles. How can I argue with that? I tried at first. But you know, Solly is as stubborn as his papa!" At this, Reb Weiss made himself chuckle. "And you. You see Solly is a good pious man. He don't yell at you because you stay away from shul, and you want to come back. You have some holiness in your life. You look to make some room for the Master of the Universe. This is good. Ha Shem is so lonely in this world the way it is, Hannele. So many of you young people going to all these different ideas. The communism, the socialism, the Zionism. While the Master of the Universe goes begging!"

Solomon gently squeezed his father's shoulder. "It's all right, Papa."

Reb Weiss patted my hand as it rested on the table top. His eyes appeared watery in the candle light. "I'm sorry, Hannele. I go on and on like an old yenta. You see what I'm like. I try to keep quiet, but I'm running out of time, and there is so much wrong! But you are a good girl." He looked up at Solomon. "She is a good girl, Solly."

"I know, Papa," Solomon answered softly.

After a few moments, Reb Weiss slapped his palm on the table top. "I act like it's not Shabbos," he said. "I will rest my tongue. But for speaking. Not for singing. Here, we are not in shul. Hannele will sing *zmiros* with us!" He began a popular Shabbos niggun.

Solomon and I joined him, timidly at first, but then more strongly. Solomon's singing voice was smooth and clear. I glanced at him and he at me. Detecting something more in his expression, I looked down nervously. I lowered my voice a bit and looked only at Reb Weiss from then on, until we had finished singing and it was time for me to go home.

"You will come back and visit, Hannele?" Reb Weiss asked as Solomon held the door open for me.

I nodded, encouraged that he seemed to want me there. "I would like that. Good Shabbos."

"Good Shabbos, Hannele."

Solomon closed the door behind us and followed me on the narrow path that led around the synagogue to the street. From there, he walked at my side. The sounds from inside the houses had quieted, and many of the lights were no longer burning. Our street seemed to glow in its ethereal rest. Truly, time felt suspended on Shabbos. The sense of otherworldliness was so strong, I felt I could almost believe with my whole heart.

"Papa likes you," Solomon said, taking care to keep his voice down. "And believe me, if he didn't, you'd know."

"Really?" I knew how like an eager child I sounded just then. "I've always been afraid he didn't. You know."

He nodded. "I understand."

By now we had reached the doorstep of my house, where we stood together. I sighed and leaned back against the door, staring down at my Shabbos shoes. The tan leather was practically perfect, unscuffed. Their little heels and fashionable buckles seemed out of place.

"What is it?" he asked. "You look troubled."

I shook my head. "Nothing. It's nothing. I'm fine."

He didn't answer for a few moments. "Hannele?" His soft voice matched the stillness of the air.

"Yes?"

"I wish I could make life so that you had never been hurt and would never be again."

I stared at him. "I have not been so hurt. And as for the future, well, there's nothing that can be done about that." My voice was tinged with a bitterness that made me wince, yet I found impossible to suppress. I really was angry.

His expression was sad. "You're referring to me, aren't you? About Chava…and all that."

I shrugged. I always tried to avoid the topic of his betrothal. Besides, why should it really bother me? Neither of us has control over it. I didn't answer.

"If you think you're the only one who feels bad about this, Hannele, you're wrong,"

"What do you mean?" I felt myself becoming suddenly belligerent, wanting to stop, yet unable to. "Don't you want to be the Rebbe?"

Solomon remained quiet for a moment, then sighed. "Sometimes, Hannele. Sometimes I do. I want to serve the Master of the Universe. I want to do His will. But other times…" He made a gesture of frustration with his hands.

"Other times what?" I hated how I was acting, but I was driven to press some kind of assurance from him. Some kind of assurance that for the times we were out of each other's sight, that I still mattered. It was impossible not to believe that when he was married and had a woman to be with all the time and to…do everything with, well, I'd become a faint memory.

"There are other things. I mean, do you believe that He…" Solomon pointed toward the sky, "…would want of me to give up our friendship?"

The plea in his question moved me. It reassured me of my place in his life. But in spite of that, my cynicism had already been set in motion, like a swirling of dead leaves in the wind. I let out a huff. You would think that someone of

Solomon's intelligence and access to God would understand. Didn't he see that our friendship had its proscribed end in the Book of Life? Wasn't God always forcing us to give up one thing for another?

"Please answer, Hannele." Solomon seemed upset too. Only he was more good-natured than I and didn't show it in such an obnoxious way.

I shifted my weight from one foot to the other and looked past Solomon, into the dark stillness. "I would hope not," I said. "But apparently, He does."

He took a deep breath. "I don't want us to fight, Hannele. We should not fight. Especially not on your birthday."

"I don't want to fight either," I muttered. "I can't help it. I just…don't like the way it all works sometimes."

"Me too." He pushed his hands deep into the pockets of his black coat. Several moments of awkward silence passed. "I guess you should go in," he said.

I shrugged. "I guess."

"But maybe we can have a lesson tomorrow evening. I still need to know more Polish for when I go into the army."

I caught my breath. "Maybe you will not have to go!"

But Solomon shook his head. "I'll have to go. I can defer only so many times."

"Never mind." I half-turned, as if to go inside. "I don't like to talk about it."

He smiled at this, keeping his side of the decision not to fight. I did not have so much hope for myself. Then he looked serious. "I will miss you, too, Hannele," he said softly.

My cheeks heated and I was glad the darkness hid their high color. "I'll see you tomorrow night?"

"If Ha Shem wills."

I nodded but then neither of us moved to leave.

"You first, Hannele."

I sighed. "All right," I said. "And thank you again for my gift." At the mention of my beautiful prayer book I was able to smile.

"You're welcome."

Only then did I turn and go in, feeling his eyes on me until I was safely inside.

The house was quiet. I'm the only one who stays up later on Shabbos eve. Mama is tired from teaching all week and Auntie Sylvia and Uncle Leo are always anxious to sequester themselves together in their room, the honeymoon couple that they are, sitting through Shabbos eve supper each week, casting each other special little looks.

I liked to sit up in the kitchen and read while I waited for Maria, the Polish woman who came to turn our lights down on Shabbos. Maria was a large round woman with dark, stringy hair, and her cheeks were so full, her eyes disappeared behind them when she smiled. She and my grandmother had known each other most of their lives and Maria was trusted with the honor of being our *Shabbos goy*, doing all the things on Shabbos for us that we were prohibited to do. And even when my grandparents had moved to their apartment in Warsaw, Maria continued faithfully to come to the house to turn down the lights so that no one in our household would ever have to risk violating the Sabbath laws against using electricity.

Maria was a kind woman and always stayed a little extra time to chat with me in quiet tones before she left, taking with her a small offering of Shabbos food as a thank you for her services. She loved to hear about the books I read, and she loved to talk about her children, two daughters and a son. I could tell by the way she spoke that her son Vlas, was her favorite. I think her adoration of Vlas surpasses even that of Auntie Sylvia's of Yoav.

I had met Vlas on a couple of occasions and realized then that Maria had described her son truly through a mother's eyes. He was five years older than I and tall, with dark hair combed down with some sort of hair grease, and a very strange-looking face with a long neck and pointy nose, which gave him a bird-like appearance. But what he lacked in handsomeness he made up for in talent. He could play a violin to charm the angels from God's side. Maria had had him play for us once several years ago, and even then I knew he'd probably be a great violinist one day. Now he was in the army, but until then he had been playing here in Wolensk in the theater ensemble at the renovated warehouse down by the river.

Maria had been very excited last week because Vlas was coming home from the army. I had to admit I was jealous of the way she went on about him. Certainly, I had never heard Mama or Papa make such a fuss about me. But then, I had no exceptional talents like he did. Loving books and baking good challah don't seem to be the sort of gifts that elevate a human being in the minds of others.

From my bedside table, I picked up the latest novel I'd been reading and went into the kitchen. I fixed myself a glass of tea and sat down at the table to read. A little while later the door opened. I set down my book and looked up to greet Maria. But it was Vlas, not Maria, who came toward me, a wide grin on his strange face. The light reflected the shine on his hair. "Hello," I said.

"Hello, Hannah." Vlas's blue eyes registered amusement at having surprised me. "I'm sorry if I startled you. I know you were expecting my mother." He stood behind a chair in such a way that he seemed to want me to invite him to sit. "She does not let my sisters go out of the house at night anymore. Since the Endecja, you know."

I nodded. "Yes. I know only too well about them. But it's all right. She had told me you were coming home. I'd just forgotten."

He grinned. "So, I can see how much I matter to you," he said, obviously making a joke. But I felt odd about it just the same. "She had to leave unexpectedly for Bialystock. My Aunt Irena fell quite ill and wanted her sister there. But she asked to be remembered to you and wanted me to give you this for your birthday." He pulled a small package out of his pocket and set it on the table.

"Thank you. Maria is very sweet." I reached for the package and unwrapped the tissue, revealing a small bottle of perfume. I smiled and set the delicate glass bottle on the table. "Please thank her for me."

"I will." Vlas remained standing behind the chair, his hands on the back of it, eyeing my glass of tea. Clearly he was not in a particular hurry to turn the lights down and go home.

His presence made me nervous and I felt eager to have him turn down the lights and leave, but I could find no polite way to rush him on without seeming terribly rude. So I offered him tea, which he accepted quite eagerly and drank with excruciating slowness, in silence, gazing at me between sips. The way he stared at me, I felt suddenly naked and looked down to make sure I hadn't changed into my nightgown and forgotten, the way you do sometimes in dreams. But, thank God, I was still in my dress. "How…how is your music?" I asked.

Vlas straightened his shoulders, obviously pleased at my interest. "It is going well," he said. "I play in the army orchestra. We perform for all the highest officers. They made me first seat."

"That's wonderful!" I said, knowing I sounded too enthusiastic. "You must have improved a great deal."

He sat up straighter, as if an invisible hand had administered a shock to him from behind. "I do believe so," he said. "Perhaps you will come to my home and I'll play for you."

I shifted in my chair, uneasy at the thought of being in Vlas's home without Maria there. He was acting quite strange, and I sensed he had more in mind than just playing violin. But I did not want to offend him by directly refusing. "Perhaps sometime I could." I picked up my glass and drank my last sip of tea.

"How old are you now, Hannah?"

"Today I am nineteen," I said, relieved at the change in conversation.

He nodded. "That is what I thought. Will you be going to university?"

I shook my head. "No. My mother and I decided it was too dangerous to go there right now because of the Endecja." Actually, Mama had used my education money to pay our way here with Uncle Leo. So I wouldn't have gone to college anyway even if it had been perfectly safe. But Vlas didn't need to know this.

He frowned. "Yes. It is terrible what they have been doing, starting trouble in the university and everywhere else. I am sorry, Hannah. I feel responsible too. It's wrong to treat the Jews that way. It makes Poland look very bad. We must resist such poisons."

I nodded, remembering that day in the marketplace. I had never forgotten those shouts and that horrible sound of people punching each other, like raw meat being pounded by a hammer.

Then we were quiet again while he finished his never-ending glass of tea. "That was good, Hannah. Thank you."

"You're welcome." I picked up our glasses and washed them at the sink, the whole time aware that Vlas was watching me. I left them to dry and picked up my book. "I'm ready," I told him.

Vlas rose from his chair and pushed it in, taking great care not to make a sound as he did so.

"Don't forget this." I handed him the package of food from dinner.

"Thank you." He accepted the food and stood there, watching me. Actually, appraising might be a better word. "You've grown into a beautiful woman, Hannah."

My face burned and I edged back. So much for my theory of never being noticed by anyone else but Solomon! "Thank you," I mumbled. Now that it had actually happened, I didn't drink it in as I had supposed, but instead, felt uncomfortably suspended between being flattered and frightened. I hurried past him out of the kitchen while he turned off the light behind me.

A slight panic rose in me as he followed me into the living room and switched that light off as well. The Shabbos candles on the dining room sideboard had burned down almost to nubs in their silver holders, so the house was almost in complete darkness. I went to the front door and opened it for Vlas.

He stopped in front of me and stood very close then leaned in toward me, bringing with him the smells of wool and soap. "Good night, Hannah," he whispered. "Good Shabbos. I will see you soon?"

"Uh...yes." I said. "Good Shabbos."

He remained a moment longer, so close that I could feel his breath on my face. Then he turned and started down the front walk to the street.

I closed the door behind him quickly—so quickly, I almost slammed it. With my hand still gripping the knob, I leaned against the door, releasing a loud sigh. Tension drained from my body like a balloon releasing air.

I made my way in the darkness to my room and closed myself inside as if entering a cocoon. I undressed, put on my nightgown and got into bed. I settled in just as Masha jumped up and climbed on me, kneading the blanket over my stomach with her front paws. I reached up and scratched her behind her ears, hoping that petting her would relax me. I felt so strange. The way Vlas had been staring at me haunted my mind. "What's happening to me, Masha?" I whispered, getting only the gentle vibration of her purr as a response.

~~~~~

'You have grown into a beautiful woman, Hannah.' These words have been going around and around in my head since Vlas said them. They were there when I went to synagogue the next morning on Shabbos. They were there through lunch afterward. I could not even nap after lunch like I usually do, and instead, went for a very long walk during which I revisited every nuance of the sound, enjoying the warm ripples that passed through me. I felt flattered and desired. I didn't even care that Vlas wasn't Jewish or that he was so strange-looking. He's a passionate musician, I thought. What does it matter what he looks like?

The only time I became afraid was when I saw Solomon after Shabbos. During our lesson at the kitchen table, he paused and studied my face. "You seem different tonight, Hannele," he said. "Distracted. Are you all right?"

My blood ran cold and I shook my head. "Yes, I'm fine." And then I felt so horribly guilty. I had lied to my best friend! What was to become of me now? But if I had told him the truth, how would he have reacted? He probably would have gotten up and stomped out of the house, refusing to have anything to do with me ever again! How could I take such a chance?

In spite of that, I still could not stop thinking about what Vlas had said and the way he had acted toward me. Yes, he made me nervous, but that must have been because I was completely inexperienced with men.

On Monday morning, my feelings were still as strong as on Shabbos eve. Thinking about them certainly provided a distraction and took the boredom out of doing my chores after everyone else left for work. On Mondays, I do the wash and straighten the house, go to market and prepare supper. Since Mama and I moved in, this has sort of evolved as our system, and I see it as my way of working off my guilt and indebtedness to Uncle Leo for taking us in after Papa left for America.

I was sweeping the front hall when a knock on the door interrupted my reveries.

It was Solomon. My skin prickled with foreboding when I saw him. It could not be good, his coming by on a Monday morning when he should have been at the yeshiva, sitting next to his study partner arguing points of scripture.

He never came by on a Monday morning. Maybe he had figured out why I had seemed distracted the other night and had come to confront me. "What is it?" I asked, gripping the broom handle until my fingers hurt.

"Don't be nervous, Hannah. May I come in?"

"Of course." I let him into the house and closed the door after him. "Would you like some tea?"

He nodded. "Yes, please." He sounded frighteningly docile.

I led him into the kitchen, set down my broom and put the kettle on. I waited a moment, thinking he might say something, but he was sitting at the table, staring down at his hand resting on the wooden surface. I looked at it too. I always liked Solomon's hands, the fingers wide and strong looking. You can see the skill in them, for he does all the repair work on the synagogue himself. You can hear the blows of his hammer ringing down the street when he works. I wonder how many Talmud scholars know how to swing a hammer like that.

When he remained silent, I went about slicing some rye bread I'd baked the day before and set it on a plate in front of him with some butter and pickled herring. I was certain he'd had breakfast, but he was a young man and I'd seen him eat large amounts of food. "Second breakfast," I said, hoping to break the nerve-racking silence with my offering.

He smiled though his eyes reflected sadness. "I'm sorry, Hannele," he said. "Thank you."

I brought our tea and sugar to the table and sat down across from him. Then, as I slid my chair into place, suddenly I knew why he was here. I felt the strangest sensation as the knowledge flooded my consciousness, as clearly as if he had spoken the words. His presence had nothing whatsoever to do with Vlas. I brought my hand to my cheek, the way people do when they feel distress. "You got it today, didn't you? You got your call-up notice."

He nodded. "But listen, Han —"

"You got it fixed, didn't you?" My voice was rising, shrill. "You told me about the fixer in Bielsk. You said you could probably get your term fixed!"

"That's what I'm trying to tell you," he said. "Papa and I are going to see him today. It is said that no Jews he helps do more than five months' basic training."

In spite of his assurances, my breaths began to come in short, sharp gasps and I turned away, mortified at my display of panic. I had been so foolish, convincing myself that Solomon would never go into the Polish Army, even though he had always told me he'd have to. I had convinced myself that they would not want this skinny, pale yeshiva boy with his beard and earlocks and mystical visions. But really, looking at him now, in this moment, I saw how I'd told myself a bunch of lies. Though Solomon was somewhat pale from being indoors so much, he was not skinny or weak. He had grown up playing his share of sports with the other boys. And I had spotted him more than once or twice up on the roof of the synagogue, shirtless, replacing broken shingles. He had as finely muscled a torso and arms as any other athletic boy. Was I really this blind?

I gripped my chair, fighting the sick feeling rising in my stomach. "Solomon, that's almost half a year! What will I...I mean, how will I..." I stopped myself before I spilled over into a ridiculous blubbering heap right in front of him.

His shoulders sagged. "The time will pass quickly. You'll see." He reached for my hand, but stopped, closed his hand into a fist and pulled it away. A flash of anger passed over his face.

I became guilty and afraid. "Are you angry with me?"

He shook his head. "No, I'm not angry with you. Why would I be?"

I shrugged, hiding my relief. "Why don't you have some bread?" I pushed the plate toward him.

"Thank you, Hannele." He picked up a thick slice, buttered it and took a large bite.

I watched him, wishing I had the appetite to join him so he wouldn't eat alone.

When he had finished, he let out a heavy breath and sat back in his chair. "You take good care of me."

My face heated. "Thanks," I muttered and took a quick sip of tea. Silence fell over us again and we both filled it with more sips of tea.

He finally said, "I need your help. Will you look after Papa while I'm gone? I mean, I know there will be others to help him, but... He is fond of you."

I set down my bread. "He is? I mean, I didn't know. Of course I will. I...I'm really glad he feels that way."

He nodded and some of the strain that had been in his face appeared to lift. "Thank you. You share a great burden with me."

Overcome by guilt, I avoided his gaze. He was praising me when I had lied to him just the other night. He doesn't see me clearly most of the time. "When do you go?" I asked, not really wanting to know, but needing to change the subject.

"Soon. After this coming Shabbos."

I nodded and stared at my empty tea glass. "Why, Solomon? Why does God make Jews go into the Polish Army? They don't want us!"

"I don't know, Hannele. I don't think it's that simple."

I looked at him a moment, then away.

He cleared his throat. "I promise I'll come back."

"You'd better."

My remark pulled a wan smile from him. "May I use your bathroom?" he asked.

"Of course."

I washed our breakfast things while he was gone. When I finished and left the kitchen, I expected him to be standing in the front hall, waiting for me. But he wasn't there. Nor was he in the bathroom.

Then I saw him standing in the doorway of my bedroom, peering in. When I approached, he asked, "This is your room?"

"Yes. It was Devorah's room first."

Masha jumped off the bed and came over to be petted. I knelt and picked her up, and Solomon gently scratched her under the chin. I was aware of how close we were standing. He peered again into the room.

"You may go in," I said.

He shook his head. "I cannot. I…should go."

"Okay." My cheeks burned. I set Masha down and followed him to the front door. When I opened it for him, I felt something on my shoulder.

His hand.

Solomon was touching me.

I shivered. He had never touched me before, not even to shake hands. I stood still, letting his hand rest there. It was the first time really any man had touched me besides Papa or Uncle Leo.

His hand felt strong and warm. "I swear to you, I'll come back," he said. "To you and Papa."

He spoke as if he were making a promise to a girlfriend.

I was not that to him. But perhaps it was better that he said such things than not to say them at all. "I know you will," I said.

He didn't answer. He kept his hand on my shoulder a moment longer, then moved it away. I felt a stab of disappointment, but said nothing. We stared at each other.

"Will I see you later?" he asked.

I nodded.

He smiled, but didn't go to leave.

"You first this time," I told him, forcing a smile myself. Usually our parting ritual brought lightness and humor with its promise for the next time. But not today.

After a brief hesitation, he turned and left.

When he had gone, I wandered about the house, unable to pick up my chores again just yet. I had much to think about, too much to feel, and I was overwhelmed. I went into my room and sat on the bed next to Masha, stroking her.

In the last few days I had gotten more bad news from Papa, turned nineteen, been noticed and flattered by Vlas, and was now faced with Solomon going into the army for five whole months.

Five months! Maybe if there hadn't been anti-Semitism there, I wouldn't have been so disturbed. I prayed Solomon would be able to defend himself. I prayed he wouldn't get hurt. I prayed he'd come back alive. Not everyone felt about Jews as Vlas did.

Yes, that was it, why I felt so upset. I tried not to think about the fact that Solomon had touched me. It had only been his hand on my shoulder. But it had been an act of incredible boldness on his part.

I lay on the bed and stared at the ceiling. Through my open window I could hear small children laughing in a nearby yard, and then a mother scolding. Then quiet. The breeze lifted the curtains, softly floating with a whispering sound, that familiar whisper of promises. Promises of everything that was changing. Inside and out.

~~~~~

Solomon was obligated to spend his last Shabbos at the Rebbe's compound. He even was bringing Reb Weiss with him! He told me of his obligation last night. Of course, I had stupidly assumed that Solomon would be here. Horror must have shown on my face because he was so apologetic and begged my forgiveness. After only seconds I found it impossible to feel hurt or angry with him. His sorrow showed me what an important a part of his life I was.

In that moment I felt our friendship was invincible. Not even his impending marriage could touch what we had. So secure did I feel, in fact, that I was able to shrug and say, "What can you do? I'll see you afterward, right?" And Solomon, clearly relieved, had smiled and said, "Of course." And just before he left my house, he turned to me and said, "Please don't worry, Hannele. Shabbos will always be ours."

I went to sleep that night with some peace in my heart. The feeling lasted through most of the morning while I began Shabbos preparations. But in the afternoon, it vanished when I stepped out into the street and saw Solomon helping Reb Weiss onto a waiting cart driven by a young Hasid, a cloth vendor from the marketplace. My strength drained from me and resentment stirred in my heart with my small taste of what it would feel like when he finally left for good. I turned and went back into the house rather than experience the agony and humiliation of watching Solomon pass my house on his way to his bride's home.

I stood at the kitchen door, staring at the mess of the various stages of food preparation. I didn't feel at all like observing Shabbos, especially when images of Chava serving Solomon his Shabbos meal and tea assaulted my mind. I saw him smiling and enjoying it, even looking forward to his wedding night. And then, "Hannah? Who's she?"

I almost left everything and went to collapse on my bed, but I also knew that Auntie Sylvia and Mama would be home soon and would both go at me like a couple of pecking hens if they found this mess. So I forced myself to continue.

Only when the kitchen began to fill with the familiar aroma of challah baking was I glad that I'd gone on. Mama came home while I was grating potatoes for kugel. She washed her hands and put on an apron to help.

I dumped the grated potatoes into a large bowl, mixing them with browned onion, eggs, and flour, listening all the while to a story Mama told about one of the children in her class. I giggled at something she said and looked up.

Yoav walked into the kitchen, commanding the earth as he moved, confident as God, sweeping up all our attention with his grand entrance. "Yoav!" I said, then realized what a sight I must have been in my apron, hair pinned back, smudges of flour on my face. Why couldn't he have warned me? I put down my wooden spoon and went to him. If I had been a dog, I'm sure my tail would have been wagging furiously.

He leaned down casually to let me kiss his freckled cheek. "Hey, molecule brain," he said, ruffling my hair like the dog I felt I was.

I stood where he left me as he went to greet his step-mother. I was, as always, disappointed by his way with me. Stupid... I always hoped for something different. I went back and picked up my spoon to continue mixing.

"All of you wait right here," he said. "I have a surprise for you."

"Where would we go?" said Auntie Sylvia as Yoav left the kitchen. I looked at Mama with raised eyebrows, and she at me.

The door to the kitchen opened again a few moments later and Yoav reappeared. Behind him was a young woman. She was — to my dismay — slender, with clear pale skin and blonde hair brushed so soft it gleamed. She smiled tentatively, looking at us as if uncertain we would like her. "This is Ruthie," Yoav said. He put his hands on her upper arms and gently pushed her toward us, introducing her to each of us with a proud flourish in his voice. Inside I sneered. I'd seen men in the livestock marketplace showing off geese and cows almost the same way!

I forced myself to smile back at her, even though once again I felt my life force draining from me, taking with it any last hopes. My heart began to pound and I looked down, pretending that my kugel preparation was of greatest urgency. Unfortunately, Auntie Sylvia volunteered me to show Ruthie to my room where she would stay with me. To be nice, I even introduced her to Masha, whom she immediately sat down with and stroked, scratching behind her ears, putting Masha into cat heaven.

I wondered who else God planned to take away from me that day.

Later, I went to shul with my prayer book though neither Solomon nor Reb Weiss was there. At least I could hear the beautiful prayers and catch a few glances at Aaron Levi.

During Shabbos dinner, I did my best to appear normal even though I really just wanted to go lie on my bed and cry. I did not join in the kibitzing and curious questions being showered on Ruthie by everyone, including Mama. Instead I devoted my energy to getting through the rest of the meal until I could get away from Ruth and Yoav. They kept exchanging flirtatious looks across the table as if they found each other more delicious than the meal.

After dinner Ruthie and Yoav went for a walk. I wasn't invited and wouldn't have gone anyway. So I stayed behind and insisted on doing all the cleanup myself. Then Mama came into the kitchen to have a glass of tea with me before she went to bed. We sat at the table together, kibitzing about this or that and listening to Auntie Sylvia giggle from the other room. Mama and I rolled our eyes at each other and chuckled. We both knew this was the signal that Uncle Leo and Auntie Sylvia were heading upstairs to their room. Auntie Sylvia always went in front of Uncle Leo who pinched her behind, something he did often and made no effort to hide. If there were other people around who weren't family, Uncle Leo would pretend to be picking a piece of lint off the back off his wife's skirt, remarking about how much he hates dirt. I have to say for Uncle Leo that though he is not a particularly religious man, he certainly fulfills the Talmudic obligation of a man to satisfy his wife at least once a week on Shabbos.

So Mama and I sat, sipped our tea and picked at a plate of almond cookies and honey kleikach left on its plate on the kitchen table. Mama kept saying, "I've got to stop eating these things. Oh, just one more little bite." This is why she is much heavier than she used to be. I do the same, and will probably follow her one day to fatness. Finally, she yawned and came to kiss me good night, leaving her glass for me to wash, which was what I was doing when I heard her call me from the kitchen door. I picked up the dishtowel to wipe my hands when I turned and saw her.

"Someone is here to see you," she said.

My heart squeezed and my mind went into a flurry. Who could it be?

Solomon appeared in the doorway. I stared at him.

"Good Shabbos, Hannele," he said.

"Solomon! I...I...What are you doing here?"

"Hannah, don't be rude," Mama said.

I looked at her. "I'm not. I mean, I didn't expect him."

He smiled. "I'm glad to see you, too."

"Solomon," Mama said, "Go sit and have some cookies."

He bowed his head to her politely as she made to leave the kitchen and bade her, "Good Shabbos." Then he went and did as she said while I fixed him some tea and sat down at the table with him.

The room looked different, as if Solomon had brought the real Shabbos with him and what had been before was people going through rituals that had no real meaning to them. I felt happier, yet embarrassed at what had been a frail greeting. Then, as usual, my cheeks flamed. Good he was here, but what about all the Shabboses to come when he wouldn't be? What then?

"I was worried about you," he said. "I felt like I hurt you by leaving."

I cleared my throat and wondered why I felt a strange tightness in my chest. "No, you didn't hurt me."

He sipped his tea, and his Adam's apple slid up and down. He seemed nervous. "I just wanted you to know I'd come back."

The tension in my chest began to radiate outward, even up into my throat. I pictured him hurrying back here, all that distance in the dark. Perhaps he'd even gotten up and left the table early! "I'm going to get you into trouble, you know."

He shook his head, giving me the terrible feeling I had let him down. "It is not like that, Hannele. And I will be going back there tonight." He watched me for a moment while he sipped his tea. "My going into the army came at a bad time."

I sighed. "When would have been a good time?"

He shifted in his seat. "Well, certainly not right after that letter from your father."

I tried to laugh in an effort to lighten the mood, but the sound came out more like I was choking on a chicken bone, so I stopped. "Oh, that. I'm not so upset anymore. He'll send for me. I know he will. He would have before, but…" I stopped because I could see by Solomon's expression that he didn't believe me. His disbelief was, in fact, like a force that filled the room, making me feel as if I were lying to him. "He loves me," I said. My voice sounded sharper than I meant for it to, so I tried to soften it. "He does, you know. And I have no reason to complain!" When I finished, I gulped my tea, which had not cooled, and burned my tongue. I set down the glass and put my hands in my lap because they were shaking.

He'd been watching me this whole time in that strange way he had, his eyes looking as if all the goldenness were melting, about to pour onto his cheeks. The corners of his mouth turned downward within the confines of his soft dark beard. "All right."

I took another sip of my tea in spite of my shaking hand and burnt tongue. I did not wish to continue speaking about Papa. It would just make me feel sad, and how tired I was of feeling sad. "Really, you need not worry. Drink your tea." I tried to make my voice light, happy.

He eyed me but did not speak further. Amid the silence, I served us each a second glass of tea. Something strange was in the air, a dark, heavy feeling I had carried most of my life and did my best to ignore.

After a little while, I heard the clock chime in the front hall. I remembered then that Vlas would be here soon to turn down the lights. I felt a strange skip in my heart as a sense of anticipation rose, suddenly eclipsing my hurt over Yoav's and Aaron's indifference. When had I grown to be so fickle, so *meshuggah* over men? I had always believed myself to be steadier in heart, after having nursed my devotion to Yoav since I was a little girl. But when he walked into the kitchen this afternoon with Ruth, so proud and happy, so smitten with her, I saw the futility of such wholeheartedness. What did I have left now that he had crushed my heart?

I wiped my damp palms on the skirt of my dress under the table.

"Thank you for the tea, Hannele." Solomon's voice moved through me like a child's tender touch.

"You're welcome." I worried my tea glass between my hands, feeling utterly transparent under his gaze. "I...I'm glad you came over."

"Me too." He shifted in his seat and swallowed. "You know, I can't really go anywhere."

"What do you mean?"

He tilted his head. "I'm not sure. But the words came."

The door to the kitchen opened and Vlas walked in. His eyes widened when he saw Solomon.

"Good Shabbos, Vlas," I said. "Please, meet Solomon."

"Good Shabbos, Hannah," Vlas answered as he nodded politely to Solomon.

Emanating suspicion like smoke from a fire, Solomon nevertheless stood and offered his hand to Vlas.

"Vlas is here in his mother's place while she is caring for her sister in Bialystock," I told Solomon, who scrutinized the newcomer with an expression in his eyes that made me a little nervous. "How is Irena?" I asked Vlas.

"The same," he replied. "Though, by God's grace, she is no worse."

"We will say a prayer for her tomorrow," Solomon told him.

Vlas set a hand on the back of a chair and bowed his head briefly. "Thank you."

"Would you like some tea, Vlas?" I asked.

He shook his head. "No, thank you. I must get home."

"All right." I rose from my chair and picked up the empty glasses. I carried them to the sink and busied myself, glad for the distraction. Behind me, Solomon and Vlas stood in silence, I imagined, watching each other, each wondering to himself what place the other had in my life. In spite of my intense discomfort, there was a shameful thrill in the thought that I could elicit a bout of silent jealousy in two men at the same time, a talent I never in my life imagined I could ever have!

When I had finished with the glasses, I turned back around. Vlas and Solomon would both leave in a few moments and I would be alone in my bed with Masha in the darkness, not knowing what Vlas would have said or how he would have treated me had Solomon not been there.

Solomon and I left the kitchen and Vlas turned down the lights behind us. I opened the front door as he did the same with the lamps in the living room. Solomon waited, standing close to me.

Vlas bid us both good night politely, his demeanor making me feel as if Solomon and I were the master and mistress of the house, leaving us to our Shabbos bed.

When he had disappeared into the night, Solomon turned and faced me. "He likes you. As a man likes a woman, I mean."

Heat swept my cheeks. "You are wrong, Solomon. He does not."

He sighed, a sound I seemed to inspire him to make rather frequently. "With you, I am always wrong, I know. But I am right even though I am wrong. I have seen men like him before. He is selfish and arrogant. And deep down he hates Jews. He'll have his way with a Jewish woman to prove something."

I stared at him. Never in all the time I had known him, had he ever spoken that way about another person. The vehemence in his words gave me a chill. "He's never been anything but polite," I said. I couldn't help feeling that Solomon must be jealous and it made him say such things about Vlas.

He reached for me, then curled his hands into fists and jerked them away. "Please be careful. I'm so afraid for you. I don't want anything bad to happen to you. You're very…" he hesitated.

I braced myself for what he would say, unable as I was to accept such an outpouring of affection from him.

He sighed, his distress palpable in the cool spring air. I shivered slightly and pulled my sweater closer around me. "Special," he said finally, his voice stumbling out in a whisper.

It was my turn to sigh then, a sound he, too, inspired me to make often, though for a different reason. "Solomon…" Tension now gripped me behind my eyes. I searched for words, but I had none. Why must he say such kind and loving things to me? "You're always so worried," I whispered. "I'll be fine."

He bowed his head and the blackness of his hat made him seem to disappear in the dark. Then he looked up again. He seemed at times, like now, to be an old man. "I wish you could keep me here by this," he said, "but there is too much beyond my control."

I shook my head. "You say so many things I don't understand," I said. His mysterious words frustrated me, and I began to feel angry.

"This time I think you do."

"I don't. Solomon, why do you do this?"

He sighed again and pushed his hands into his pockets as he always did. "I just wish I didn't have to go."

At this, my anger vanished. He had voiced what I felt too. "And you think I do wish it?"

Solomon bowed his head. "No, Hannele. I know you don't."

Neither of us spoke after that. I felt suddenly very tired, very weary. Yoav and Ruth would probably return soon from their walk and I wanted to be in bed, pretending, at least, to be asleep. "Shall we have one last lesson?" I asked him in Polish. "Tomorrow evening?"

He nodded. "Yes. Tomorrow," he answered as he had been taught. "I would like that very much." He had learned the language very quickly, almost too quickly, making me suspect a few times that he'd spoken it all along and had asked me for lessons to give him an excuse to be with me. But either way, it didn't matter. He was my best friend. And though the future frustrated me and made me want to say many times, "Let's forget being friends anymore," I just could never do it.

He pushed his hands deeper into the pockets of his long black coat and stepped back. "Hannele?"

"Yes, Solomon?"

"Good Shabbos."

"Yes. Good Shabbos."

We stood there as usual, I waiting for him to walk away, he waiting for me to go inside and close the door. After several moments of this, we finally grinned at each other.

"You first," he said.

I chuckled. "All right." Slowly I turned and went in, closing the door behind me.

I went into my room, using only my knowledge of where everything was to help me get ready for bed in the darkness. I found Masha curled up on Devorah's bed and lifted her, sitting on my own bed to pet her. After several minutes I heard the front door open and close. I set Masha down and got up to greet Yoav and Ruth. In spite of my earlier intention to feign sleep, I would be a terrible hostess if Ruth had to grope about our room in the dark as she got ready for bed.

"How was your walk?" I asked when they saw me, surprised and annoyed at myself that I still searched Yoav's eyes in the dying Shabbos candlelight for any sign of affection from him.

"Just wonderful," Ruth answered. "Your town is quite nice."

Yoav leaned over and kissed Ruth on the cheek. He embraced her and they stood locked together while I waited, feeling like a complete idiot and intruder. Finally they pulled apart. "Go ahead with Hannah," he told her. "I'll be right out here." He indicated the velvet-covered sofa on which Auntie Sylvia had left Yoav clean bedding. He reached out and ruffled my hair. "Good night, monkey face."

If he had pulled out a knife and had stabbed me twenty times in the stomach with it, I don't think it would have hurt as much as him calling me such a name in front of his girlfriend! I clenched my teeth. There was no point in saying anything. There never was with any of these people in my family. "Come, Ruth," I said, struggling not to sound brusque. "It's late."

Ruth followed me into the room and I picked up Masha, who had returned to her customary resting place on Devorah's bed.

"Thank you for letting me stay in your room with you," she said. Her tone was sweet and genuine, making it more difficult to hate her.

"You're welcome," I mumbled and started to unbutton my blouse. "Do you need any help? I know it's very dark in here."

"No, thank you, Hannah. I've grown up not using the lights on Shabbos so I'm used to finding my way in the dark."

I settled under my covers and could hear her doing the same. There was silence for a few moments.

"Boys are terrible teases, aren't they?" I heard her say suddenly.

Some are, I wanted to say, *but Solomon isn't. He's very kind*. Since she did not know him, such a statement would have been meaningless. "Yes, I suppose," I said instead. I lay in the dark, stroking Masha, wondering, as I had so many times whether *I* was the problem. Maybe I was wrong to feel so hurt. Maybe I took offense where none was intended. No one's family could be that cruel. Some of the fault had to lie with me. After all, I was the intruder here, wasn't I?

What a mess everything was! As my eyes grew heavier, the last question in my mind was, if I was one of God's chosen people, what exactly was I chosen for?

~~~~~

On the last day before Solomon went into the army, he asked me to meet him at the edge of the *puszcza*, the primeval forest on the outskirts of Wolensk. The forest is so large that if you went into it near our town and kept walking all the way to the other end, you would come out in Bialystock, quite a few kilometers from Wolensk.

Nervously, I waited for Solomon in the meadow that borders the forest. We had never done anything like this before and my stomach tingled even well before I saw his black-garbed figure in the distance, making his way toward me. Until now, our friendship had been limited to sitting in our kitchens and occasional walks back from the postal station. I felt now like we were somehow going against the entire world just by being out here together in the daylight.

Solomon approached me, looking nervous and sheepish both. Certainly, he seemed to feel the same way I did. He motioned to me with his hand. "Come, Hannele," he said and went ahead of me.

I followed him along the edge of the meadow, in the warm sunlight, feeling a sense of daring and intrigue I had never before experienced. He led me into the forest through a large gap between two tremendous pines. Almost instantly, the world became darker and cooler, and so quiet I could hear the soft bed of dead pine needles crunch under my shoes.

Solomon led me in a bit farther, then stopped at a tree so thick and huge, we could both lean our backs against it at the same time and still not be on opposite sides. I breathed in the loamy scent of the mushy pine needles and black earth. Above our heads, only narrow slivers of sunlight penetrated the forest's canopy. An occasional breeze bent the treetops, and they swayed like the bodies of men at prayer. We looked at each other and smiled.

A mischievous gleam came into his eyes, one I'd seen before, but not for a long time. "What do you think?" he asked.

I sighed. "It's beautiful in here, Solomon. So different than how it seems from outside."

"Yes, it is. I've spent a great deal of time in here. I wanted you to see it."

I smiled at him, though I knew my cheeks were burning an embarrassing pink.

He glanced at me, then away, and we continued to lean against the tree, listening to the undulating stillness of the forest.

After a while the light filtering through the trees began to slant and fade. Solomon stood up, away from the tree. "I have something else for you to see." He started back the way we had come and I followed him out of the forest, across the meadow, farther down along the river where anyone hardly ever goes. There, sheltered by a growth of trees, was the old mill, built probably a century and a half before, abandoned for a larger building when the population grew. I'd heard of the place, but had never seen it. I suspect it was used now on summer evenings as a meeting place for young lovers. I guessed that Aaron and Eva had come here, too, at some time.

Solomon pushed open the rickety door and stood aside for me.

I brushed past him. Inside was dark and cool, and smelled of rotting wood. I stepped gingerly across the dirt floor toward the old wheel and millstone. I ran my fingertips over the rough, speckled surface. How long it had been since I had explored like this! Not since I was a little girl.

He came closer, watching me, his face silhouetted in the meeting of shadow and light. I couldn't see his eyes, but his quiet nearness made me suddenly, uncontrollably nervous. I crouched where some old planks had been nailed across the open rickety floor. "Look! The river passes right beneath us!"

He knelt nearby and we watched the water swirl and gurgle past.

"It's amazing, isn't it?" I said and looked up at him.

His gaze trapped mine. "Yes, Hannele," he murmured. "Amazing."

I wanted to look back at the water, but couldn't pull my gaze away, held by the rich melting amber of his eyes. I stared until I felt a terrible ache. I felt like I was disappearing and that I could fall right through spaces between the boards, float away with the rising water. I blinked rapidly and looked back down, refusing to raise my head again.

"We must not come here again, Hannele," Solomon said.

"Why?"

"Please, don't make me explain."

I felt my cheeks burn anew, then waited while he rose and gestured for me to follow him. "Come," he said. "Let's go back."

I nodded and followed him as far as the edge of the shtetl, where he let me go ahead of him. I walked home, glancing back every few minutes, afraid, always afraid that if I didn't, Solomon would disappear.

The next morning, I woke up with that same tightness in my chest and throat that I'd been feeling lately. Only this time it was in my stomach, too, and all I could take at breakfast was some tea. When I finished it, I put some food together in a package for Solomon to take along on his journey to the army base on the outskirts of Warsaw somewhere, and left the house.

Outside, the day was brilliant, the kind that makes you feel guilty if you stay inside, that perfect weather, not too hot or cold with the kind of breeze that whispers only of good things. Only today, life didn't feel like it held the good things promised by the breeze.

Solomon answered the door at my knock and I almost stepped back in my shock to see him in an army uniform with shiny buttons and a smart-looking cap. "Hello, Hannele," he said. A strange little smile came to his lips, and the look in his eyes seemed to say, "Yes, I know how different I look." Then he stood aside for me to come in.

"Hello." I stared, knowing I shouldn't, but I couldn't help myself. He looked so different, strange, and several moments had passed before I realized that his earlocks no longer hung down on either side of his face! I had never seen him without them! What was happening? "Solomon!" I exclaimed softly, "Your *payos*! They're...gone!"

"Not completely." He bowed his head, showing me how he had cut them, leaving just enough of his hair to tuck them invisibly behind his ears. "I'm not ashamed of who I am," he added. "I just don't want to take any chances."

I sighed. Solomon's ingenuity brought a surge of pride in me, but at the same time, the sight of him without his *payos* was disturbingly unnatural, the kind of thing that made me shudder inside about the ugly nature of human existence.

Solomon closed the door behind me and ushered me in. Reb Weiss sat in a chair at the wooden table, his thick gray hands covering his face. His poor old body heaved with the pathetic huffs of old sobs. Solomon went over to his father and knelt down, putting his hands on the elderly man's shoulders. "I will be all right, Papa. I promise." Then he held him, rocking him as he would a child.

The sight of them together sent a pang through me that came from some invisible depth somewhere, and I turned away just slightly, waiting, feeling very much like an intruder.

"Sha, sha," I heard Solomon say in a low soothing voice. "The time will pass quickly, you'll see. And Hannah is right nearby."

"I know. I know." Reb Weiss's voice was thin and old with sobs. "Listen to me. I *pisch* like a baby! But I never thought to see my scholar look like a soldier. What kind of world is this? So many changes! So many changes! May Ha Shem bless you and keep you, Solly. My precious son!"

I heard Solomon stand up and turned to look at him and his father. He leaned down and kissed Reb Weiss's sagging cheek, then put his hand on the elderly man's shoulder. Reb Weiss reached up and put his hand over it and they stood like that a moment. Then he gave Solomon's hand a couple of pats.

Then Solomon came over to me. He was looking at me intensely "Will you keep him company a while?"

I nodded. The rush of intense feelings had been made bearable by an onset of numbness. And I could only look at Solomon from this eerie neutral plateau. His army uniform now seemed a dream costume of some sort.

"I will miss you, Hannele."

Strange tremors came around my eye sockets, and I blinked several times.

"Will you miss me?" He sounded like a pleading child. "Please say you will if it's true."

"Of course I will! You're my best friend! Why wouldn't I?" And what I said was true, only I was so terrible at saying such things that brusqueness helped them come out.

Solomon smiled. "Am I really?"

"Yes!" Then I held out the food I had packed for him. Fresh bread, cold chicken and various sweets. "This is for you. For your trip."

"Thank you." He accepted the package. "You take good care of me."

In my head I thought, *Until Chava does.* But I said, "You're welcome, Solomon. Please come back safely. And write to me."

"I will. I promise." Solomon nodded. An unexpressed embrace seemed to hang in the air between us. Shouldn't friends embrace at times like these? I thought maybe he would put his hand on my shoulder like he had the other day. I was now waiting for that, too. But he didn't.

Images followed on my words of Solomon in his uniform, being beaten up by some large, ruddy-faced Polish peasant. I shook them away. "Please," I said again. Five months! It may as well have been five years.

A faint smile came to his lips. "I guess I'll go first," he said. He turned and carried his package to the front door where his satchel waited. He picked it up and opened the door, letting in light from the brilliant spring morning. I watched him step out the door, leaving darkness again as he closed it behind him. And then he was gone.

I stood quietly in the spot where Solomon had left me, picturing in my mind the image of him walking down the street in his uniform, satchel in hand. He was still nearby, near enough that I could see him if I only opened the door and looked out. Near enough to hear me if I called to him. But soon, very soon, he would not be.

This situation was unbearable — Solomon going into the Polish Army as a Jew, and his old father sitting there sobbing, and me, wondering and worrying about his safety, and waiting. All my life was about waiting, it seemed. Not finding a career. Not getting married and fruitfully multiplying like a good Jew should. Just waiting. Waiting for Papa to send for me. And now waiting for Solomon to come home from the army. Waiting for the old Rebbe to die so Solomon could marry Chava and take his place. Waiting for him to end our friendship.

Once again, I felt drained of all my strength and wished nothing more than to go home and collapse on my bed. Then

I heard a sniffle behind me. Reb Weiss! The poor man! How selfish I was being! I turned and went over to him. I wished I could say something to comfort him, but no words would come. Gingerly, I sat down in the other chair.

He was the picture of misery. One hand covered his face, while the other lay, palm down, on the surface of the table, the fingers gnarled with rounded, arthritic knuckles and tough skin.

Softly, I put my hand over his, not certain if I was doing the right thing. But when I did so, suddenly there were words to say. "Solomon is a strong man," I said, not knowing where the words came from, but knowing somehow that they were true. "He'll command respect in the army as he does here at home."

Reb Weiss uncovered his face. His eyes appeared tired and watery from years of studying scripture by dim candlelight. "From your mouth to His ears," he answered, pointing a finger toward the ceiling. "Where Solly is going, they don't look for scholars of Toyreh."

I smiled and we sat together for a little while with my hand still resting on his. These moments with Solomon's father were comforting and I found myself wishing that I belonged here and that Reb Weiss had found me along with Solomon on his doorstep. I don't think I would have minded the poverty if I could have had a father like Reb Weiss.

"Hannele," he said, "I am going to make some tea. You will have some, yes?"

I nodded. "Yes. "I'd like that."

With a quick pat on my hand, he stood up went to the small stove. I watched him prepare the glasses for tea, his movements slow and deliberate. Solomon moved that way too, not slowly, really, but deliberately, as if every small detail were worthy of his complete attention.

We chatted a little about the cheyder students while waiting for the water to boil. When it did, Reb Weiss went to rise again but I stopped him. "Please, let me."

"Thank you, Hannele," Reb Weiss said, patting my hand again. "Solomon has to do many things for me lately. I do not get around so good as I used to."

"Please don't worry. I'm happy to help you." I prepared the tea and brought our glasses to the table.

"You are a good girl, Hannele. I see why Solly is so devoted to you."

I glanced away, as I always did when praised. "He is a very good friend to me."

"I must have done something good in this life to have been blessed with such a son," Reb Weiss said. He put his sugar cube between his teeth and took a sip of tea, his silvery gray *payos* swaying slightly. I had seen Solomon do this countless times. How like his father Solomon was in some ways. Reb Weiss shook his head sadly. "He is too good for this world." He looked at me with his watery eyes. "Ha Shem is very lonely in this world, Hannele."

I did not answer. I thought angrily for a moment that of course He is lonely because He abandons us, but I was afraid of offending Reb Weiss who would surely send me away.

After our tea I washed the cups and swept the floor.

"I am grateful for your help, Hannele," he said after I had set the broom in the corner. "I used to be too proud to accept help. But now I have no choice. The Master of the Universe teaches us whether we wish to learn or not."

"I will help you any way I can," I told him as I pushed my chair into the table. "I must go to my uncle's store now. But I will come by later."

Reb Weiss smiled, though his face looked painfully like a gray empty sack. "You're a good girl, Hannele."

I left and began my walk to Polaski Street. A refreshing breeze lifted the clothing hanging on lines in different yards, flapping them like banners, and the world was greener now with approaching summer. But it all felt strangely hollow. Even Reb Weiss's little apartment had seemed drabber and darker. I tried only to think about tonight when Mama and I would go to the moving pictures. If you see enough moving pictures, you have a whole other world to think about, full of beautiful people who love each other forever. A much better world than this one. I mean, what kind of god would force a pious Jew like Solomon to leave his old father alone to serve his term in the anti-Semitic Polish Army? I sighed and looked ahead of me as I made my way to town.

~~~~~

Vlas turns down the lights in the living room, plunging us into the fading half light of the dying Shabbos candles, then takes my hand... "Come, Hannah," *he says.* "Sit with me." *He pulls me through the darkening room toward Auntie Sylvia's sofa, bringing me to sit very close to him. Suddenly, his hands are on my back, rubbing.* "You've grown into a beautiful woman, Hannah," *he whispers in my ear. His voice is slithery and hot in my ear.*

I know he's telling me that so I will give myself to him. But I love to hear those words. It's wrong for me to let him do this, perhaps the most wrong thing I could ever do. But I'm so tired of feeling so alone all the time, that I don't care about right and wrong anymore. I've given up.

"Hannele, how could you do this?" a voice says from somewhere in the darkness. It's Solomon, and I pull away from Vlas, terrified that Solomon will hate me.

Vlas disappears and Solomon sits down in his place and puts his arms around me. "You're mine, Hannele," he says. "Don't you ever go near him again. Don't you know that's the way it should be?"

I smile, joyful that Solomon has finally said something, that he's finally taken a terrible burden away. I'm so happy I can't stop smiling. "Yes, Solomon. It is."

Then Solomon holds me tight and caresses my hair. I feel so safe and happy. I smile more in my joy…

Sudden light pierced my eyelids. I opened my eyes, my lips still curved in a smile. Solomon was gone, and I was in my bed. I looked around the small bedroom. No one was there except for Mashele, curled up in a dark ball on Devorah's old bed.

I looked up at the ceiling and shivered. The dream had felt so real. I had even been smiling when I woke up. But of course it was just that—a dream. Solomon was in the army. He'd left two days ago. Was it really only two days? Never before had two days seemed such a long time. And besides, Solomon would never say anything in real life like he'd said in my dream.

Then I remembered Vlas had been there too. In real life, Vlas wouldn't be taking my hand and touching me the way he had been. That kind of thing between Jewish women and Polish men didn't happen in Wolensk. Probably because the last Jewish woman to have an affair with a Pole had been forced by the Jewish elders to leave Wolensk. Can you imagine? Sent into exile by her own people? You'd think we'd know better than that after all our history!

Even so, in spite of all its unreality, the whole dream, from start to finish, stayed with me all morning, and into my work in Uncle Leo's store. So strong was it that even the special used book corner Uncle Leo had let me have in the store couldn't distract me.

Usually, I can get lost in the world of my books. In some of them, you can find a world just like in the moving pictures. There are many love stories written in Yiddish with girls like me in mind. And the time passes so quickly when I read them. Sometimes I can get so absorbed while reading someone can be calling my name and I won't even hear them! I collected so many of these stories over the last few years that Uncle Leo let me take a small corner of shelves to sell them for a couple of groschen apiece. Some of the customers have even brought in books they don't want any more just so I can sell them for pocket money. I guess it's my way of dealing with not having become a librarian in Warsaw. I tried to work at the library here, but the Wolensk library is not as large and there is already enough staff.

So I content myself with my used book corner, which I keep well dusted and alphabetized by author, which was what I was doing when Uncle Leo called my name from the cash register. I looked up at him. "Yes?"

"Would you do something for me?" he asked. "I need you to go across to Levi's store and pick up the shirts I ordered and bring them home. I can't leave here just yet."

My chest felt then as if someone had flung a rock at it. Going to Levi's meant seeing Aaron who worked regularly for his father and would certainly be there! So nervous did I become that I didn't even bristle at his request like I usually did. Not that I mind running errands for Uncle Leo, it's just that I hate the way he asks, as if I don't know he only asks me because he doesn't trust me to look after the store in his absence. "Yes," I said as calmly as I could. "I'll go." My voice sounded thin and papery as it always does when I'm nervous.

"Thank you, Hannele," he said. "I will see you at home then."

I nodded, thinking he might have noticed I had started shivering. But when I looked up, Uncle Leo was already busy with something else. "Yes, at home," I repeated.

I went into Levi's store with my stomach lurching. I looked for Aaron behind the cash register counter, but I didn't see him. In the corner of the store by the back was a small podium used for tailor fittings. Jack Pearlman was standing on it in a new suit. That's when I saw Aaron. He was crouched down, pinning up the legs of the trousers.

"Hello, Hannele," Mr. Pearlman said.

"Hi, Mr. Pearlman."

"Aaron," Mr. Pearlman said, "You can finish my trousers later. You shouldn't keep a pretty girl waiting."

I smiled at him, knowing my cheeks had flushed a deep pink. "It's all right," I said. "I'm not in a hurry." I began to shiver and turned away, concentrating my attention on the glass case underneath the register which held an assortment of cuff links. I remembered that case well, having bought my father a pair of them for his birthday several years ago. On top of the case was a small rack of ties.

Then I heard Mr. Pearlman thank Aaron and go into the back to change. Then Aaron stepped up next to me at the counter.

"Hannah?" Aaron said my name as if he had never seen me before. He set down his little box of pins and took his tape measure from where it had been dangling from around his neck. He set them on the counter. He smiled, looking at me the same way as Vlas had the other night. For one brief moment I wondered if they were actually one soul sharing two different bodies.

"Hello," I said. "I came for my uncle's shirts."

Aaron raised his eyebrows as if I'd said something in a strange language.

"He ordered two shirts?" I said. "Leo Goldman?"

"Oh, yes. I'll get them." He disappeared in the back room for a few seconds then came out and put a brown paper package on the counter. "They're already paid for," he said.

"Okay." I picked up the shirts.

Mr. Pearlman came out then and asked Aaron to let him know when his suit would be ready. We both bid him good-bye and he left.

I, too, should have left. But like an idiot I stood there, struggling to find a question to ask Aaron, or anything to say, just to be able to stay there a little longer. After all, when would be the next time? But I couldn't think of a thing, I was so nervous. "I guess I should go."

"How have you been, Hannah?" Aaron asked suddenly.

Joyfully I abandoned my pretense of leaving. "I've been fine, thank you. And you?"

"Very well, actually. I received some photographs from my cousin who immigrated to Palestine." He sounded very proud and excited. "Would you like to see them?"

I couldn't believe that Aaron Levi was offering to show me his photographs. How could I refuse? "Oh, yes!"

Aaron went in back again then came out with a package in his hand. He brought it over and stood close to me, his shoulder touching mine as he showed me each picture. "That's Emil there." He pointed to a young man on a horse. "He lives on a kibbutz now." The terrain in the background looked very rocky and dry, but the man on the horse was smiling as if he felt free.

"Your cousin looks very happy," I said.

"He is." Aaron set down the photograph and looked at me. "I tell you, Hannah, Palestine is the place for our people now. Poland is dead. Our people are dying here. There is nothing but death now."

An eerie shiver ran through me at his words. What about the people like Solomon who were alive with their love of God? Didn't they mean anything? "Do you really believe that?" I asked.

"Yes."

"Will you go to Palestine too?"

"I am waiting on my papers," he said. "My mother and father wish for me to be at home a bit longer. They are afraid now, you know…after what happened to Shmulek."

I nodded and continued to stare at the photograph of his cousin. The wide open spaces and seemingly endless sky of this rugged country made me wonder whether Solomon had ever thought to go to Palestine. He's never spoken of it, not once, and I knew he would never leave Reb Weiss to go anywhere.

"I can't wait to go there," Aaron said. "I want to start a new life."

"I wish you luck."

"Thank you." Aaron glanced at his wristwatch. "Excuse me a moment. I must lock the front door."

"Oh, I'm sorry. I didn't realize how late it was. I won't keep you." Sick with disappointment, I made to leave.

He reached out and squeezed my shoulder. "Don't go now, Hannah. Wait with me a few minutes? We'll leave through the back door."

"What?" I said almost dizzy from the feeling of his hand on my shoulder and his wanting me to stay there, alone, with him. "All right, yes!"

He took his hand away and went to lock the front door and then led me to the back room where there were two chairs and a small table. "Have a seat," he said.

I sat down, praying that I did not look as nervous as I felt.

He sat down in the other chair. "I'm sorry, Hannah, I should not have invited you back here. I forgot about your boyfriend."

"Boyfriend?" I was genuinely puzzled.

"Yes, the Hasid."

I almost jumped up off the chair! He thought that Solomon was my boyfriend! . I did not even know when he would have seen us together, but it was possible. There were those times when Solomon met me in front of the postal station. Did we appear so intimate?

I did not answer right away, and realized suddenly that the way he had said, "the Hasid," seemed derogatory and I wanted to retort, "Where's your girlfriend, the starlet?" But I was so enthralled by Aaron and being here with him that I said nothing in Solomon's defense. "Oh, you mean Solomon," I said with a forced chuckle. "No, we're good friends, that's all." A sudden guilt gnawed at me just then, but that, too, was overshadowed by my feminine enslavement.

Aaron grinned. "Well, then, I guess I'm not sorry." He leaned forward in his chair, closer to me, so close that I could smell the faint scent of cologne. He reached up and touched my cheek.

I blinked as the room tilted to one side, then the other. The feel of his breath on my face was intoxicating.

"May I, Hannah?" he whispered.

I blinked again, fighting with my body not to fall off the chair. "You want...to kiss...me?"

"I know it's fast, Hannah, but I can't help it. When you walked in the store, it was like I'd never seen you before. You've gotten so pretty. And then you listened to me go on about Palestine. Most girls get bored by that." He reached out and took my hand.

"What about Eva?"

Aaron glanced away for a moment. "We...uh...broke up. It's been some time now." He looked into my eyes. "So? May I?"

I nodded, even though I knew I should not have. I mean, what kind of girl would allow a boy to kiss her after merely giving her a few pretty words? Certainly a weak one of low moral fiber.

He leaned forward and kissed me, a tentative peck on the lips, at first. Then he paused, as if waiting to see what I would do.

And what did I do? Nothing. Nothing but wait for him to kiss me again, which he did, longer, this time, with his whole mouth. I felt as if my insides would explode from the excitement as the mysterious world of what men and women do together began to reveal itself to me, the feel of it and the taste, the softness of Aaron's hair as I reached up to touch it.

So intoxicating was it that not even a distinct sense of doom could tear me from these kisses. I could not stop. I could no more have moved from that chair than I could have sprouted wings and flown to America to see Papa. Even the fact that Aaron was going to immigrate sometime soon to Palestine did not compel me to get up and leave. Only when I knew that I absolutely must get home or my lateness would be questioned, was I able to pull away from Aaron and tell him so.

He grinned at me. "Will I see you again?"

Mutely I nodded. Of course he would!

Aaron led me out the back door. Once outside, he kissed my lips one more time. "See you soon, Hannah."

"Yes, soon." I forced myself to turn and walk down the alleyway, around the corner and back to the main street. I practically floated home, a smile on my lips the whole way.

That evening I could barely eat my supper my stomach was so tight inside. I could think of nothing else but that hour or so I had spent with Aaron. I still could not believe that he had wanted to kiss me!

"Hannah, why is it you pick at your food like a little bird?" Mama asked me. "You're a young lady, not a sparrow."

I looked up at her. "I don't know. I'm just not very hungry."

Mama furrowed her brow. "Since when are you not very hungry? You love Auntie Sylvia's cooking!"

"She is tired from working with her books," Uncle Leo said.

I looked over to him. He was actually smiling, and I felt confused. Who could understand Uncle Leo? He made me feel most of the time like a burden he couldn't wait to get rid of, and then, in a moment here and there, he seemed to be actually nice.

Mama released a sigh of obvious frustration. She did not know my life and was not happy about it. "You may be excused if you wish."

"Thank you," I answered, glad for the chance to escape to my room where I could lie on my bed and think only of what had happened that afternoon, telling Masha about it in hushed whispers as I stroked her.

All the next day I waited, my stomach in knots, my hands shaking, for Aaron to come see me. Surely he would, now that we had shared something so sweet and intimate as kisses. All the time I worked in the store, I looked every few seconds to the door, hoping to see him coming in, maybe with flowers or something like that, wanting to take me to the moving pictures where we could sit in the dark, holding hands the whole time. But he didn't. He must have been busy, I thought. But even so, if I was important to him at all, he should have come. Didn't he realize the next evening was Shabbos? The afternoon was a time of preparation. No time for a secret tryst.

But then I remembered I would see him at shul, and then maybe we could go for a walk after supper, holding hands and kissing good-night. Until then, I was content to remember over and over, those kisses. Was there anything better than that in the whole world? I didn't think so.

~~~~~

"Solomon, you're back so soon!" I am weak with gladness.

We are standing in my kitchen. He smiles, tall and handsome in his army uniform. "I told you, Hannele, the time would pass quickly," he says. I almost reach for him, but then I frown and turn away. I can see into my bedroom when I turn. "It's Shabbos," I say. "You will be at the Rebbe's for Shabbos."

Solomon puts his hands on my shoulders. "I would not let Shabbos pass without seeing you. Ha Shem has made a space for us. Don't you know that?"

When he says this, I feel happy enough to float into the clouds, and I turn to embrace him.

But when I do he is gone.

Panic grips my being and I opened my eyes to look for him…

A pair of eyes were staring into mine. "Solomon!" I whispered and stared back. The eyes blinked. Green and almond shaped. Masha.

Masha's front paws kneaded my chest over the covers. She mewed for her breakfast. I wanted so badly to remain under the covers a while longer. I felt shaken by my dream, and yet still wanted to lie there and think about the other day in Levi's store. But I could not, in conscience, let my cat go hungry. "All right, Mashele, I'm getting up."

I shoved the covers off and sat up, pushing my feet into my slippers, as I did first thing each morning because my feet were always cold, even in summer. Masha followed me into the kitchen. "What has happened, Masha?" I said to her as I took some chicken liver from the ice box and mashed it up on a plate. But Masha only mewed again as I put the plate down on the floor, next to her water bowl.

As I filled the tea kettle at the sink, I looked out the window to the synagogue. A sudden pang stabbed my chest when I thought of how far away Solomon was. He would probably find some nice Jewish family to invite him to Shabbos dinner. And they would probably have a beautiful daughter. "What a baby you are, Hannah," I said to myself as I put the kettle onto the stove. When had I let this happen? How was it that Shabbos and Solomon for me had become so deeply intertwined? Is that why I dreamed of him and not Aaron?

That evening after shul, I waited outside the synagogue for Reb Weiss, who was coming to our house for Shabbos dinner. I stared at the synagogue door, watching for Aaron. I was sure he would come right up to me, letting the world know what was now between us. I straightened my shoulders when he came outside with his father, waiting for him to notice me. But when he did, he only smiled and gave a slight wave with his hand. I stared at him, my skin prickling cold over my whole body. Why didn't he come over? I waited, staring at him, as if willing him to approach me. Then he and his father headed in my direction, and I felt a surge of hope. That is, until I realized they were walking in the direction of their house.

"Good Shabbos, Hannah," Aaron said to me as he and his father passed.

My shoulders sagged. "Good Shabbos. See you next week?"

"Yes, next week," Aaron said, but there was no sign in him of the ardor he had shown me just a couple of days before. Maybe he felt strange with his father right there. A small light of hope burned.

Then Reb Weiss came over and took my arm so I could help him with the short walk to my house.

During the meal, thankfully, no one in my family started with me about my future as they had when Solomon was here. In fact, they were quite pleasant. We had just finished when Reb Weiss closed his eyes and began to chant the Grace After Meals. We joined him and when we'd finished, he began to sing: "Bim, bam, bim bim bim bam, bim bim bim bim bim bam." The melody of Hasidic song.

The sound came out so slowly and tremulously at first that only I, who had sung zmiros before with him and Solomon, realized that's what he was doing. He tapped the palm of his hand on the table top in time to the singing. There was a compelling joy in the sound, and soon, I joined in with him, followed by everyone else, Mama, Uncle Leo and Auntie Sylvia. I, too, tapped my hand on the table as the spirit of the Shabbos songs drew me out. As I sang I looked at Reb Weiss, who had surprised us with the zmiros, seeing again, how much Solomon was like his father. This made me feel, for a few moments, that Solomon was here with us rather than in some horrible army barrack somewhere.

When it was time for Reb Weiss to leave, he thanked everyone for Shabbos dinner and for the company. I hoped that Uncle Leo or Auntie Sylvia would say something to him about being invited the following Shabbos, but neither did. I knew that I would have to see what I could do.

I walked Reb Weiss back to the synagogue. He held my arm at the crook of my elbow. Walking was difficult for him and he limped from an injury he had received as a boy when a cart overturned on him. But at the same time, there was a strength that emanated from him the way the earthen scent of pine emanated from the trees and the floor of the primeval forest. "Just leave me at the front here, Hannele," he said as we neared the synagogue. "I must see that all is well here before I can sleep." He winked and patted my hand before releasing me. "Good Shabbos, Hannele. You do a mitzvah looking after an old man like me."

I smiled. "I would do it whether it were a mitzvah or not. Good Shabbos, Reb Weiss." God, how I wished it was a few hours earlier and that we had the whole evening to do again, just the same.

"Tonight we will pray to Ha Shem that he will keep our Solly in his arms, yes?" Reb Weiss said.

"Yes." I nodded, feeling suddenly very sad. "Reb Weiss, would you like me to wait for you to finish?" I wanted so much to stay there with him. "Is there anything you need me to do?"

"No, Hannele, thank you. I will be only a minute in here. But you will come see me tomorrow, yes?"

I nodded. Tomorrow seemed very far away. "Yes. Tomorrow."

I walked slowly home, enjoying the cool night air. But as I approached my front door I remembered that Vlas would soon be here. I felt my stomach tighten, especially when I remembered what Solomon had said to me about him. But now Solomon was not here. I would have to get used to his not being here. Even though he was coming back from the army, the day would come when Rebbe Zalman died and Solomon took his place. As a Hasidic rebbe with a wife and followers, he would exist in an entirely separate world from me, even though he would be living just on the outskirts of the Jewish quarter. I would need to have my own life.

When I went into the kitchen, Mama and Auntie Sylvia were busy doing dishes and putting leftover food away. I felt a bit guilty for having enjoyed myself walking Reb Weiss home while they worked. "I will finish," I told them, "There is only a little bit left."

"All right, Hannele." Mama rubbed her lower back with one hand. "You are younger and stronger." She smiled then kissed me good night.

Auntie Sylvia kissed me on the cheek. "Good Shabbos, Hannele." I knew by the tone in her voice that she was happy to be free to go to bed with Uncle Leo. I smiled to myself and shook my head as I went to finish cleaning the kitchen from dinner.

When I was done I settled down at the kitchen table with my book and my tea, but I found it difficult to concentrate. My eyes looked at the words, yet two whole pages could pass by without my remembering any of it.

The house had been slumbering in Shabbos quiet for quite a while when I heard the front door quietly open. Vlas walked into the kitchen. I looked up when he came in, my heart giving a sudden thump in my chest.

"Hello, Hannah. Good Shabbos," he said.

"Good Shabbos." I set down my book.

He stood, watching me.

"Would you like some tea?"

Vlas looked puzzled. "Yes, I would. But is it all right?"

I furrowed my brow. "Yes," I answered, not understanding his hesitance. "Of course."

He smiled, looking relieved, then seated himself politely, almost primly, at the kitchen table.

I made him a glass of tea, struggling as I did so to keep my hands steady, especially when I served him.

"Thank you," Vlas said. He sipped his tea, eyeing me as I sat back down in my chair. "Hannah, what I meant before to say…is it all right for me to be here with you, alone like this?"

I looked at him. "I don't understand."

"Well, you are engaged," he said. "Was that not your fiancé I met last week?"

"Oh!" I exclaimed, as understanding flooded in. How could I have forgotten? "No!" Then I giggled, a strange sound more like choking. "We're not…we're…Solomon is my dear friend." But immediately when I saw the expression on Vlas's face I wondered if I should just have allowed him to continue believing that Solomon was my fiancé.

"I see," he replied. The Vlas I had known before seemed to return instantly, and I realized that I had opened some sort of invisible gate.

I sought quickly for another topic. "You know, Vlas," I said, "I have been meaning to tell you how well you play violin. You should be in an orchestra in Warsaw."

Vlas raised his eyebrows as if such praise had come directly from God. "Thank you, Hannah!" He leaned forward in his chair. "I am so happy you said that! I have been considering trying to get an audition there, but I have been afraid. Now I know I must try!"

I smiled. "I hope you would go no matter what I said. How could a few words from me be so powerful?"

Vlas's eyes had that look in them, the one I had seen the first night and I immediately felt the accompanying flutter in my gut. "That is the power of a beautiful woman."

My face began to burn and I looked down at my empty tea glass.

Vlas reached out and put his hand over mine. I wanted to pull it away, but felt that I could not. "Hannah," he said, "Does it bother you that I am not Jewish?"

"I...I don't think so." Truthfully, I had not thought of it because I had never imagined myself to be involved with a man who was not Jewish. Now, with Vlas sitting here holding my hand, I did not know what to think. I did not seem to have any standards anymore, if I truly had had them to begin with. "We are both human beings, are we not?"

Vlas smiled. "It would seem so. I see Jewish women who are very pretty."

His remark seemed odd, but I said nothing.

"When I was seventeen, I knew a beautiful Jewish woman in Warsaw," he continued, seeming to take my silence as encouragement. "She was a widow. An actress. I played in the theater where she worked. She was very kind to me. She taught me about love."

I caught my breath and almost pulled my hand back, but he was squeezing it now. My cheeks were burning again and I knew, with horror, that I was blushing.

"I'm sorry, Hannah. I did not mean to embarrass you. I am trying too hard to convince you I am not prejudiced."

"I already knew you weren't prejudiced."

He began rubbing his fingertip over the top of my hand. "There is just something about you, Hannah," he said and leaned forward. "You must have men fighting over you."

I laughed. How utterly ridiculous he sounded. "I could not imagine such a thing."

But Vlas was not laughing. "I could," he said.

I stopped my giggling and stared again at his hand on mine. Was it possible that Vlas really liked me as much as he seemed to? "I must wash the glasses," I told him.

Vlas released my hand and I stood up. I went to the sink, all the while very conscious of him watching me. I should tell him about Aaron, I kept thinking while I washed the glasses. Why I didn't when he took my hand, I don't know. And how was it that after all this time, I was suddenly noticed by two men in one week? Was I giving off some kind of scent or something?

When I finished and turned around, I saw that Vlas had risen from his chair. He was watching me with glassy eyes and a strangely swollen expression. I wiped my hands on the dishtowel and set it down. "I'm finished."

Vlas stood still as if he had not heard me, but then gave a small start. He stepped aside for me to pass and followed me out, turning off the kitchen light.

I had such strange feelings and was shaking so badly by then that I went straight to the front door and opened it while he turned off the chandelier over the dining room table and a small table lamp in the sitting area.

Then he came over to me and picked up my hand. "I hope we will be able to spend some more time together, Hannah. I will be here a few more weeks."

"I guess we will," I answered, still not telling him about Aaron.

Vlas held my hand to his lips and kissed it. "Good Shabbos."

"Good Shabbos," I whispered back and waited, with my insides all twisted up, for him to let go of my hand. I was spinning all at once up to heaven and back down again to *gehinnom*. Guilt and excitement and hurtling from girlhood made the night look blurry and unreal. And yet, in the background, were Solomon's words of warning and his plea to be careful, telling me I was special.

When Vlas had gone I closed the door and paced quietly in the hall before going into my room. If I was so special, why wasn't Solomon marrying *me* and not Chava? Then I stopped. Who'd just thought that? Solomon and I didn't feel that way for each other. We had completely different and separate lives ahead of us. I wished I had someone to talk to about all these things. Marta came the closest, and I didn't think all these uncertainties and subtleties would be within her mental grasp. She would probably just give me some kind of straightforward solution which I would be completely unable to fulfill, such as stay away from Vlas and Solomon both and wait for the right man to come along.

Finally I went to bed and lay, just before falling asleep, petting Masha and telling her everything that was happening. Because next to Solomon (whom I couldn't possibly tell), Masha was the best listener I knew.

~~~~~

"What are you doing, Hannah?" Mama asked. It was close to bedtime and she had come into the kitchen for her nightly cup of tea, only to find me busy at work.

"Baking," I answered simply.

Mama picked up the kettle to fill at the sink, eyeing me all the while. "Baking? On Monday night? What are you baking?"

"Almond cookies," I answered, hoping that brevity would exasperate her and not make me explain to her my desperate plan to bring almond cookies to Aaron the following day.

Mama sat down at the kitchen table as I dropped the small fragrant balls of dough onto a baking sheet. "What's his name?"

I looked at her, my eyebrows raised in genuine surprise. "What makes you ask that question?"

Mama sighed. "Why else would you be baking almond cookies at this hour, five days before Shabbos? For your health? Come, Hannele, I was your age once, unbelievable as that may be." She furrowed her brow. "You are so secretive, just like your father."

I narrowed my eyes at her. "Papa is not secretive!"

Mama raised one eyebrow. "He's not? That is why he had plans to immigrate to America with that friend of his, David Rosen, for two years before bothering to tell us?"

I plunked my spoon into the bowl of dough and put my hands on my hips. "Mama, I already knew that!" I picked up the baking sheet and shoved it into the oven, slamming shut the oven door.

"All right, Hannah, I'm sorry." Mama was silent while the water in the kettle began to hiss and bubble. "Would you like to have some tea with me?"

Her invitation soothed the upset she had roused in me the moment before and I accepted. I usually enjoyed having tea with her before bed. While she prepared the tea I dotted the second baking sheet with drops of dough and pressed an almond into the center of each one.

Mama brought our tea to the table and we sat together. I was quiet as I sipped my tea, trying to ignore Mama's expectant gaze.

"Hannele, *nu*? What have you to say?" she asked finally.

I sighed, knowing that if I did not answer her she would *noodzhe* me until I did and Uncle Leo and Auntie Sylvia would come into the kitchen the next morning and find my lifeless body on the floor, noodzh-ed to death. Well, perhaps I exaggerate a bit, but Mama can be extremely annoying at times. "Aaron Levi," I said.

Mama raised her eyebrows. "Oh! Well! He's a handsome boy! Good family. Ambitious." She nodded toward me to show she was impressed with my taste. "I did not know you liked him."

"I've always noticed him. We spoke the other day when I brought him some buttons from the store."

Mama made a strange twist of her mouth and a sudden darkness came into her face. "Just make sure that almond cookies are all you give him," she said.

"Mama!"

Mama held up her hand. "Hannah, just listen. You are a beautiful young woman. And you are at that age now." The kettle began to whistle and Mama rose to pick it up off the stove.

I watched her pour the tea. Her dark hair was laced with threads of gray and her face was fleshy, the skin of her cheeks and forehead red and dry. How much she had changed from the woman she had been in Warsaw with her red lipstick and French perfume and dates in fancy restaurants. Now she looked more like a frumpy Hasidic wife and went out only with me to the moving pictures once in a while or to play cards. Back then she had dated a different man almost every night of the week. She was never with one more than a month or so, always finding a complaint about him. He didn't brush his teeth properly or he had terrible table manners. Always something. After a while I realized she was still in love with Papa and wouldn't admit it. To her, no one would ever be as good as him.

She brought the glasses of tea to the table and sat back down. The warm, cakey aroma of cookies filled the small kitchen. I switched the baking sheets and sat down with her.

"I worry about you, Hannele."

I did not answer, but shrugged as I sipped my tea.

"Hannele, nu?" She was in one of her rare authoritative moments.

I flashed my eyes at her. "I will only give him the cookies, Mama."

Mama scrutinized me. "Men take whatever they can."

"All men?"

She picked one of the cookies off the baking sheet and dunked it into her tea. "All the ones I've known."

"Including my grandfather," I said. "He took from all of us." I picked up a cookie and tasted it. The nutty, buttery flavor filled my mouth and I closed my eyes for a moment as I felt a surge of hope along with my enjoyment. When he wasn't busy yelling and fighting, Zayde used to tease and tell me Bubby's almond cookies made him want to marry her. A part of me must have believed him, for I dared to think that these cookies, which were almost as good, might have a similar effect on Aaron. I would settle for a crush if not a marriage proposal.

"You are still angry with your grandfather?" Mama asked. "You must let the dead rest. After all, he gave, too."

I furrowed my brow. "He gave grief. He was cruel. He yelled. He kept us all afraid of him and enjoyed it. You're angry too, Mama. You just won't admit it." I looked down, feeling guilt mixed in with my bitterness. I hadn't missed him when he died. I daresay I had been relieved.

"I have anger sometimes," Mama said quietly. Then she shook her head and brushed away a few crumbs. "These are good, Hannah. Soon you will bake as well as Bubby did."

"Thank you." I stood to take the other sheet of cookies out of the oven. "Mama, do you think Solomon is like that, the way you said? I don't."

Mama ran her fingertip along the rim of her glass. "Solomon is a special young man. I am very fond of him. And in spite of things I have said in the past about his...situation and its effect on you, I'm glad you have him for a friend."

I furrowed my brow again as I scraped the cookies off the baking sheet onto a clean plate and began to clean up from my baking. I had expected her to rhapsodize on Solomon's qualities the way I saw them. I was terribly disappointed. Somewhere inside of me I had been hoping she would say that she would have liked to see me and Solomon together. That would have somehow given me permission to have made the almond cookies for him, rather than for Aaron.

Mama helped me by drying the baking things as I washed them and putting them away, then washed our tea glasses as I wrapped up the cookies for the next day. I did, however, leave a small plate of cookies for Auntie Sylvia and Uncle Leo on the kitchen table with a note, just before following Mama out. After all, I had used their kitchen. Leaving them a few almond cookies was the least I could do, was it not?

~~~~~

My legs felt like lokshen noodles boiled in water as I neared the door of Levi's store. My hand had barely the strength to open the door, but I did. Aaron looked up when I walked in with the package of almond cookies I had labored over the evening before. The sight of him made me almost lose my breath. I prepared myself to be gathered into his arms and kissed again.

"Hannah, hello." He sounded horrifyingly disappointed, as if he were surprised and puzzled that I would be there.

The store was empty of customers, and as it was time to close, Aaron went to lock the door then came over to me. We stood amidst the racks of jackets and slacks. Aaron's father, Solek Levi, had the distinction of having brought the ready-made suit to Wolensk.

"So, Hannah," he said, "Did your uncle order more shirts?"

I furrowed my brow and waited for him to start calling me molecule brain or monkey-face or to ruffle my hair. "No!" I said. "I mean…" I held up the cookies, wishing in that moment that I had made them instead for Solomon, who was a devoted fan of my baking and cooking. "I…I wanted to bring you these. They're almond cookies. I made them."

Aaron still looked puzzled. "You made me cookies?"

I looked at him, slightly less awed than I had been moments before. "Yes," I answered, not seeing what was so difficult to understand and wishing more with each second that I had not done this. I set the cookies on the nearby counter. "I hope you like them." I turned and began to walk to the door.

"Wait, Hannah."

I stopped immediately and turned back around. His expression had changed from one of puzzlement to something resembling sheepishness. "That was very nice of you," he said. "Um, I am sorry I did not come to see you. It was a…busy week."

I smiled as a surge of hope restored me. "Really?"

"Um, yes. Really."

My awe returned. "I thought maybe I had done or said something wrong."

Aaron shook his head. "No, Hannah. You're a nice girl."

An awkward silence followed, such as I had never felt before in my life.

"I liked your photographs," I told him, desperate to break the silence. "Palestine seems like a wonderful place."

"It is! In fact, I received a letter from my cousin just yesterday to tell us he is now a father of twin boys."

"Oh! Mazel tov! That is wonderful!"

Aaron's handsome face beamed and I could see that he, too, was relieved for the change of topic. "Their names are Adam and David."

"That really is wonderful, Aaron."

Aaron nodded. "It is. And now I have two more reasons to go there as soon as I can."

I looked down. "Yes, I suppose you do."

Then we were silent again, the only sound being people passing by the window of the store.

After several moments, Aaron said, "I think I must go."

I looked at him, with a nagging sense that he wanted to get away from me. But this didn't make sense since he had just finished telling me I hadn't done anything wrong. "All right," I said.

"Come." He took my arm and led me toward the back. "Have a seat. I have a couple of things to do, then we can leave together."

Wordlessly I obeyed. I touched my arm where his hand had been while I listened to the sounds of him moving around in the shop, the gentle scrape of broom bristles against the wooden floor, the clinking of the cash register.

When Aaron appeared in the doorway to the little back room where I waited, he was holding the package of cookies. He held them out. "Thank you again for these." He came over to the table and set them down. "It's the first time a girl ever brought me cookies."

I smiled back into his dark eyes, though inside I felt completely a mess of nerves. "Really?" It was difficult to believe he didn't have girls bringing him cookies every day.

"Really." He stood a moment in front of me where I sat in my chair, then kneeled down. He leaned forward, his hands on my shoulders, and kissed me on the lips.

If I had had any doubts about whether I had been right to come here, they were gone in that moment. *He must love me*, I thought when he did not pull away, but instead put his arms around me, caressing my back as he kissed me more. I understood even more why men and women make such a fuss about each other. I even understood why women were made to sit separately from men in the synagogue. If I were sitting next to Aaron in the synagogue, prayer would be forgotten.

Gingerly, I rubbed Aaron's back over his shirt, exploring the bulges of muscle there. Our kissing grew more heated and after several minutes, Aaron reached up and started to feel my breast. I pulled away then, still breathing heavily. "I'm sorry," I said.

Aaron too was breathing heavily and looked away from me, giving me the impression he was collecting himself. But then he looked up. To my relief, he was smiling. "I'm sorry, too. I got carried away. It's just that you're the prettiest girl in town."

I stared at him. His words were very hard to believe, even though I wanted nothing more! There was no way I could be prettier than Eva Schulz! "Th...thank you," I managed to say. "But you don't need to be sorry, Aaron. It's me."

He sighed and put his hand over mine. "It's getting late anyway. Come, I'll walk you home."

"All right." I stood and my spirit rose with me.

We walked from town together. I wanted to make conversation but after a couple more questions about his cousin's life in Palestine and Aaron's rather brief answers, conversation lagged. Perhaps it wouldn't have if Aaron had asked me a question or two about myself, but he didn't, and I didn't offer anything. After all, he probably wouldn't have been interested in the latest Yiddish romance novel I'd read or what other types of goodies I'd baked. Or how I looked after Solomon's father and sat with the elderly man, drinking tea and talking about Toyreh and the sad state of Polish Jewry with and all its ideological divisions.

Aaron wasn't religious so we couldn't talk about Sabbath observance the way Solomon and I did. I suppose we could have spoken about Zionism, though I really didn't know much about it and Aaron had basically exhausted his view on it when he'd told me that Poland was a dead place for Jews. Our lives were so completely different. Aaron's ardent desire to leave made me feel like a provincial shtetl Jew, something I never felt with Solomon. Well, I decided then and there, I would study up on Zionism and Palestine so that next time Aaron and I saw each other, I would be able to converse with him. Come to think of it, I remembered that Yoav had left some of his books upstairs in what was now Mama's bedroom. I would go up there and retrieve them and begin reading as soon as possible.

Aaron left me at my front door with a smile and another thank you for the cookies. He didn't say anything about when we would see each other again, but I had every intention of going to his father's store the following afternoon. I watched him walk away until he disappeared around the corner. I went into the house, still smiling. However, as I closed the front door behind me, my joy was tinged with the eerie sense that even though Solomon was away in the army, he had been watching us.

~~~~~

Zayde must have been lying to me about Bubby's almond cookies, playing on a little girl's gullibility, for the next afternoon threatened to pass without Aaron calling on me at Uncle Leo's store. And I was certain he knew I was here.

"Why do you stare out the window that way, Hannah?" I heard Uncle Leo's voice from behind the cash register. "The scenery does not change as it does when you're on a train."

I sighed and turned back to my task of straightening the spools of thread. The next I knew, Uncle Leo had come to stand next to me. "You're a good worker," he said. "I don't think the thread display has ever been so color coordinated as it is now."

I frowned. If I was such a good worker, why was he so anxious to be rid of me?

"You may go if you'd like," he said. "I know it is difficult to stay inside at this time of year."

My gaze had been locked on the door of Levi's store when he said this, making my stomach surge painfully. "Thank you, Uncle Leo. I suppose I would like to be outside."

"I knew it," he said. "I was young once."

I resisted the urge to roll my eyes as I stood up. I checked on my book corner one last time to make sure that everything was in order then said good bye to Uncle Leo. I opened the door and went out, my eye trained on the door of Levi's. I had gotten halfway across Polaski Street when I spotted Eva Schulz approaching the door ahead of me. She disappeared inside, and I froze where I was, just missing a horse cart full of hay which was passing by. "No!" I cried out loud. This could not be. I ran to the door and tugged, but it had been locked. I peered inside, but no one was there. Terror filled me. "No!" I cried again. How horrible this was!

I turned and rushed through the narrow passageway between buildings to the back entrance of the store, stopping there and staring at it, willing it to open and for Aaron to come out and bring me inside. But the door remained stubbornly shut in my face.

With shaking breaths, my face burning like the fires in Gehinnom, I continued to stare at the door, no longer feeling like a human being but some kind of frightened animal, trembling and gasping for breath. I knew I had no dignity whatsoever, but could not have cared less. My beautiful dream of holding hands in the moving pictures, Shabbos dinners together, and maybe riding horses across those pebbly deserts in Palestine was sinking in its grave like an old forgotten widow.

I did not know how much time had passed before the back door opened, nor could I have cared. My entire world in that moment had shrunk to the vision before me of Eva emerging from the back room, giggling and patting her wavy blond hair with one hand while Aaron kissed her cheek. A choking sound ripped from my throat, causing Aaron to look up, clearly startled to see me.

"Hannah?"

Eva stopped giggling and looked at me.

I turned and ran with my hands clamped over my mouth, forcing back the horrible nausea which churned in my stomach.

People stared at me as I rushed by them, choking on sobs as I ran, but I didn't care. Just like the day Papa left and I screamed and screamed and didn't care who knew of my despair, so it was as I made my way to my house, stopping only when I had slammed my bedroom door and fallen onto my bed, my face pushed deeply into the pillow.

After several moments I heard a knock on my door.

"Hannele?" I heard Mama say.

When I didn't answer, she just walked in. I did not look up, thinking that maybe if I ignored her she would go away. But really I knew better. I felt her sit down on the edge of the bed. She began stroking my hair with one hand, the way she used to when I was little. Her touch was comforting, and I lifted my face from my pillow and moved it to her lap.

"There, there, Hannele," she crooned, "Everything will be all right."

Her hand on my hair calmed me, eased the hysteria and finally, I lay quietly.

"Hannah," Mama began softly after letting me calm down, "you look as if you've just witnessed a pogrom. You must tell me what happened."

I rolled over and looked up at her. "I don't want to talk about it." My voice was thick and gummy from crying.

"That is no answer."

I sighed. It was simply too painful to repeat. So I said: "Human cruelty, Mama. That's all I can say right now."

"I wish you would stop these games." Her voice turned a bit sharp. "Why can't you just tell me what happened?"

"I will. But please, not just now."

She sighed and I could feel her frustration. She did, however, continue to stroke my hair. "I don't know when you became so difficult," she said. Then she was silent.

I wriggled closer to her so my head rested against her belly. She had become more pillowy in the last few years and I savored this moment, for God alone knew when it could happen again. I closed my eyes. "I'll be glad when Solomon gets home."

"He is a good boy," she said. "I have noticed that. He's...different."

"Yes," I agreed, as the image of Aaron and Eva coming out the back door, flushed with their animal closeness. I winced. "Different. That is the right word."

~~~~~

The next day, I woke with a terrible headache, a piercing pain in my forehead, right between the eyes. The pain was so intense it made my stomach churn. It was all I could do to get out of bed and feed Masha, after which I fell right back in.

Mama came and put a cool cloth on my forehead and made sure the curtains were closed to the light of day. "Your uncle can go one day without you there," she said. She came over and pressed her hand gently on the cloth. The pressure was soothing. "I'll come home early today."

"I'll be all right," I muttered. "But please go see Reb Weiss for me. Will you, please, Mama? I promised Solomon."

Mama stroked my hair. "Yes, I will. I'll tell him you don't feel well. Solomon is lucky to have a friend like you."

Yes, I thought sarcastically. *How lucky he is!* But I knew if I said that to Mama she would start in on me. "Thank you."

I rolled back over, covering my eyes, pressing the cloth down on them firmly. It was the only thing that eased the pain. I never wanted to leave my room again. I wished I could just stay huddled up in here, safe from all the horrible ways of people. But I knew that what I wished was impossible. Everything I've ever wished has been.

Masha jumped onto the bed and curled up with me and my terrible headache and mixed up life. I stroked her for a few minutes until I felt sleepy. Oh, good, I thought, hoping that I could sleep straight through the whole day and night, only to wake up when Shabbos was only a few hours away.

~~~~~

Uncle Leo can be such a *schnorra*! I know I shouldn't be so angry at him, seeing as how he took me and Mama in the way he did, even if he did so for fear of Zayde coming back from the grave to punish him if he didn't. And certainly, if I go on feeling this way I risk spilling out more of that hatred that got me into so much trouble in the first place. But I can't help it. He always makes me feel like I'm an imposing greedy child.

You see, I stopped into the store the next morning after beginning my Shabbos preparations because I needed to make sure it was okay for Reb Weiss to come to Shabbos dinner as he has the previous two Fridays. Auntie Sylvia reminded me about it before she left for the bank, giving me the depressing feeling that Reb Weiss had only a certain number of invitations to our table allowed and that they were almost used up. I didn't want to go anywhere near that part of Polaski Street on any mere chance of seeing Aaron, but I had to, because really, I wanted to do the right thing. Thank God I had woken up without a headache, because it would have been impossible to go. But I went.

"Are you sure that Reb Weiss does not want to visit another family this week?" Uncle Leo said when I asked him. "Surely you wouldn't want to be greedy with his time."

I felt a shadow close over my heart at the way he said that because I knew what he really meant. His face always turned bright red when his thoughts and his words didn't match. It took me several moments to find my response. "Reb Weiss likes us," I said quietly. "And...well...I promised Solomon I would look after him."

Uncle Leo reached up and scratched his head of tight graying curls. "Hannah, does Solomon expect us to feed his father every week?"

Now I couldn't help but simply stare at Uncle Leo. "No," I said, my voice shrinking. "He never expected anything like that. But if it's not all right with you, I'll see if the Pearlmans—"

"No. No. That won't be necessary." The redness in his face flushed deeper. I had shamed him into magnanimity. "He can come, of course. You know that. I just thought...well..." Uncle Leo scratched his head again. "Are you sure there's enough food?"

Again, I stared at him. Uncle Leo has a gift for making me feel angry, disgusted and guilty all at once! But I never forget he is my gracious host. I nodded and put on a photograph smile. "Of course there is, Uncle. Don't worry a moment."

Uncle Leo nodded and I excused myself to go to the postal station, sneering at Levi's storefront as I hurried away. I was expecting another letter from Papa. Certainly, the news would be the same, yet I longed just to see his blocky slanted scrawl on the paper, the one thing that connects us, aside from my ever-burning hope of going to see him in America some day.

Of course, Papa's letter said exactly what I had expected it to say, only today, Solomon was not there, standing nearby, looking at me sympathetically. I crumpled the paper into my pocket and went to the butcher to buy the chicken for supper. I had the evil thought of buying two, just to give Uncle Leo a rise. But of course, I didn't have the guts to actually buy two chickens. So by the time I got home with my letter and my chicken, I could feel no really good reason to have Shabbos. Only Reb Weiss's presence and his expectation of observance made it matter.

I didn't tell anyone about my letter this time. I just took the crumpled paper and stuffed it in a rubbish bin outside someone's house on my way to see Reb Weiss and tell him about dinner. He was happy to see me and waved a piece of paper at me. "Hannele," he said, "The Master of the Universe is taking care of our Solly! He spends Shabbos with a nice Jewish family and he does good in his training. He says to 'Please tell Hannele that I am well and staying out of trouble and please to send her my fondest regards.'"

He handed it to me to read, which I did, then set it on the table. What a relief he was doing well, yet an aching emptiness nagged me. He also apologized for not having written a separate letter since they didn't give him much free time, but that he would as soon as he could. That made me feel better! Still more than four months stretched ahead before he came home. And look at what had happened in his absence already!

That evening I didn't go to shul. I lit the candles with Mama, shrugging away her curiosity, then waited until the evening prayers would be finished before I went to meet Reb Weiss and walk him to our house.

During dinner, I scrutinized Uncle Leo, waiting for him to say something embarrassing that would make Reb Weiss not feel welcome, but thankfully he didn't. My vigil was wearing me down a bit and I found that a few extra sips of Shabbos wine took the edge off. Come to think of it, after half a glass, nothing bothered me, not Aaron Levi, not Papa's letter, and not the fact that Solomon hadn't been there outside the postal station, waiting for me with his loyal concern. My God, life was just a series of things with sharp edges, wasn't it?

After an entire glass of Shabbos wine, I became considerably more cheerful and talkative. The whole world seemed softer and shinier, making what had happened two days before with Aaron seem a million years ago! Why hadn't I tried this before?

A while later, after I had walked Reb Weiss to his apartment and came back, the shiny, swimmy feeling had mostly worn off, but in its place resided a calm evenness, a sense of relaxation for which I was very glad. I don't think I had ever felt so calm in my whole life, and I certainly didn't want to go back to being the mess of nerves and horrible emotions I had been before dinner.

So when Vlas came in and found me in the kitchen with my book, which I was really just staring at rather than reading, I did not feel as nervous as usual around him. I invited him to sit and have tea, speaking to him in quite a flirtatious way, exaggerating my movements as I prepared his glass, which I set down in front of him, leaning over just a bit too close. Then I sat down, plunking my elbow on the table and resting my cheek in my hand. I smiled at him and he grinned back at me, though his eyes showed just slightly his momentary loss of assurance.

"Hannah," he said, "You seem so different this evening. What has happened?"

I giggled a bit and rolled my eyes. "I don't know. I guess I'm just so tired of the misery there is in life. There should be good things, too. Don't you think?"

Vlas looked down. "Oh," he said. "I thought maybe it was because you liked me."

I raised my face away from my hand. Oh, no, I had hurt his feelings! "I do like you!" I said quickly.

At this he grinned again and reached for my hand, rubbing it with his fingertips as he had done the week before. "Is it really possible you have no boyfriend?"

Boldly, I leaned toward him. "Is that so hard to believe?"

Vlas lifted my hand to his lips. "Absolutely," he whispered back, his breath puffing warmly into my palm as he dotted Valentino-style pecks on my skin.

I had flirted my way into something more serious, and I felt some of my boldness wear off. I became aware of the open curtains above the sink. The kitchen lights were burning brightly, putting us in stark view from the darkness outside. I became afraid that if someone saw us, by tomorrow I would be following that other fallen Jewish woman out of Wolensk. "We had better go in the other room," I whispered.

"Yes. Yes. The other room."

I got up and brought the empty glasses to the sink, pulling the curtain closed before washing them. As I worked, I suddenly felt hands on my shoulders. I let out a tiny gasp and pretended to be intent on rinsing the glass as he pressed his body against me. He started kissing the side of my neck. I turned off the faucet. "Someone could walk in," I said under my breath.

"We will be very careful," he whispered back. He took my hand and led me out of the little kitchen, turning down the lights as we went. He did the same with the living room lights and the house filled with darkness, punctured only by the fading glow of the Shabbos candles on the sideboard. Vlas put his arms around me again, this time from the front and nuzzled my hair. "Take me to your room, Hannah," he murmured.

I looked up into the darkness, toward where Mama, Uncle Leo, and Auntie Sylvia were upstairs, absorbed in their own Shabbos worlds of love and sleep. I could not imagine they would be sleeping so soundly if they knew what was happening just below them. How could I allow Vlas into my bedroom? What was I doing here, standing like this with him as he began to kiss the side of my neck and rub my back? I thought of Yoav and of Aaron, both of whom had cast me off with their cruel indifference. I thought, too, of Solomon, whom I did not want ever to have a chance to rip my heart to pieces as they had. I would not be left behind this time. I could still experience that which other women experience and not be left behind.

In that moment, I turned my back on my childish, girlish dreams of love and romance. I sneered at the image of my white marriage bed as I tilted my face up to Vlas and let him kiss me on the lips. I took his hand and led him to my room, closing my bedroom door as softly as I could behind us.

"Come to the bed," Vlas whispered.

In the darkness, we made small steps, I, leading only because I knew my way around my room. "Here."

Vlas laid me back on my bed, underneath him. He began kissing me, this time in greedy gulping motions with his lips, making me feel like I was a bowl of food to a man who had not eaten in days. He put one of his arms around me, while with the other he undid his trousers and lifted my dress.

I did not stop him. I had always thought I would stop any man but my husband from doing that.

"Hannah," Vlas murmured, "Let me in." His hand was groping me down below, and I then realized my legs were pressed tightly together. He began rubbing me and slowly I opened them. "A little more, Hannah.". He moved over me and began to push himself inside. He found it difficult and pushed harder. How it hurt! I cried out softly but Vlas continued to push until he tore through.

I grabbed onto Vlas's shoulders and dug my fingers into them, trying to bear the pain. Why had no one told me about the pain? "Vlas, please," I begged, when I could no longer endure it. "Please stop. It hurts! Please!"

Vlas tried to keep going, but then stopped when I dug my fingers desperately into his arms. In one movement he pulled away and rolled off me. "All right, Hannah," he muttered.

I sat up and pulled up my underpants. My shoulders began to shake and my eyes felt hot. I covered my mouth with my hands, stifling the scream that was churning in my throat.

Vlas was sitting up now, buttoning his trousers. "I had better go." he said quietly in the darkness.

I uncovered my mouth. "Do you hate me?"

Vlas sighed. "No, Hannah. I do not hate you." He stood up and I helped guide him from the dark room so he would not bump into anything and make a noise that could be heard upstairs.

I followed him to the front door, hoping he would say something, anything to show me how he felt. I opened the front door and held it open for him.

Vlas came and stood in front of me. "Good night."

I looked up at him, still waiting. I might as well have waited in front of the wall. How like a different person he seemed now. Before, he had known just what to say, just how to look at me. Now, nothing came from him but a quiet, wordless distance. "Good night," I replied.

He stood for another moment, and I even dared hope…but then he turned and walked from my house. I watched him as he went, yet he did not turn around, not even to wave. Reluctantly, I closed the door, standing, waiting, ready to open it again in case he turned back. After several moments of silence, I knew he was too far away. He would not turn back now.

Standing motionless in the front hall, listening to the clock, I did not know what to do. I could not go into my room. Not yet. I didn't really belong anywhere. There was nowhere to go. But I needed to move around. I went into the kitchen and paced back and forth in front of the sink. "Oh my God, Oh, my God," I whispered. Each time I passed the kitchen window, I saw the synagogue, and shame pierced me. So I stopped my pacing and sank down heavily onto one of the chairs. With my elbows on the table, I grabbed bunches of my hair in my fists and squeezed, hard, hard, until I thought I would pull it right out of my scalp. Was it really just hours ago that I was smiling and singing Shabbos songs with Reb Weiss and my family? Was I really that same girl, a virgin then, at that table surrounded in the glow of the Shabbos candles? No, it could not be. I was no longer that virgin. I was now bereft of that bridal gift a woman gives to her husband. And it had taken no more than a few seconds. I was a woman now. But what kind of woman?

I was gripped then with the strong urge to run to Solomon and ask him what the Scriptures said about such a woman, although I probably could have guessed. I almost did get up from my chair and run out the door, down to the synagogue. But of course, Solomon was away, somewhere in the army, and would be for the longest time. And even if he were here, how could I possibly tell him what I had done? He would hate me for sure, and I would lose him.

I sighed again, too weary to think anymore. As I stood up to go to bed, I felt the soreness down below. Oh, God! There would be blood! Did life ever cease to bring pain and sadness? I went to the bathroom where I tended to myself. Then slowly, quietly, I tip-toed to my room, tired enough now not to care that Vlas had been in my bed just a short while before.

On Shabbos morning, no one seemed to notice anything different about me. I stared at my reflection in the bedroom mirror for a long time I wasn't going to shul, so what did it matter? And my face didn't look any different. I still had discomfort between my legs, but that thankfully wasn't something anyone else could notice by just looking at me. For having lost my virginity the night before, I did not look any older or any more grown up. Maybe it didn't make you a woman if you were unmarried and gave it to a Polish man. I sighed. There was nothing I could do about it now. I had to live with my dirty secret.

I almost could not bring myself to go see Reb Weiss, certain as I was that he would take one look at me and know. But I had made a promise to Solomon, and if I asked Mama to go over there again for me, she would become suspicious. As it was, Reb Weiss, if he noticed a difference, said nothing and was happy to see me and to talk about Solomon.

~~~~~

During the week I brought a pair of nice lace white curtains to Reb Weiss from Uncle Leo's store. I found the beautiful soft panels in one of the boxes that had been delivered and fell in love with them. I managed to finagle them from Uncle Leo who reluctantly agreed to let me work a few extra hours to pay them off. If I had been in his place, I would have said, "Take them. Reb Weiss does an important service for us and he's so poor. Make a gift of them." But I am not Uncle Leo.

Until I left the store that afternoon, I thought only of putting those pretty curtains up in Reb Weiss's dingy little room. Just the thought of doing that for him made gladness sweep over my heart and I felt the happiest I had in weeks.

When I showed them to Reb Weiss, I knew immediately I had done the right thing. His grayish eyes misted over at the sight of them, and he sat quietly at the table, watching me put them up over the small window above the sink. They were not difficult to hang and immediately brightened the small, dark room. Then I opened the window to let in the warm summer breeze, which lifted them in sweet billows. The breeze was balmy and fresh, and for once, made me believe its promises might actually be possible.

"Thank you, Hannele," Reb Weiss said as I turned and came to sit across from him. "You are very kind."

I smiled but then looked away, feeling stabs of guilt at every kind word from him.

"Solly will love them," he added as he rose from the table to prepare our tea. Each day when I came to see him, he insisted that making the tea for us was the least he could do.

"Just think, Reb Weiss," I said as I watched him take out two clean glasses from the cupboard, "The time will pass quickly until he comes back."

"Yes, Hannele." Reb Weiss picked up the kettle. All his movements were slow and precise. "I pray only that I am still here to see him."

I sighed, hating when he said such things, which he did regularly. They made me feel unbearably sad. "Of course you will be here."

"There is no 'of course' in this life, Hannele."

I did not answer, and instead, rested my forehead against the heel of my hand, my elbow on the table. Delicately, I traced the rough grain of the table's wooden surface with a forefinger.

When it was ready, Reb Weiss put a glass of tea on the table in front of me.

"Thank you, Reb Weiss."

"There is nothing for to thank me, Hannele," he said. "It means so much that you come here each day."

I watched Reb Weiss sit back down, not liking how tired he seemed. He sat quietly, sipping his tea through a lump of sugar between his teeth. I could not see that without remembering the time Solomon had done that to make me smile, the afternoon our friendship had begun. Maybe *begun* was not the right word because really, Solomon and I had somehow known each other for a long time before that day, even before he had begun following me around. At least that is what it felt like.

"I am sorry to you, Hannele," he said after what seemed a lengthy silence.

I looked at him. "What is there to be sorry for, Reb Weiss?"

"I am sorry for what is past. I wish I had known of you…" He waved his hand in the air in his search for words. "Before." He reached up and stroked his beard, which, had never grizzled, in spite of his age, but had remained soft and full. Solomon's beard would one day look like that. I mean, Rebbe Solomon's beard.

Reb Weiss pointed toward the ceiling. "The Master of the Universe keeps secrets from us, Hannele. Many secrets."

He was watching me, his eyes pained. His voice grew heavy with regret, and I understood what he meant. I sighed. "Yes, I know."

"I've wished many things in my life," he said. "Things I wanted to be different. But they couldn't be. This is one of the most painful."

I stared into my tea glass, unable to bear the weight of such praise. My guilt was excruciating, for if he knew the truth about me, he would not have felt such things. "You mustn't worry," I said finally. "You've done the right thing. He's needed there."

Reb Weiss touched his beard again. "You are a good girl, Hannele. You see my son clearly." In the flickering candlelight, his eyes appeared watery. The expression in them was eerie, a strange mixture of sadness and joy. "Solly goes where he is needed."

I looked down at my empty glass. "I know."

"Always, Solly looks to the Master of the Universe to guide him. The boy makes mistakes sometimes, and probably he will make more. But even then, his heart is with Ha Shem."

I nodded. "Yes. I know."

Then Reb Weiss put his hand gently on mine. "Still, Hannele," he said, "I am sorry. Your life has brought you much suffering, and you are grateful for such a friend. It means something to you that such a one would come to you. Maybe you even think sometimes that though you suffer, the Master of the Universe still looks over you." He squeezed my hand then, and I felt such kindness from him, I almost began to cry. "And, this I know, Hannele, it is not only the followers of the Wolensker rebbe who need such a friend."

~~~~~

That same week, two days after I had brought Reb Weiss the curtains, Mama brought home a letter from Maria in Bialystock, telling us that her sister had begged her to come and live with her permanently. She was so very sorry and would miss us terribly, she explained, but Irena was not well enough to manage on her own. And since her daughters were going with her and her son would be moving to Warsaw, she had no more family in Wolensk. I caught my breath when Mama read the letter to me and Auntie Sylvia. I had forgotten about Vlas leaving. He wanted so much to be in the orchestra in Warsaw. A wave of bitterness passed through me. I certainly wasn't reason enough for him to stay.

I felt panic, too, about what this all would mean for our keeping of the Sabbath. We really did not know anyone else whom we trusted enough to come into our home. Auntie

Sylvia asked Uncle Leo about it that night at the dinner table. Mama and I looked at each other, stifling giggles under our napkins when his face reddened and his eyes flicked back and forth. Surely, if we broke the Sabbath laws and touched the lights ourselves, his father would come from the grave and torture Uncle Leo's dreams forever.

"Well," he said, "we can look for someone. But in the meantime, my father would not have wanted some peasant coming into his house whom he did not trust and stealing from him. Having Maria here was one thing. I wasn't even happy about that son of hers coming here."

Auntie Sylvia patted my uncle's shoulder reassuringly.

My blood ran cold when he said that, though I realized he had not been referring to what happened between me and Vlas. But I knew also, with a sinking feeling, that he would not really look for a new Shabbos goy. He was perfectly happy to sit down to a good meal of roasted chicken and potato kugel whether it was Shabbos or not. The blessings, the ritual washing of hands, even going to shul to pray, were, for him, mere formalities that, when practiced, kept him from his father's angry dybbuk. After Vlas turned down our lights for the last time next Shabbos, Uncle Leo would do it himself from then on. And he would justify breaking the Sabbath laws to his father's ghost.

~~~~~

The following Shabbos, I waited in the kitchen as usual. When Vlas walked in, I stood up from my chair. He smiled at me. I did not smile back.

"Hello, Hannah." He approached me in small hesitant steps.

"Hello, Vlas. Good Shabbos."

When he had reached the table, he stood behind one of the chairs, waiting.

"You may sit if you'd like," I told him, feeling a stirring inside of me, a weakening. I gripped my book so he would not see that my hands had begun to shake.

Vlas sat down, primly folding his hands on the table in front of him. There was no sign of the confident, seductive man he had been before.

"Would you like some tea?"

"No, thank you, Hannah."

An unbearable silence followed his polite refusal of tea, leaving me nothing to do except search desperately for something else to say. Reluctantly, I lowered myself in my chair. "How have you been?"

"Well enough. I am sorry, though, for last week. I left very quickly."

"I know."

Vlas shifted in his seat and leaned forward. "I…I   have some good news, though."

"Yes? Please, tell me."

Vlas bowed his head. "I made it in. The orchestra, I mean."

I looked away for a moment, toward the window over the sink. "Oh," I said. My voice sounded small and far away. "Congratulations. I am glad for you."

He lifted his gaze. "I have you largely to thank for it, Hannah. You encouraged me. For that I am grateful."

I shrugged. "You're welcome."

"As you know, I will be living there from now on." He almost sounded as if he were asking my permission.

I nodded. "I suppose you have to."

"Yes. I have to."

"You will like it there in Warsaw. It's a beautiful city."

"Yes, I know."

"Good luck, Vlas."

"Thank you, Hannah." He put his hand up to his mouth and cleared his throat politely. "My mother misses you. She has told me many times."

I waited, hoping he would say more about Maria, but he didn't. "I miss her, too," I said. "I have known her almost my whole life."

He cleared his throat again. "I'm certain she will write to you."

I nodded. There was to be no more conversation, so I rose and rinsed my glass. "I am ready now," I said when I had finished.

Vlas looked at me questioningly, his eyebrows raised.

"I mean, for the lights."

"Oh! Yes, the lights."

I pushed my chair in and hugged my book to my chest, almost like a protective shield. I waited to see what he would do. If he came to me I knew I would not be able to tell him no. But he did nothing. This hurt and brought relief both at the same time.

Vlas followed me out of the kitchen, turning down all the customary lights. I then held the front door open for him to let him out into the balmy night.

He stopped in front of me. "Good night, Hannah," he said. "I mean, good-bye."

"Good-bye," I said.

Vlas hesitated, looking as if he might speak. But he seemed to decide the better of it because he turned slowly and walked away.

~~~~~

Autumn, 1938

"You are a good girl, Hannele. You see my son clearly."

"Yes, Reb Weiss," I answer. "I know." I am glad my back is to him so he will not see me clench my jaw. How many times can he say these words before he tires of them?

"Hannele," he says, "Please turn around that I may look on you."

I sigh and put down the dishtowel and glass. I unclench my jaw so that Reb Weiss will not be offended and turn as he asked, but when I do, I cannot see him in the shadowy light. I see a uniform, its large buttons glowing. There is a man standing right in front of me. My upward gaze sees first his dark, soft beard, then his dark golden eyes. "Solomon!" I whisper. Joy rushes through me. "Solomon!"

Solomon smiles and I feel his arms around me, holding me against him, strong and sure.

Then, suddenly, we are in my bedroom, in my bed. My clothes have disappeared. *But so have his, and he is above me, surrounding me…*

The heaving of my own breaths woke me. I sat up, holding the blanket to my chest, as if someone had walked in on me and Solomon in the throes of passion. However, in the moments that followed, my consciousness registered my surroundings. The room was dark and quiet. Only I was there, in my nightgown, which clung to my damp skin.

I looked out the window to see if the light in the sky would tell me I had overslept, but it was not yet dawn. Even Masha was still curled up in the other bed, making that strange groaning snore she made when asleep.

I pushed the blanket down and lay back, waiting for my body to cool, as the shadows of my dream still played about me. How strong it had been! My stomach was clenched up tight inside as it was each time I had such a dream, and there had been several in the five months that Solomon was away. Then, as the room lightened and my breathing calmed, I remembered that today was the day. Solomon was coming home today! He had said so in his last letter.

In a mere few hours he would be back. My stomach squeezed and jumped inside. Sleep would not return though my eyelids were still heavy, and I could only watch the drowsy darkness continue to fade. Finally, when Masha stirred and looked up at me with expectant, hungry eyes, I rose, put on my wrap, and went to the kitchen to prepare her breakfast. She followed me at my heels, mewing.

"Which dress should I wear today, Mashele?" I asked her as I put some herring on a plate for her. She adores herring and I gave it to her special to celebrate. But she ignored my question, crying hungrily until the plate of herring was on the floor. She attacked the rare offering, forgetting my presence completely. I didn't mind. My excitement overshadowed even my worry that Solomon, the observant person that he was—both with people and with his faith—would see me and immediately know about my sin. "I'll bring over cookies and mandel bread and some other things, Mashele," I said. She answered only with the slurpy sound of her chewing on dead fish. I just continued to babble as I put the kettle on for tea. "What do you think, Mashele? Should I put my hair up or leave it loose? It is so much longer now."

I sat down at the table with my tea and some bread and butter. The kitchen was nice and quiet, as no one else was up yet. I nibbled at my bread. Eating was not so easy because my stomach was still tight inside, but I ate anyway, washing the bread down with my tea. I wondered if any other girls had a life like mine. Did other people have such a strange friendship as I did with Solomon? I doubted it. Perhaps my capacity for strangeness made Aaron not really want to be with me. But then again, he immigrated to Palestine last month as he had so long dreamed, and hadn't even taken Eva with him. Even she, so beautiful and lithe, had to find herself a new boyfriend, which she did quite soon after Aaron's departure.

After breakfast I stood at my mirror, *futzing* with my hair, winding it around my fingers, lifting it up off my neck and back down again as if it would tell me how to fix it. Then I sighed. "He's just your friend, Hannah," I said to myself. "Why such a fuss? How long now until he leaves again, this time for good?"

I decided on a simple twist, then picked out a nice dress. Then I stared at my reflection for a few moments. My face was a bit fuller as I had gained some weight over the past few months. Admittedly I'd spent a lot of my time eating. Every day I brought cookies and pastries with me to Reb Weiss and the two of us sat and ate them together with our tea. That time with him had been a great comfort, and although I was glad for Solomon to be coming home, I was sad about not visiting Reb Weiss each day.

I frowned at my slightly chubby appearance. I looked like I had fallen apart over the last few months. Stray wisps of hair stuck out no matter how much I brushed it. Wrinkles stayed in my dresses even when I pressed them. My stockings bunched at the ankles, resistant to my constant straightening tugs. I tried to smooth myself, but to no avail. Oh, well. Good thing I wasn't a girlfriend, or Solomon would be very disappointed. Still, I wanted to look presentable. Solomon couldn't come home to a complete mess, could he?

At the door to Reb Weiss's small apartment, I hesitated before going in. My heart pounded so that my hand shook. "Hannah, stop it!" I whispered to myself. I knocked softly then opened the door, peeking in cautiously, the need to wait for someone to answer the door no longer a concern. Inside, I could hear murmuring voices and an old man's sobs. I looked in a bit farther, allowing my eyes to adjust to the shadowy room.

A knot in my chest tightened when I saw him. His back was to me, and he was kneeling, but I could see Reb Weiss in front of him, leaning forward, his old hands on Solomon's uniformed shoulders. I felt suddenly like an intruder and almost closed the door, determining to knock properly and wait, but they both had seen me.

"Hannele!" Reb Weiss called, "Come, see who is home!"

Solomon rose and turned to me, smiling like in my dream of only a few hours ago which was still, I realized as he drew closer, unsettlingly fresh. I felt immediately, agonizingly shy, and I imagined he could see the images of us from my dream world. I could manage only to smile and feel my cheeks burning.

"Welcome home, Solomon," I said.

Solomon held out his hand. I took it and he squeezed mine warmly. "Hannele, I missed you."

I looked down at the heavy boots he wore. "I missed you, too." I squeezed his hand and smiled.

Gently he pulled me toward the table. "Come, sit with us."

Like an obedient child, I allowed him to lead me to the table where I set down the small basket of bread and cookies.

Reb Weiss was smiling and wiping his cheeks with a handkerchief. He looked at me, radiating joy. The small space around us was filled with a sense of jubilation and we did not speak.

Solomon pulled out the other chair for me, but I shook my head. "You sit down, Solomon. I'll make tea."

He smiled at me, his eyes glowing, as they often did, like pools of melting honey. "Very well. Until you are ready to sit."

I smiled back but turned quickly away, lest I looked too long into his eyes.

"Hannele has taken very good care of me, Solly," I heard Reb Weiss say behind me. "She did not miss one day."

"Hannah is a good friend," Solomon said quietly.

I turned to put the glasses on the table and set out the bread. My eyes met with Solomon's as I did so, and I bowed my head quickly, my cheeks burning.

Solomon rose and gave me his chair. There was a small footstool in the room, which he brought over and set down by his father's feet. My heart squeezed in my chest at the sight of Reb Weiss with his hand on Solomon's shoulder.

We sat, drinking our tea as Solomon told us of his time in the army, filling in the gaps he had left in the few letters he had had time to write. He mentioned nothing of anti-

Semitism and I dared not ask, even though I found it unimaginable that he had encountered none.

"There is something that I did not tell you in the letters," Solomon said after he had finished telling us about his training.

I felt my body stiffen at these words. My hands tightened around my glass of tea. I was certain he would speak of some pretty girl in the home of the family where he had spent Shabbos.

"What is it, my son?" Reb Weiss asked.

Solomon sighed. "I met some people in a town nearby the barracks," he said. "They were German Jews. Refugees." Solomon bowed his head, and I did not want him to go on although I knew he must tell us. "Horrible things have happened to them. Their house was burned down by Nazis. Their business was taken away. The husband had been badly beaten. Jews in Germany are murdered every day. They are forced to wear yellow stars stitched onto their clothing. Many are put into prison camps." He looked up at us. "If this Hitler makes war, we too, will be in danger."

He fell quiet after that, and the three of us were silent as his news sifted downward, deeper into our souls, dampening the happiness of his return.

How strange that such horrible things and good things could all be happening at once. First, Solomon was home safely, and then last night at supper, Uncle Leo asked me to mind the store by myself for a while because he and Auntie Sylvia were going to go visit Devorah. They were staying away through Shabbos and Uncle Leo was trusting *me* with the store. I did not want to let him down, although, after what Solomon had told us, I felt a panic and wished to stay here with him and Reb Weiss. I thought fleetingly that with such terrible things happening so close by, Papa would certainly arrange to bring me over to be with him as soon as possible.

I rose then and collected the empty glasses to wash. When I had finished and turned back around from the sink, Solomon, too, was standing, watching me, his hand on his father's shoulder. For a moment I did not move, feeling strongly that I would become dizzy and lose my balance if I did. How changed he seemed, and yet, I could not say exactly what was different. I saw it when he smiled, which he did now, in spite of the graveness of what he had just told us. His smile was warm and caused the skin around his eyes to crease, bringing out the golden color even more. This all made me nervous in a way I'd never felt, not even that first afternoon. "I must go," I said.

"I will walk you home," Solomon said.

"Actually, I must go to my uncle's store."

He smiled. "Then I will walk you there."

I looked at him with what must have been quite a puzzled expression for he chuckled, but then looked serious.

"Is it all right, Hannele?"

I nodded, very much wanting to stretch out the time until I had to be alone in the store. "Yes. But are you? I mean..."

Solomon chuckled again. "Perhaps the yentas will not recognize me now. And even if they did, what difference does it make?"

I shrugged, because really, I, myself didn't know anymore. I mean, Solomon was going to be the next Wolensker Rebbe no matter whom he was seen with.

Reb Weiss took my hand and squeezed it affectionately before I left. "Hannele," he said, "I hope you will still come to see me. Just because Solly is home, you and I, we're friends too. No?"

I smiled then as if the gates of heaven had opened. "Yes, of course we are, and I can still come visit."

Then we left and Solomon and I started for Polaski Street. As we walked, I found myself glancing sideways at him every few moments. He looked impressive in his uniform. There was confidence in his gait that had not been there before, or had I just not noticed it? It felt strange and kind of intriguing to be walking beside him. Though he looked like a real soldier, I was very glad he did not have to go back there.

"How is your mother?" he asked.

"She is well. She will be happy to see you."

"And I her. And Mashele?"

I smiled, knowing he would ask about her as well. He never failed to remember either of them. "She, too, is well and will be happy to see you."

"Did Papa tell you his stories?" Solomon asked.

I smiled. "Every day he had at least one. I now know about most of his life, and about Wolensk of the nineteenth century." I glanced at him. "I enjoyed them all."

"I always enjoyed his stories, too," Solomon said.

We walked a bit farther without speaking as the buildings of Polaski Street came into view.

Solomon cleared his throat. "Hannele, I cannot thank you enough for the care you gave my father. You are a good friend."

I sighed. It felt awful to have him believe I had been so good when, at the same time, I had been so very bad. My bad feeling intensified as we passed Vlas's house. Well, what had been Vlas's house. "You needn't thank me, Solomon. Reb Weiss is so kind and good that I cannot imagine someone not wanting to care for him. Besides, I wasn't the only one who helped. Mrs. Pearlman, for example, she brought him a—"

"My father is very kind and good." Solomon said before I could finish. "But so are you."

I looked at him. "I'm not good like you say." I shook my head. "You're wrong."

Solomon smiled. "Ah! When you tell me I am wrong, I know that I am home!"

"Solomon!"

Solomon chuckled, but then sighed, and his amusement faded. "It is you who are wrong, Hannele. Do you believe that you have ever shown me only your admirable qualities?" Solomon's voice was gently reproachful. My face burned in shame and I did not answer.

We reached my uncle's store and stopped near the door. People bustled around us, talking, calling to each other, arguing. Horse drawn carts rumbled over the cobblestones, but it felt to me as though we were alone in the world, Solomon and I.

Solomon stood, facing me. He was a bit taller now. His payos were no longer tucked behind his ears, but they were still cut, no more than wisps of hair at his temples. His beard had grown longer and was neatly trimmed, and his golden eyes appeared liquid, like his father's. I had always thought that Solomon had the strangest eyes I had ever seen. But now, under his gaze, I felt like a squirmy child who had been caught stealing. They were the eyes of a man who loved God, who could see into people's souls. "No one is a saint, Hannele," he said gently. "No one. Not even the Baal Shem Tov."

"Solomon! That is sacrilege!"

Solomon grinned, and I could not help but grin as well. "I am so happy to see you, Hannele."

My stomach lurched, but I had no time to reply, for just at that moment, Uncle Leo came out of the store.

"Hello, Hannele," he said, "I thought that was you I saw through the window." He looked at Solomon and put out his hand. "Welcome home, Solomon."

Solomon accepted the handshake. "Thank you, Mr. Goldman."

"Well, I'm off," Uncle Leo said. "Take good care of things here, Hannele."

"I will, Uncle Leo. And please send Devorah my regards."

Uncle Leo looked nervously at me, then at the store. I tried not to feel insulted. After all, this was a big step for him. He didn't like leaving me alone there, but Auntie Sylvia had nagged him about it, she missed her grandchild so much.

I watched him disappear into the bustle of people. Then, suddenly, I felt a great weight lift from me, remembering joyfully that this meant Mama and I had the house to ourselves for two whole days! My first thought was that Solomon and Reb Weiss had to spend this special Shabbos with us, and I wouldn't even have to ask permission and feel guilty about it! "Will you be going to the Rebbe's for Shabbos tomorrow?" I asked, feeling that shyness sweep over me again.

Solomon sighed. He looked suddenly very uncomfortable. "Actually, I had hoped…to be with you." He looked down at his boots.

I smiled although I could feel my hands tremble a bit. "Then you and Reb Weiss will come tomorrow night? It will be only me and Mama. And Masha, of course." For a moment, I remembered how torn he felt. His words of the first afternoon came to me in an echo. He had spoken of the pain of living in two different worlds.

Solomon looked up again. He smiled, his expression both glad and pained. "I would be honored."

Some people went into the store, and I had no choice but to follow them. "I had better go in," I said. As usual, neither of us moved.

"Hannele, will you be all right? I'm concerned. I mean, about those things I told you before."

"You mean about the Jews from Germany?"

"Yes. It is very frightening."

I looked away for a moment and shrugged. There seemed always things to be frightened about. Always. "What can you do?"

Solomon reached out and put a hand on my shoulder. His touch unnerved me, but not in a bad way. However, the concern in his eyes unnerved me even more. No one had ever looked at me that way. No one but Solomon.

A Polish woman went into the store just then.

"I really will be fine, Solomon. I had better go in." I felt pressed and anxious, yet did not move.

Solomon gave a brief nod. "You first, Hannele."

I glanced again into his eyes. A joyful relief swept through me. Nothing really has changed, has it? Maybe things would get better in Germany. And Solomon was still here with his father. And they would be over for Shabbos. And we would have chicken and sing zmiros and drink tea and chant blessings. Maybe nothing would ever have to change. Knowing this, knowing that Shabbos would be here the following evening, just like it had been before, only better, I could turn and go into the store. I smiled just before opening the door with its small glass panes and jingling bells. "Welcome home, Solomon."

~~~~~

That first Shabbos with Solomon and Reb Weiss, when Mama and I were alone in the house, was the most glorious one I can ever remember. Mama and I prepared a feast of roasted chicken, potato kugel, boiled carrots glazed with honey, and, of course, my challah. The lightness of Mama's and my mood as we prepared dinner was due mostly to the fact Solomon was home, but when I set the table with only four places, leaving Uncle Leo's place at the head of the table empty of a setting, Mama and I looked at each other with guilty smiles, like children who had been let out of the classroom to play because the teacher has gone out.

The four of us sang zmiros after dinner, and Solomon and Reb Weiss stayed quite late, so late that Solomon and I did not have our separate tea in the kitchen. But it did not matter, because something that had felt broken was now mended.

After they left and we had cleaned up, Mama turned down the lights because I did not want to touch them. I looked at her and she shrugged. "There is no one else to do it," she said.

~~~~~

During the weeks following Solomon's homecoming, autumn began to pass into winter. Solomon was very busy helping Reb Weiss teach the little boys in the cheyder as well as at the older ones at the yeshiva. He still made frequent pilgrimages to see the rebbe, and their agreement stood as it always had. Solomon would marry Chava and take his father-in-law's place when the Master of the Universe had given them the signs. We all knew what those signs were, but did not speak of them, as if silence somehow muted their reality.

However, in spite of Solomon's busy schedule, he always found time to have tea, if not on Shabbos, then an evening or two during the week. Sometimes he came looking for me in the library the way he always used to and we would whisper to each other among the stacks of books.

Each day I waited guiltily for Solomon to ask me whether I had gone on any dates while he was in the army, but he said nothing. Perhaps he felt the same way I did. I never asked him about Chava either. It was like we had a tacit agreement not to discuss such things. His feelings had been clear to me that Shabbos eve when he had met Vlas. Our silence about these things felt strange to me and yet I suppose there wasn't much point discussing things I didn't look forward to happening when I had absolutely no control over them to begin with.

The autumn winds carried with them more stories like the ones Solomon had brought home from the army. The things we heard about the situation of the Jews in Germany were so horrible I felt only like screaming that they were lies. People could not possibly do such things like that to other people! Whenever anyone spoke of it, we would look at each other with wide, frightened eyes. Some of our neighbors began to move away, telling us we should go too, while there was still time.

I wrote to Papa, telling him what was happening and asking him what we should do. His reply to our letter was to wait, that he would see what arrangements he could make. The immigration quotas had tightened, he said, and we must be patient. Yet, he added, those Jews we spoke of were in Germany. We were far away in Poland, far enough away that we would be safe. He was certain of it. Mama and I had looked at each other over Papa's letter. We both felt a nagging doubt, yet also were both desperate to be reassured by the man whom Mama had called husband, and whom I called Papa. So we allowed ourselves to be comforted by the smattering of his words on paper.

Solomon, too, was worried. He did not say much, but I sensed the heaviness about him, the same one that had been there before he went into the army. One evening after supper he called on me to go walking. I knew this to be a sign that he would want to speak his mind. The evening was very cold and I wrapped in my heavy woolen coat despite Mama's objections to our going out.

As Solomon and I started toward Polaski Street, the winter wind bit at any part of our faces that was unprotected by hat or scarf. But we did not mind because we were the only people outside and could walk undisturbed. On Polaski Street, a stabbing wind coursed around us. We ducked into my uncle's storefront and pulled our coats more tightly around us, seeking to bury our cold hands by hiding them in our coat sleeves.

"Have you heard anything else from your father?" Solomon asked.

I shook my head. "He does not seem concerned. I know he would have already made arrangements for me and Mama if he thought…" I stopped, unable to finish my sentence. I watched Solomon's face, which, in the darkness with only the glow of a nearby street lamp, darkened before he turned away. I sensed that he disliked Papa and was trying not to argue with me again about him. "What does Reb Weiss say?" I asked.

"Papa wants me to leave here. He wants me to leave here and go east, toward the Ukraine. I have not had my life yet, he says."

"Solomon, it is hard to imagine there being problems here like in Germany, even with the tensions." I heard my voice rising, shrill, almost matching the wind. "Mostly we get along from day to day."

Solomon was watching me, but I avoided his eyes, looking instead around at the dark street, at the cobblestones, the shop buildings that looked like large wooden houses, the signs hanging above the doors. Everything seemed dark and lonely. Had Reb Weiss forgotten me in his fear for Solomon?

Solomon took a step toward me, his hands emerging from his coat sleeves to hold my shoulders firmly. "Listen to me, Hannele. No matter what happens I would not go anywhere without you. Do you understand?"

I looked back at him as a pain stabbed through me, the way it did every time Solomon said something that showed how much he cared about me. I lowered my head. "Yes." My voice came out in a whisper, barely audible above the wind.

"You interrupted before I had a chance to tell you that." He stood there, looking down into my face, his hands still on my shoulders. The expression in his eyes appeared to be searching inside of me, and I felt my stomach jump. "You believe me, don't you? Papa is afraid." He took a deep breath. "If things were different…" He fell silent, gazing at me with that…look he had. "I have nothing worldly to give you, Hannele." His voice grew heavy with sadness.

"I don't care about that, Solomon."

"I do. I would give you everything if I could. It tears me up inside that I can't do what I really wish in my heart, but I *can* give you my word."

I felt my eyes grow hot with unshed tears and blinked them back. Only one escaped and began to roll down my cheek. Solomon reached up and brushed it away with his thumb. At the touch of his finger against my skin, I began to shake and Solomon moved his hands away and rubbed them together vigorously. "You're cold, Hannele. Let's go back and have tea with Papa."

"I'd like that," I said, relieved that he thought my shivering had been from the cold.

With our hands in our coat pockets, we walked quickly back to Solomon's home, our shoulders hunched up to our ears, trying to protect ourselves from the winds of change which blew around us.

~~~~~

Winter, 1938-39

In spite of all our fears, we continued our lives as usual. The breath and pulse of the Jewish calendar still moved within us, perhaps even in those Jews who had largely shed religious practice to embrace modernism and communism, a godless philosophy which, in spite of my own political apathy, makes me shudder. The coming of Hanukah, the celebration of the miraculous oil and the spirit of the Maccabees, did much to lift spirits. It even brought Devorah and her two-year-old daughter, Ruchel, to stay with us for a few days while her husband, Isaac, was in Warsaw on business.

"Would you like your old bed back?" I asked her when Auntie Sylvia had ushered Ruchel into the kitchen for a special Hanukah doughnut. "I will make sure that Masha stays off of it."

Devorah smiled. She was pretty, small and slim, with large brown eyes and brown hair. Marriage and motherhood seemed to have been good for her. She had originally planned to study law, but when she met Isaac, she left school to marry him. Her manner was softer and she seemed to have lost the melodramatic edge she'd had in her teenage years. "No, thank you, Hannah. Ruchel and I will stay in Yoav's room together. I will not disturb Masha."

"All right," I said. "I will bring your bags up."

The next morning, I quickly did my morning errands and rushed back to help Devorah look after Ruchel while we prepared for Shabbos.

Just after lunch, Devorah started to peel and shred potatoes for *latkes*. I was making my challah and had finished forming the loaves. I set them aside to rise then sat at the table with my cousin, holding Ruchel on my lap while waiting for them to be ready to bake. I found myself staring at Devorah's hands while she worked, unable to believe they were the same hands that in previous years had always been perfectly manicured.

"You're impressed with me, I can tell," Devorah said as she rubbed a potato back and forth on the grater. "You probably thought I would never cook."

"I don't know." My cheeks burned. She was being so nice that I couldn't possibly tell her, *You're right. I always thought you were a horrible princess.*

Devorah smiled. "That's what love did to me. It made me give up many things I thought were important." She sighed. "I couldn't have both."

I stared at her and at her now useful hands, not knowing what to say.

"Hannah, maybe Ruchele would like to play with Masha," she said.

I smiled. "All right." I put my arms around the little girl. "Come, Ruchele," I said softly, close to her ear where a golden wisp of her hair tickled my nose. "Let's go visit the kitty." I rose from the chair and carried Ruchele to my room. "There she is." I pointed to Masha curled up in her spot on Devorah's bed.

"Kitty!" Ruchel reached out her chubby little arm toward Masha, but Masha did not look up as she usually did when I came into the room. An icy tingle passed through my skin and I brought Ruchel over to the bed and sat down gently, holding her in my lap. I reached out with one hand and stroked Masha, but she lay still.

"Oh no!" Quickly I rose and carried Ruchel back to the kitchen.

"What is it, Hannah?" Devorah asked as soon as she saw my face, "Did something happen to Ruchele?"

"No." I gently but swiftly set Ruchel down on the kitchen floor. "It's Masha." I turned and ran back out before I could hear what Devorah would say. My breath came in short bursts as I rushed back to my room, screaming inside, *Oh God, my Mashele!* "Please be up now, Mashele," I cried as I went in.

She was still as I had left her, looking peacefully asleep. I went over to her and touched her head. Nothing. I scratched her on the ticklish spot on her back, which, if touched, always makes her turn and try to bite my hand. But she did not move.

I dropped to my knees next to the bed, covering my face with my hands, unable to hold back loud sobs.

"Hannah, what is it?" I heard Devorah's voice from the doorway. I did not answer as a bitterness rose in me that I hadn't known I still carried. How was it that my cousin suddenly cared about what happened to me or Masha? It was she who had let Masha out of the house one day several years ago. And only good fortune's hand, and not Devorah's, had made Masha reappear at the door later that night, mewing to be let in.

When I had calmed down enough, I rose and picked Masha up off Devorah's bed, feeling my heart wring painfully. This would be the last time I lifted her off the bed. When I turned around, Devorah was not there. I carried Masha out into the living room.

Devorah was standing by the dining room table, rocking Ruchele in her arms, making soothing sounds. When I came in, she looked at me with dark eyes. "You frightened Ruchel," she said to me. "That was not necessary, Hannah!"

"I'm sorry." I opened the front door and ran out, not bothering to put on my coat. The December air bit through my sweater and dress as I rushed down the street toward the Old Synagogue, praying Solomon was home. I knew that sometimes when he was not at the yeshiva, he worked with students at the apartment. I knocked loudly at the door, waiting for a response. "Please be home, please be home," I whispered through chattering teeth.

Within moments the door opened and Solomon poked his head out. "Hannele! What are you doing out here like that?" He reached out and pulled me in by my upper arm and shut the door. The tiny apartment glowed with warmth. "Come by the stove and sit." He drew me over toward the table where a boy of about fifteen sat bent over a volume of Talmud. At first the boy looked at me with great curiosity, then down, quickly, at his book.

Solomon pulled out the chair he had been using and put it right by the stove. He took me by the shoulders and gently pushed me down onto the seat. "Jacob," he said, "I am sorry, but we must finish after Shabbos."

"Yes, Reb Solomon." Jacob obediently gathered his books together and bundled himself up, avoiding gazing at me, lest he offend his teacher. "Good Shabbos."

Solomon closed the door after Jacob, then came and kneeled down in front of me. "What is it, Hannele?" he asked gently. "What do you have there?"

I looked at him through the blurring of my tears. "It's Mashele." I held Masha's body slightly toward him so he could see. "She's gone!" A fresh spate of sobs overcame me and I slumped over.

"Oh. I'm sorry."

I began to choke on my sobs, which came faster and harder than I could release them. Though my eyes were closed, I could feel Masha gently being removed from my arms. I heard Solomon moving around the room and then his arms were around me as he kneeled in front of me once more. "I know how much you loved Masha."

"I did love her! I did!" I allowed myself to sob in Solomon's arms, my forehead pressed on his shoulder. I had dreaded Masha's death for a long time, and now it had happened. How would I stay in that room alone now without her?

I felt Solomon's hand on the back of my head and the other on my back. He rocked me gently, the way I had seen him do with Reb Weiss the day he'd left for the army. After a while, I became exhausted from sobbing and grew quiet. I realized then that Solomon was holding me very close.

I reached up and wiped my eyes on the sleeve of my sweater. "I'm sorry."

Solomon put his hands on my arms and held me away from him so he could look into my face. "For what, Hannah?"

"I disturbed your lesson."

Solomon smiled. "Sha." He reached out and took one of my hands. "Human needs take precedence over the study of scripture."

I sniffled and rubbed my nose with the back of my hand. "Devorah told me I scared Ruchel with my crying," I told him. "Ruchel's only two. Do you think I hurt her?"

Solomon looked down and I could tell by his expression that he was reflecting on my question. "She is going to learn that people cry and get upset. She will have to learn about death. It will hurt her more if she is sheltered from these things."

When he said that, a terrible weight lifted from me, and tears came once again to my eyes.

Solomon smiled at me. He squeezed my hand then brought to his lips, pressing them on the back of my hand.

Immediately, I began to shake, the way I had when he had brushed the tear from my cheek. He then put down my hand and rose, disappearing into the other room. I became frightened suddenly that I had offended him. But when he came out he had a blanket in his hands. He put it around my shoulders. "I will make you some tea, Hannele. Then I will walk you home. You need to rest."

I nodded and pulled the blanket around me as Solomon put on the kettle. I could still feel the impression of his lips on my hand and shivered a bit more.

While he waited for the water to boil, he came and sat down in the other chair. "I pray you didn't catch a chill. I will be very angry with you if you ever do that again."

"I won't, Solomon. I promise." Then I looked down. "Th…thank you."

"You're welcome."

When the tea was ready, Solomon brought me a glass, watching me as I lifted it to my lips.

After a few sips of warming tea, I set down my glass. "Solomon, what will I do now?"

Solomon thought a moment. "Well, unfortunately, the ground is frozen. We must wait until it thaws to bury her."

"But what about until then?"

"I will take care of her, if you leave her here with me."

I looked at him. "Solomon, how can I ask you to do that?"

"You didn't ask, I offered. I will act as your *chevra kadisha*. A mourner is not supposed to deal with such matters."

I watched his face and bit down on my lip. Could it be true what he was offering to do for me? "Are you sure?"

"I am sure Now please don't worry another moment."

I looked at him, still uncertain. How could I expect him to take care of such a thing?

"Hannele, that day I told you I was going into the army and asked you to look after my father, you did not begin to know the burden you shared with me and the relief it brought when you agreed."

"I was happy to, Solomon."

"Well, I am happy to do this for you. Is that not what friends do for each other? Share their burdens?"

I sighed. I did understand. Now. "Yes, Solomon. Thank you."

"Now listen. It is almost the Sabbath, and you are not supposed to mourn on the Sabbath."

I slumped my shoulders. "Yes, I know. But how can I not?"

A look of sweet humor came into Solomon's eyes. "This is how. You must remember that Mashele was a good Jewish cat, and that she would not have allowed it."

I raised my eyebrows at him, taken aback at first by the irreverence of this remark. But then I giggled as I pictured Masha turning her back on me with her tail in the air, the way she always had when she was mad at me. "All right." I sighed. "I will do my best."

"Good." He squeezed my hand.

We were quiet for several moments when Solomon looked at me. His eyes had that appearance of melting, his special gaze meant just for me.

I became nervous and looked down.

"Come now. I will walk you back. Keep the blanket around you." Solomon put on his coat and walked me to my house. "Go in quickly," he told me when we had reached my door.

"Will you come by later?"

"Yes, of course. I want to make sure you're all right."

"Good." I sighed in relief and opened the door. Then I looked back at him.

"Go now."

I stepped inside and took off the blanket, handing it to him. "Thank you."

"Go in!"

"Yes, Solomon." I closed the door and turned, bracing myself for more reproaches from my family. I took a deep breath and walked toward the kitchen, remembering as I did so, all that Solomon had just done for me, remembering that just a little while ago, Solomon had kissed my hand. His comforting friendship made me feel able to face anything more Devorah might say to me. Thankfully, she was up in her room, playing with Ruchel. When she finally did come back downstairs to work in the kitchen, she acted as if nothing had happened.

That evening, Solomon told me his solution to the problem of Masha's burial. Just after he had left me at my house, he went and found some scraps of wood from which he had made a small box. He put Masha in the box and set it discreetly in a corner of the yard of the synagogue, by a fence to wait out the winter. We were to bury her as soon as the ground had thawed enough. Solomon treated Masha as if she had been an important person and I was grateful. I had to struggle however, to remember what he had told me about friends sharing each other's burdens in order not to feel horribly guilty for accepting so much help from him.

As far as my family, nothing more had been said on the matter of my having frightened the baby. Auntie Sylvia had hugged me, expressing her sympathy for my loss. Even Uncle Leo was sympathetic, although he did manage to get in his two zlotys by mentioning that I probably wouldn't want another pet for some time to come. That is: No more cats in the house!

In her own way, Mama, too was a comfort. She had come into my room as I was changing my dress. She sat on the edge of my bed and brushed my hair for me. We both stared at the empty space on Devorah's bed. Gently she ran the brush through my hair. "Don't worry about Ruchel," she said. "Devorah is a new mother. Every little thing is cause for terrible alarm. I know. I was that way with you."

I looked at her. "Thank you, Mama."

"You're welcome, Hannele. I hate to see you suffer."

~~~~~

Spring, 1939

I miss Mashele so much I can't stand it! It's been months since I found her lifeless body on Devorah's old bed, and I just cannot accept that she's really gone. In the same way I used to forget that Solomon was in the army and expect to see him, I forget all the time that she's not there and that her body is in a little wooden box in the synagogue yard, waiting for the ground to thaw. Every night and early morning, I swear I can hear her breathing from the other bed and I start to pull the covers off me to go and prepare her breakfast. Then I remember and lie back down. Then, there are times when I think I see her out of the corner of my eye, a dark form, close to the floor, sweeping by and disappearing around the corner. I even dared to tell Solomon about these things and he said not to worry about it, that it's good I loved Masha that I would miss her so much.

I've never considered myself to be a terribly intuitive person, but everything is changing. I can feel it, as if Mashele's death marked the end of a whole era.

It certainly provoked a change in Solomon. Ever since the day I brought her dead body to him and he let me cry in his arms, I feel like he sees me as a girlfriend rather than just a friend.

I don't know anymore where friendship ends and courtship begins. He no longer keeps that unspoken rule we used to have about not asking each other about that part of our lives. Now, almost every time we see each other he asks whether I've "met anyone?" That's how he says it. And I always answer "no." Which is true, even though there are some very handsome boys in Wolensk. Like Jack Rubinstein on whom I have developed a crush. Jack's father has a geese farm and I always stop in the livestock market while on my errands to speak to Jack and admire his fluffy honking geese, bulging in downy puffs from their crates. Jack is friendly to me, but hasn't asked me on a date. Actually, I would feel funny about going if he did ask. I'm not a nice girl anymore and he would probably find that out somehow and not want to see me. Also, with the way Solomon is acting so jealous, I wouldn't want to face the barrage of questions from him I know he would give.

Actually, Solomon's jealousy is annoying. Especially when *he's* the one who's going to be married. I mean, if anyone should be jealous, shouldn't it be me?

And anyway, what is he thinking? Does he somehow believe that I could be his girlfriend? If it weren't for this strange invisible glue that keeps us in each other's lives, I would be tempted to tell him not to do this anymore, straddling these two worlds anymore the way he does. He's been doing this since I've known him, but now that he's getting older and closer to taking on certain responsibilities, the tension is getting worse and worse. In fact, he gets depressed at times and there are dark circles under his eyes. Reb Weiss (I shudder even to say this) does not feel well much more of the time and Solomon now has most of his father's responsibilities. I try to help as much as I can, but still, I don't know what to say to Solomon in these times and sometimes feel the need to get away from him.

And as if things aren't bad enough already, Solomon insists on reading the newspapers every day. The pages are covered with ghastly reports on the plight of Jews in Germany. I can't bear to look at them. I've tried to tell him to stop. I've even gone so far as to beg him to throw the paper in the rubbish, but he is so stubborn and won't listen. Solomon takes all the weight of the world's problems onto his own shoulders, as if he had some sort of control over them. So when I say something, he just looks at me and tells me he is worried about me too. Why, I don't know. It's too late to do anything about me or anyone else. Hitler is threatening to make war and the immigration quotas have shrunk almost to nonexistence at this point. My world of waiting has simply deepened, as now I am waiting to bury Mashele, and waiting to see what our fate will be. I have given up on Papa bringing me over to America, and can only hope that if Hitler does try to come into Poland, our army will be able to drive him back out.

I can certainly say that this was one of the ugliest winters I have ever lived through, one iron cold day after another relentlessly dragging on with nothing but ills.

But now, finally, those days have come when the sun's warmth is strong enough to melt the snow, bit by bit, turning the ground to mud. Today is the day Solomon and I are to bury Mashele.

Solomon came to the door just as I finished a glass of tea. On waking up this morning, I'd had the strange feeling that this was the day. When I opened the door, he was standing there, looking at me sympathetically, a small wooden box tucked under one arm, and a hand shovel sticking from his coat pocket. "It's time now, Hannele," he said gently. "And don't forget your prayer book."

We decided to bring Masha to the meadow at the edge of the forest. Solomon set the box down and knelt to dig the hole among the tall brown grass. When he had covered the box with earth, he stood and softly uttered some prayers in Hebrew, his body swaying, as it always did when he prayed. He then told me to recite the Mourner's Kaddish from my prayer book.

We marked the site with some stones, although we both knew that the summer grasses and wildflowers would cover it, making it difficult to find again. I didn't care. I wanted to be able to pass by here and not see her grave. I stared down at the small pile of stones. It was so difficult to feel anything, thinking that Mashele was down there, underneath all that.

Solomon came and stood next to me, then reached out and put his hand on my shoulder, a warm pressure that caused me to shiver lightly. "How are you?"

I shrugged. "I am all right, I suppose." I pushed my hands deeply into my coat pockets. "Mashele will be happy here, I think."

"Yes. I believe she will."

Then I looked up at him. "Thank you, again, Solomon."

He smiled. There were moments like these when certain tensions between us faded into the background, and we were simply two people who happened to be friends. "Come," he said, "Let's go back."

I sighed as a cold morning wind passed around us, blowing my hair against my cheek.

Solomon offered me his arm and the moment of simplicity passed. Gingerly, I took his arm and we started back. We walked without speaking. We had never walked arm in arm like this before, the way older men and women who had been married a long time do, or young people who were courting, in the first blushes of love and anticipation of their life together. We were not a couple. We were strange. I stared straight ahead, clenching my teeth to stop them from chattering.

"Hannele," he said, "I'm sorry for the way I've been acting lately. I get so scared. I'm frightened for our futures. I hate not knowing what will be."

I looked at him. The kindness in his voice washed away the ills of winter. I, too, was frightened. I just tried to do other things besides think about it so much. "It's all right, Solomon. Really."

He smiled at me. "We'll be warm inside soon enough," he said, having noticed my chattering teeth. "I'll make you some tea."

I nodded, saying nothing. I knew the chattering was not from the cold. I was a rugged Polish girlchik. Even the deadest of winter did not chill my bones. No. When my teeth chattered, I knew it wasn't from the cold. It was never from the cold.

~~~~

September 1939

I have decided to go to America… I can't go one more day without seeing Papa. I pack my valise and walk out of the house. Mama and Auntie Sylvia and Uncle Leo watch me walk out and don't even try to stop me. They don't say anything at all. They just watch me go.

As I head down the road that leads out of Wolensk, I'm thinking that I should say good-bye to Solomon. We'll miss each other. We're such good friends, but he has Chava now, I remember bitterly. He'll be fine without me.

I walk along the road and everything has a strange pinkish glow about it. My valise is heavy, heavier than when I first packed it, and it's difficult to walk, but I push and push, so I'll be on time for the boat to America. I need time to find where it is, and to buy my ticket.

Then I hear the loud rumbling of a truck. Maybe whoever is driving will give me a ride to wherever the ship is, but I should be careful because all around me there are hateful people who might try to kill me. I look over my shoulder as the rumbling grows louder and louder. *The truck never seems to pass, moving right along side me, never stopping, and the whole ground beneath me begins to quake...*

I opened my eyes as the picture on the wall above my bed fell onto my legs. The rumbling did not fade with the dream. I looked in confusion around my room, which was just becoming visible in the gray light of dawn. There was no road, no truck, no early morning thunderstorm, but the rumbling grew heavier, louder, now permeating the entire room in deafening sound and movement.

I sat up quickly as the roaring passed over and around us, then began to fade. The perfume bottle that Maria had given me a long time ago lay on its side on the bureau, rattling, then grew still. I picked the fallen picture up from my blanket and stared at it, just as Mama appeared at the doorway, looking like a frightened child.

I looked up at her. The expression on her face was begging me for an explanation. "Airplanes," I said to her when I realized I recognized the sound. I had heard airplanes before, but never so close, as if they would scrape the roof! A nauseous feeling began to churn in my stomach. Nothing good could come from those airplanes.

Mama stood in my doorway, hugging herself while I quickly dressed. I hugged her, and we stood there for a moment, then went together to the kitchen.

Uncle Leo and Auntie Sylvia were already there, still in their bedclothes and robes. Uncle Leo was turning the knob to the radio, trying to find a human voice among the static sounds and Auntie Sylvia was staring at him, chafing her hands. She barely glanced at us when we came in.

I went to prepare a glass of tea, keeping my gaze from Mama's frightened face as she stood, huddled by the table while Uncle Leo honed in on a broadcast. The words stabbed at us through the static like tiny daggers. Hitler. Luftwaffe, Hitler's air force. Nazi party marching into Poland. War.

Auntie Sylvia jumped up from her chair and grabbed her husband. "Leo! Yoav! My God! He's right there!" She began to wail and Uncle Leo grabbed her up in his arms.

"We have an army, Sylvia," he said, trying to hold her down. "He will not reach Yoav. I promise!"

But nothing he said helped. Auntie Sylvia kept wailing and struggling in his arms. Finally he managed to drag her out of the kitchen and upstairs while Mama, shocked from her childlike stupor, went to get something to calm her.

Alone in the kitchen, I hugged myself, shivering. I looked around, lost. My gaze fell on the tea kettle, which was on the verge of whistling. Though I didn't feel hungry, I sliced some bread, doing all the things I would normally do, pretending it was a morning like any other. Pretending we were not about to be caught in war.

In a few minutes, Mama was back and sat with me at the table, her eyes red.

"How's Auntie Sylvia?" I asked.

Mama shrugged, and stared down at the slice of bread I put in front of her. She was back in that place.

After breakfast, she left to dress while I washed the dishes. In a moment however, I heard her say my name behind me. I turned. She stood there with Solomon just behind her. At the sight of him, my blood froze.

"Solomon! What is it?"

"It's Papa," he said. "He is not well and is asking for you. Can you come?"

I pulled off my apron and threw it over a chair. "Of course I can."

We left and walked quickly toward the synagogue. Our street, which was usually busy at this hour with people going to work and hanging out their washing, was quiet, and you could almost feel people cowering inside their homes, waiting to see if the planes would return.

"What happened, Solomon?" I asked, hurrying to keep up with him.

"It's his heart. It doesn't work right."

Unthinking, I reached out and grabbed Solomon's arm. "I didn't know!"

"He tries to keep it a secret."

"Why?"

Solomon kept looking straight ahead as we approached the synagogue and took the path around to the back. At the door, he stopped and turned to me. "He never wants anyone to fuss," he said.

I looked up at him. "He told you this?"

Solomon shook his head. "No. I just know him."

He opened the door and held it for me. The small apartment was dark, except for one lamp in the corner. I thought briefly how unkind it had been for the builder of this place to have made it so dark.

"Come, Hannele." Solomon closed the door behind us. He touched my elbow lightly as he passed.

I followed him into the bedroom. The light from the other room just reached in, outlining the beds in gray shadows. There was a strange odor in the air. As my eyes adjusted to the dimness, I could see Reb Weiss's form on one of the beds.

"Solly, you are here?"

"Yes, Papa. I brought Hannele."

"Hannele?"

"I am here, Reb Weiss."

"You can go to him," Solomon whispered behind me.

Cautiously I made my way to his bedside and kneeled down.

"I am not so good today, Hannele." He lifted his hand slowly toward me.

I took his hand. "I know," I said softly. "You will be, though." I bit down on my lip. Between the strange odor in the room and the painful sound of Reb Weiss's breathing, as if a heavy weight were pushing down on his chest, I grew dizzy. The pain of biting my lip kept me from succumbing.

"I wanted to see your sweet face, Hannele." Reb Weiss formed his words slowly. Speaking was difficult, but he seemed determined. "But it is so dark in here, I can't see a blessed thing!"

I chuckled in spite of myself. "You must rest now, Reb Weiss."

Solomon came closer to the bed. "Hannele is right, Papa. Listen to her."

Reb Weiss closed his eyes and I thought he was going to sleep. But then he opened them. "Solly," he said, "If they come here, you hide the Toyreh."

"I will, Papa."

Reb Weiss's hand slackened. "I can rest now." His breathing softened and his eyelids fluttered closed. Solomon touched my arm and I stood up from the bedside, following him out of the room, the sound of Reb Weiss's snoring softly behind us.

In the other room, Solomon led me to a chair. I sat and watched him light the tiny stove and put up water to boil. Then he came and sat in the other chair. We were silent. There seemed to be nothing but the promise of death in the air around us.

My hand rested on the table. Solomon made a movement in his chair, and then I felt his hand on top of mine. "I am here, Hannele." His voice was soft.

I looked up. His eyes reflected the dim lamplight, their honey color melting, as always. "I know."

After we had our tea, I washed the glasses while Solomon looked in on his father. "He's still sleeping," he told me as he came to stand next to me at the sink while I dried my hands and folded the raggedy dishtowel. "My father loves you. You've brought him happiness."

I looked down. "Do you really think so?"

"Of course. I would not have said it."

"I love him, too." But then I looked up as the tone of his words sunk into my mind. "Solomon, you talk as if he's dying!"

"Hannele…" Solomon gently put his hands on my arms. "He is."

"No!" Then Solomon's arms were around me. He held me against him. I felt his lips pressing on the top of my head. It could not be true! God could not be so cruel! How many times in the last year had I almost slipped and called Reb Weiss *Papa*? He had been kinder to me than my own family. I held onto the sleeves of Solomon's shirt, crumpling them in my fists. His black vest absorbed my tears.

For a long time we stood there like that. When I looked up at Solomon, his eyes were wet. Oh God! I remembered again my selfishness. "I'm sorry," I said.

Solomon's arms were still around me. "Why do you apologize?"

"Reb Weiss is your father, and yet, you comfort me." I shook my head and wiped my face with the back of my hand. "I'm a nuisance."

"No, Hannele," Solomon reached out and pushed back a lock of my hair, causing me to shiver slightly. "I beg you not to say such a thing."

"But it's true."

"Stop." Solomon closed his eyes. He took his arms from around me and put his fingertips to his temples. His movement commanded my obedience, reminding me that his father was in the next room, dying. That I had once again been selfish with him, and that he, once again, had responded with patience and forbearance.

I sighed. "Have you eaten anything?"

He shook his head, opening his eyes slowly.

"I will go get you some food." My heart squeezed at the look in his eyes. "In the meantime..." I went over to the small window above the sink and pushed it open. A cool breeze rushed in, lifting the white lace curtains.

When I turned, Solomon was standing by the table with what looked like a bundle of clothes in his arms. "Will you bring this to your home and hide it?" He held it out. "It's the Scroll. I took it from the Ark this morning."

I reached out and took it from him. "Of course I will. But Reb Weiss said —"

"I know. But there is no *if* about it, Hannele. They will be coming."

I shivered and hugged the precious scroll. I turned to protest once again, but when I looked again at Solomon, he had sunk down onto the footstool. To speak again would be wrong. So I went to leave. As I passed by him, I put my hand on his shoulder. "I won't be long," I told him softly, penitently.

"Please, don't be."

"I won't. I promise."

Back at home, I hid the scroll in my dresser underneath my sweaters, then went and quickly gathered together some leftovers from the previous night's supper as well as part of a loaf of bread and packed the food into a basket. I walked back to the apartment behind the synagogue and knocked quietly on the door, afraid to just open it as I had taken to doing.

After a few moments, the door opened and Solomon stood there, watching me. The rims of his eyes were red, and there was an eerie calm about him. He reached up and raked his fingers through his hair, pulling off his yarmulke as he did so. "Hannele," he said softly, "Come, say good-bye."

~~~~~

I knew that God was going to separate me and Solomon one day, but I didn't know He would do it in such a cruel way, and that I would have to watch. It's horrible enough that Reb Weiss was gone, to have heard the thud of the earth being dropped on the pine box that held his body. I felt like something in me died with him. I didn't realize quite how much I had grown to love him, and now I'd never see him again.

But with that, Solomon didn't need me anymore. He had his future wife and mother-in-law who had taken over him in his mourning. The two of them are always there, even after the rebbe himself has come and gone, fussing and arranging platters of food on the small wooden table which groans under the weight. Don't they even notice that?

And Chava. I knew her the moment I saw her, reddish-gold hair, delicate and sweet. It was at this first glance that I realized with a quite sickening feeling, Solomon's steadfast determination to fulfill his commitment. Why wouldn't he be determined? What man wouldn't want such smooth cheeks and eager virtue? That's just what I meant about love not being real and about how God takes people away from us in all sorts of soul-destroying ways. Finally, I couldn't take any more, so I stayed out of Solomon's way, taking refuge at the kitchen table, reading. I feel a bit guilty doing that, but I'm positive that Solomon does not notice my absence.

Even though I haven't been going there, I stare at the synagogue from the kitchen window for long periods of time, especially after meals when I am washing the dishes, just as I am doing in this moment, staring at the large, square wooden synagogue in the glow of the streetlight. Mama had a terrible headache and had gone to lie down. I had almost finished Mama's and my dishes—for Uncle Sylvia and Uncle Leo rushed off to see Devorah in Bialystock for a couple of days—when I saw the rebbetzin and Chava leave. Solomon was there too, helping them into a waiting wagon drawn by two horses which then passed down the street with loud grinding of the wooden wheels and clop-clop of hooves. Solomon stood, watching them, while I watched him. I thought he would turn around and go back inside when they had disappeared. But instead he began walking toward my house. Guilt overwhelmed me that I hadn't been to see him in two days, but…

I don't know if he saw me watching him from the kitchen window, but quickly I dried my hands and went to the front door, opening it before he had had a chance to knock. Not having seen him in two days, I lurched inwardly at his appearance. He was unsettlingly pale and disheveled, the circles under his eyes almost as dark as his clothes. And I was too glad to see him. Two days seemed suddenly as long as the five months he'd been in the army, and suddenly, my angry jealousy seemed pettier than I had thought. After all, Solomon had come here, hadn't he?

"Where have you been?" he asked. "Have you abandoned me?"

"I…No…" I said. "I…thought you didn't need me anymore."

Solomon sighed, then reached up and rubbed his hand over his face. "Don't do this, Hannele. Please."

"Do what?"

He gestured to me. "This. I know why you've stayed away, but you're wrong. I need you." He looked down. "I've missed you."

I glanced past him to the synagogue, unable to look Solomon in the eyes now. I was chastened and reassured both. At least for the moment. "Come in and rest awhile," I said. I seated him in the living room, something I never feel at liberty to do when my aunt and uncle are home, and went to make some tea. When I came out of the kitchen with the tray, Solomon was sitting very still, looking down at his hands.

I set the tray on the low table and sat down next to him, reaching over to serve him his tea. It was then my hands started shaking and I fought it. Solomon's grief was horrible to look at, and I didn't know what to do or say.

"How have you been?" he asked me.

I shrugged. "All right. Just sad."

Solomon nodded. He said nothing and sipped his tea, not bothering with his usual lump of sugar. I sat, holding my glass, still not knowing what to do or say. We were both quiet all the way through drinking our tea. When our glasses were empty, Solomon set his down and turned to me. "You don't understand what it means to me that you're close by," he said. "You make it bearable to stay there."

I nodded, clenching my teeth at the unbearable sweetness of what he was saying. I had not been very loyal these past two days, although I had felt fully justified.

Then Solomon reached out and picked up my hand. Gently he squeezed it and held it, our joined hands resting between us on the velvet seat. I glanced at him, seized with the strong urge to just cuddle up against him and hold on. But I didn't dare.

"Hannele," Solomon began after several minutes, "The rebbe, he wants me to go there as soon as *shiva* is over."

I felt my body tense, and anger and jealousy flooded back over me. Reassurance was always temporary. My place in Solomon's life was doomed and had been since the beginning. Why did I always try to think something else? "And will you? Go, that is?"

Solomon sighed heavily and squeezed my hand. "I don't know. I don't know anything. There is a war coming. We're trapped now. I don't know, Hannele. All we have is this moment."

I didn't say any more and set my empty glass on the tray. Just when I did, Solomon moved closer to me, still holding my hand, and with his other, gently touched my cheek, at which I started to shiver.

"Hannele," he said, his voice low, almost a whisper. "I don't know if anything I do is ever right. I've never been more confused in my life. But one thing, maybe the only thing I know is that I won't abandon you. I give you my word. I said it before and meant it. As impossible as it is for you to believe, I'll find an answer. You must have faith."

At this I felt a surge of anger. I had had faith before and it had never been rewarded. "God is cruel, Solomon! Don't you see that? You never believe me!" Then I started to cry, unable to control myself. I thought Solomon would get angry at me and leave, but he didn't. He pulled me to him and let me cry, even though he was probably the one who needed to cry.

"Hannele, Hannele. You see everything through the wrong eyes." Then he was quiet while I sobbed. How patient and gentle he was with me, the hateful, willful thing that I am! He can love everyone. And that's exactly why he was going away, Chava or no Chava. I knew. That was his fire, the fire that had destined him to be the next Wolensker rebbe.

When I had calmed down, Solomon smoothed back my hair from my face. The way he was looking at me with his melting eyes made me want to cling to him and run away from him all at once. He leaned over and pressed his lips to my forehead. When he pulled away, he looked at me, touching my cheek again with his fingertips. I tensed, expecting him to kiss me on the lips, his face was so close.

"You're so pretty, Hannele," he whispered.

I shook my head. "Thank you. But I don't think so. Chava is pretty."

"Not like you." Then he sighed and sat back against the sofa. He pulled my hand to him and laced his fingers through mine. "Is it okay if we just sit here like this for a while?"

I nodded. "Of course." I settled more comfortably into the cushion. We sat quietly, listening to the grandfather clock, its ticking marking the passing of these moments. We sat for what seemed a long time, just like that. For me, though, it would soon be gone forever. Those moments were the sweetest I ever had in my whole life.

~~~~~

That night I dreamed of blood. Screams and cries. I could hear flames, great roaring tongues of fire, orange and red, licking at the old, sacred wood of the synagogues. And there was only terror of death pervading the whole world.

When I woke up, I hadn't really been dreaming. Mama's cries and wails were filling the house, under which the ground was vibrating.

I jumped from bed and ran into the hallway, almost colliding with Mama who had been on her way to my room, her hands tangled into her hair in fists. She took them from her hair and grabbed me. "Hannele, don't look outside! Don't look!" She grabbed wildly at me, but I fought her off and ran to the kitchen. "Hannah, get away from that window!"

The desperation in her voice ripped through me, but I was paralyzed, unable to tear away from the sight. Dark billows of smoke rolled skyward from a pyre that had once been a beautiful wooden synagogue! I couldn't see which one it was. At the street level, a line of army tanks rolled down the street through the smoke. Mama grabbed me once again, touching off my screams. "Solomon!" I screamed. I struggled with Mama trying to twist away from her to go to the door, but she held onto me with strength I had never imagined was in her.

"No, Hannah!" she screamed. "No! They'll kill you!"

"Mama, please!" We struggled some more until I gave up and wrenched away from her a final time. Mama sunk into a chair, sobbing into her hands, while I stared out the window, rubbing my raw throat.

The tanks had passed and there were lines of soldiers marching in their wake, seeming oblivious to the smoke. The soldiers wore dark green uniforms and their heavy boots clopped ominously on the dirt of the road, making a racket nearly as loud as the tanks. Lines of rifles pointed in the air, and flags, red with a white circle emblazoned with a strange black symbol in the center, flew. I had seen that symbol in the Yiddish newspapers and my heart thundered with terror before my mind even formed the words: Hitler was invading Poland and we Jews were doomed.

"Hannah, please." Mama's quivering little voice came from behind.

"Mama, what about Solomon?"

"How can you help him now?"

I continued to watch the burning synagogue. A gust of wind blew smoke away and I saw that by a miracle, Solomon's synagogue was not burning. But there were soldiers attacking the building, smashing the windows with their rifle butts and tearing away pieces of the beautiful carved moldings. I turned away and covered my eyes. *They are coming, Hannele,* Solomon had said when he gave me the scroll to hide. Was he in there? Had they killed him? I fell to the floor in a useless sobbing heap. Ashamed and terrified. This was how I would face death.

~~~~~

They are sadistic bastards, these Nazis. I never knew God created people capable of such cruelty! I'd never believed human beings to be the nicest of creatures to begin with, but I could never have imagined the very existence of such ones as these. For two weeks they terrorized us. They smashed and looted Uncle Leo's store. They pulled all the bottles and packages of everything off the shelves and tore most of my books to shreds. Then they gave the store to some Polish man, a Volkdeutsch, he is called because he is of German ancestry, and forced a group of us to clean it up. I told him it had been my uncle's store and he said I could work there. It is humiliating, but we need the little bit of money he pays me for food. Mr. Pearlman, who now has to clean the street each day, waits for me and walks back to the Jewish Quarter with me because he is afraid for my safety. He was always a very nice man.

At night we can hear them marching up and down the streets, singing and shouting. "Death to Jewish pigs!" they yell. One day they beat an old Hasidic man nearly to death and cut off his beard. They set fire to several homes, and on another day, they gathered a group of Jewish men and women (thank God I was nowhere nearby, I would have been one of them) and made them dance naked right in the street at gunpoint!

I think frequently of killing, maybe swallowing all the pills we have in our medicine chest in the bathroom. But then Mama would have had to face the Germans all alone. Uncle Leo and Auntie Sylvia were trapped in Bialystock, although I think they wouldn't care what happens to Mama anyway. I couldn't do that to her and so I will suffer along side her. At least she and I are together.

The only sliver of hope I have is that Solomon might still be alive. The same day the Germans arrived, we learned, several people had fled into the nearby *puszcza*, the primeval forest. It is deep and dark, with a dense canopy of pines and other trees. I cannot imagine what it must have been like for Solomon to have been in that synagogue apartment when the Nazis began to smash and burn the synagogues. I only pray that he made it out alive.

Then, one day, the Germans were gone. Simply gone. Their tanks rolled back down the streets the way they came, the same soldiers marching behind them, with flags and rifles. And in their place came the Soviets, with their tanks and soldiers. You should have seen the fuss! Most of the people of the Jewish Quarter went running out, yelling greetings and waving scarves at them. I thought some of them would run up and kiss the soldiers and the tanks as they moved down the street!

The air all around us smelled of their burnt fuel, but the gasoline stench was infinitely preferable to the smell of a burning synagogue. Mama and I did not go out into the street to greet the Soviets, both of us preferring to stay in the house and breathe a bit of relief. Instead, we stood and watched the whole thing from the kitchen window.

I still didn't know if Solomon was alive or dead, and our lives had been ripped apart in a mere two weeks by the Germans. We had been living on potatoes and matzo meal fried with onions.

I looked at Mama. She felt my gaze and smiled faintly at me. Then we just stood and watched.

Beyond the marching soldiers and gas fumes stood Solomon's synagogue. By a miracle of biblical proportion, the once majestic wooden building was still intact. The broken windows had been taped and missing, chopped-out shingles made the Old Synagogue look quite ragged. God, how I wanted to go in there. But even if I were to go outside in the first place, I could not bring myself to see what had become of the beautiful prayer hall. Mr. Pearlman told me that the Germans had looted it, taking for themselves the silver plated cover on the door of the ark and had chopped up the ornately carved wooden screens and benches on which the men sat to pray. How could they have done such things?

It didn't matter anyway. No one was going to have a chance to repair the synagogue, for within hours of their arrival, the Soviets abolished all religious institutions and boarded up the synagogue doors and windows, including Solomon's apartment. What would it be like for Solomon to come back and see all this? I doubted that Solomon would be back at all.

And what a rag tag looking bunch they were, the Soviets! The Nazis had been crisp and polished, even in the midst of all their vileness. These Russians wore tattered great coats, their boots scraped and dull. They walked around with their rifles hanging loosely from their shoulders and cigarettes hanging from their mouths. Of course, we'd prefer none of them were around. But better these than the Germans.

That evening, Uncle Leo phoned to tell us that he and Auntie Sylvia would be back by the following evening, providing the trains were running on time. Mama, who had answered the telephone when it rang said, "The train, Leo? But you have a motorcar." She listened to his answer, then put her hand over the earpiece and looked at me. "They've taken his car!" she whispered to me. I covered my mouth to stifle giggles. Mama tried to reproach me with her expression, but then had to cover her mouth, too. She turned back to Uncle Leo, and I went into the kitchen for some more cookies, all the while picturing Uncle Leo—who absolutely hates dirt almost as much as he hates spending money—brushing off the seat in the train before sitting down. Oh well. In times like these, such is practically the stuff of comic Yiddish theater.

All schoolteachers were instructed to go back to their jobs, so the next morning Mama got us both up early so I could have breakfast with her. I soon saw why she wanted my company. She was a nervous wreck!

"I don't even want to go out there," she said. Her brown eyes were glassy with fear and her hands trembled around her tea glass. "What if they grab me right off the street and deport me? It's happening now, you know."

I sighed and shrugged. Mama's hysteria could be contagious and I wanted none of it. "Don't worry, Mama. They need you to teach school. And besides, if you just agree with everything they say, you'll be fine."

Mama looked at me. "I don't agree with them. I believe in God."

"Sha! Just agree on the outside."

Mama nodded quietly, though her face was chafed and strained. She finished her tea and set down the glass. "How do I look?"

"Beautiful. Maybe you'll meet a nice communist and get married."

Mama shook her head as she rose from the table and picked up her purse. "What a mouth you have on you, Hannele."

"Just go. I'll do the dishes."

"What are you going to do?"

"I don't know. I'll find something. Read a book. Tidy the house for Uncle Leo. He'll like that after riding the train."

Mama and I looked at each other and grinned. But then she became serious. "Don't go out there if you don't have to, Hannele." She reached out and smoothed my hair back in a motherly way. "These soldiers look so unsavory. They seem quite fond of their vodka from the looks of them."

I rolled my eyes. "Don't worry, Mama! I have no reason to go out. You'd better go. If you're late, you know what happens!"

"Don't even joke like that!" She kissed me on the cheek and left. From the kitchen window I watched her go up the street, looking straight ahead of her, clutching her purse. No one bothered her, so I turned away and fixed myself a second glass of tea. I was still in my nightgown and bathrobe but was in no hurry to dress or to do anything else.

I was about to sit down at the table when a sudden knock on the front door echoed through the house. A simple knock on the door had a meaning for me it hadn't before. In my stockinged feet I padded to the front door and leaned close, still holding my heart, which felt like it was trying to claw its way out of my chest. I pulled my bathrobe tightly around me. "Who is it?" I said, trying to sound older and stronger than I was.

"Hannah? It's Solomon, Hannele."

As if an imposter were lying to me to gain entrance, I cracked the door and peered out. But he had been true. The first I saw of him was his eyes. No one else had eyes like Solomon. "Solomon!" Quickly I opened the door the rest of the way. "Solomon!" Out of habit, I glanced at him, then at the street, looking for spying yentas, then drew him inside.

I had imagined many times what I might do if I saw him again. And here he was. And I did none of them. I stood and stared at him, my hands over my mouth. We never do what we think we will in any given situation. I just felt overwhelmed with the basic truth that he was alive, standing here in front of me, dark circles under his eyes, emanating a haunting sadness. Aside from that, however, there was nothing in his seemingly well-fed and only slightly rumpled appearance to indicate he'd been living in a forest this whole time. A nagging ache told me where he had been. At least part of the time.

"Hannele." His usually clear gentle voice trembled. "I'm so sorry. There was no time." Suddenly, he dropped to his knees and grabbed my hand, holding it to his cheek. His beard was soft and warm against my skin. "If I'd led them to you with the scroll here, what they might have done to you!" He sobbed and rocked back and forth, pressing my hand to his cheek.

I felt horrified that he should act like this! Who am I that he should humble himself like that? "Solomon, no." I reached and grasped his shoulder, trying to pull him up. "Please, Solomon." Anything else I could feel, anger, fear, even joy at seeing him alive, was washed away by his great sorrow. "Don't do this. You did nothing wrong. I understand. I'm just glad you're alive." I squeezed his shoulder, still begging him with my touch to stand up.

Solomon closed his eyes and pressed his lips to my hand. Then he held it again to his cheek. "Thank you, Hannele. I was so worried about you. And when I saw you were alive and well, I prayed you would forgive me for fleeing."

"There's nothing to forgive, Solomon. They would have killed you. They're horrible beasts."

Solomon opened his eyes and looked at me. "How beautiful you look, Hannele."

I felt my cheeks burn, then realized, oh my God, that I was in only my nightgown and robe. I had to go and dress! "Have you eaten anything?"

"No."

"I'll give you breakfast. I...I just have to get dressed."

Solomon nodded and kissed my hand again before letting it go. "Thank you."

"For what?"

"For being my friend."

"I'm the one who should thank you." I turned and went to my room, closing the door behind me before I took off my robe. Quickly I put on a blouse and skirt and went to the kitchen, where I found Solomon seated at the table, waiting for me. He stood up when I walked in, but I gestured for him to sit back down.

He waited quietly while I put bread in front of him and prepared tea. He lifted off his yarmulke and raked his fingers through his hair in an agitated manner, and I noticed that he did not go to the sink and do the ritual washing of his hands before eating as he had always done.

As I waited for the water to boil, I sat down, watching Solomon as he tore unceremoniously into the bread and stuffed a large hunk into his mouth. When he had swallowed, he sat, breathing heavily. His eyes searched the room, seeming to appreciate its warm quiet. Then he looked at me. "So much has changed, Hannele," he said softly.

"Yes, I know."

"I abandoned you. When I had given you my word I would not."

I shook my head. "No, Solomon. It's not like that. They could have…" I hesitated, almost choking on the words themselves. "Burned you."

The water boiled and I rose from my chair to prepare tea. I put Solomon's glass on a small plate with a cube of sugar, the way he liked it.

"Thank you," he said when I set the tea before him. "You take good care of me."

I smiled and sat down again, my hands around my glass. "Where did you go?"

Solomon took a sip of his tea. He sighed as he set the glass and his sugar cube down. His face had a strange look. "Into the forest. I was there for days. There were others, too." He sighed. "I've never been so cold and hungry and frightened in my whole life. Except when Papa found me on the doorstep."

"You remember that?"

Solomon nodded. "Yes. I do."

"Then what happened?"

"Well, we stumbled around for days, not knowing which direction we were going. I didn't want to go far away. I wanted to get back to you. Two of us, this other man and I, when we came out of the forest there was a farm. It turned out we had gone east where there were no Germans. A Polish farmer let us stay there and fed us in return for help with their wheat harvest. They were very kind. But at first, they were afraid of us." He touched his beard. "They see this, and they become afraid." He sighed again. "We are strangers wherever we go, Hannele. Nowhere is home."

Then he looked at me, his gaze resting intently on my face. I had never seen such an expression on another human being's face. I couldn't even describe it, but it made me feel beautiful and terrified at the same time.

"How did you get back?" I asked softly.

"The farmer came and told me about the agreement between Hitler and Stalin, that Russian soldiers were marching through to take their place. When the news spread that the Germans were leaving, I knew then that I could come back…to you. It was very late yesterday when I reached Wolensk. I did not know if the synagogue would be open for me to come in. I stayed the night at the rebbe's home."

I stiffened slightly at this news. Sudden jealousy nagged at me. "Oh."

"Hannele, I thought about you all the time. I was so worried something terrible had happened to you and I could not bear it if it had. Tell me what happened."

And so I did. I told him about Uncle Leo's store and working for the Volkdeutsch. And how horrible and ghastly the Germans were. I told him about the old Hasid and the people being forced to dance, and the old woman who had to scrub the cobblestones of Polaski street on her knees with a toothbrush.

When I had finished, Solomon put his hands over his eyes and sat there, saying nothing. When he looked up finally, I felt a shiver run up my spine. His face looked so creased and chafed. His eyes were bloodshot, and I could see what he would look like as a very old man.

"Have you had enough to eat?"

Solomon nodded. "I have. Thank you."

I picked up his empty glass. "I'll wash these things and then we can go into the other room."

"Yes, Hannele." He waited quietly for me to finish.

When I had I dried my hands, I turned to him. What were we going to do? I felt suddenly nervous, the way I had when I'd been alone in Levi's store with Aaron.

"May I see the scroll?" Solomon asked.

"Of course. It's…in my room." I looked at him to see his reaction, but he only nodded. I led him to my bedroom. He did not stop in the doorway as he had before. I pointed to Devorah's bed. "You may sit if you'd like. That was Masha's favorite seat."

Solomon smiled faintly and sat on the edge of the bed, watching me go to the bureau. I took the scroll out of its drawer and laid it on the bed next to him. Tenderly he opened the cloth and caressed the velvet cover. "Papa taught me to read from this scroll," he said. "Thank you for keeping it safe." His sadness was palpable, filling my small bedroom.

"You're welcome, Solomon."

"I have not been back there yet." He looked at me. "Will I be able to go back?"

I stood in front of him, chafing my hands together. I had so dreaded this moment. "No," I said softly. "They've nailed it all shut. I'm sorry."

Solomon nodded. Then he looked down to the scroll. He cradled it, stroking the velvet ornately embroidered cover like he would a child's head.

Strangely, I thought of the day Masha died and I had sat with her little body in my arms, sobbing. Although now, I couldn't imagine what Solomon felt, having lost Reb Weiss only a few weeks before, escaping from the Nazis, and freezing and starving, only to come back and not even be able to return to the only home he had ever known. What do you say to someone who has gone through all this? How do you deal with the helplessness of not being able to make it even a bit better? I felt as ineffectual as Mama did in times like this. I shivered and swallowed, my throat feeling suddenly very thick and pained.

"Will you still keep it here?"

"Of course I will."

"Thank you, Hannele. It's best if you put it back now."

I leaned down and Solomon gently placed the scroll in my arms. Even though it was a small one, it was quite heavy with its wooden handles and the immense amount of rolled up parchment on which the five whole books of Moses had been meticulously inscribed all by hand. I went and placed it back in the drawer, covering it carefully with my sweaters, in such a way that no one could ever guess that such a sacred relic was hidden underneath them.

When I had closed the drawer and turned around, Solomon was leaning over with his elbows on his knees, his hands covering his face. His shoulders were quaking, and I realized he was sobbing, quietly. I had never seen him cry before. I stood and watched him, flooded with the same horrible helplessness. Why did I not know what to do? All I knew was how he had held me when Masha died. Perhaps that's all you can do when someone has died.

I inched over to the bed and sat down next to Solomon. Gingerly, I placed my hand on his back, between his shoulder blades.

At my touch, Solomon lifted his face and looked at me. "Hannele," he whispered, his voice heavy, his throat thick with his tears.

"I'm here, Solomon." Slowly, I moved my hand so that my arm was around his shoulders.

Without hesitation, Solomon turned and fell against me, his face buried into my neck. I put my arms around him as his sobs escalated into deep guttural sounds that seemed to emanate from a great invisible well within him.

I rocked him gently as I had seen him do with Reb Weiss, as he had done with me. I stroked his hair, noticing with each stroke how soft it was. Like a baby's hair. How many times had I looked at Solomon, never imagining how soft and beautiful his hair was? I was suddenly trapped in the awareness, even as I held him in his grief, that the person in my arms was no longer the strange yeshiva boy who had befriended me, following me around all those years. Solomon was a man, undeniably. He felt strong in my arms. I felt a womanly stirring down below, and I became frightened. Frightened that I wanted to be holding him like this. Not wanting to let go. People who loved each other destroyed each other.

After a long while, I felt Solomon grow calmer. I thought he would move away from me but he didn't. He remained in my arms, his forehead pressing into my shoulder. He took several deep breaths then raised his head. He had been pressed against me for so long, the air close around us. His warm breath caressed my face.

"Thank you, Hannele."

I did not answer because I had begun to shiver.

He reached up and touched my cheek. "Are you cold?"

"No."

Solomon held his hand against my cheek and gently brushed his thumb across my lips. "I don't feel as if I have any beliefs anymore, Hannah," he said. "I only know what I feel when I look at you."

I felt the stirring again in my womb. The sensation traveled upward, like an invisible stream, warming my breasts. I began to shiver uncontrollably. To my horror, my teeth chattered.

"Hannah, what is it?"

"Nothing. I'm sorry."

Solomon pushed back a lock of my hair. "Your hair is so pretty. It's as soft as I imagined it would be."

"Thank you," I whispered.

He gazed into my eyes again and I saw his focus drop to my lips.

My heart jumped. I was frozen in place, in a tortuous suspension between wanting to pull back and desperate for what could come next

He kissed me. Tentatively at first, merely pressing his lips on mine. Then with his lips parted, seeking deeper kisses. I let him in. Our tongues touched and a small jolt of surprise passed between us. I even reached up and tentatively caressed his beard with my fingertips. It, too, was as soft as his hair.

Solomon kissed my cheeks and my neck, then my lips again, all the while stroking my hair and my back. Then he stopped suddenly and hugged me. "Hannah," he whispered into my hair, "Hannah."

I hugged him back, my cheek resting on his shoulder. I felt my body coursing inside with that feminine desire to be taken, surrounded by the man she loved, both inside and out. I felt like I belonged with him. No feeling had ever filled me with as great a terror as did this desire.

Gently he laid me back on the bed underneath him and sought my lips again. I stroked his back, even dared to let my fingertips follow his shirt below the waist of his trousers. When my fingertips touched his skin, Solomon let out a soft moan and began to fumble with the buttons of my dress. He undid several buttons and began nuzzling my bare skin, kissing it softly and gently touching one of my breasts over the brassiere. "Hannah, you're so beautiful," he whispered. Then he reached up and slipped the strap off my shoulder.

For a moment I remembered Vlas. The experience had been brief, turbulent, over in moments with no pleasure. Solomon's mere kisses had been pleasurable, soft and worshipful. Unlike anything I'd ever experienced. Now, he fondled my bare breast in his hand. Exploring it with a touch full of...wonder. Like touching me was the most incredible thing *he'd* ever experienced.

Heat radiated all through me. My eyelids fluttered. The world blurred. Down below, more heat pulsed. I felt...slippery.

Solomon moved against me in such a way that if we had been undressed, he would have been inside of me. Then he lowered his head and began to suckle on my nipple. I stiffened slightly, feeling very exposed, but he was very tender. I had not imagined how this would feel. The sensation made me breathe heavily. Another brief memory of that first time with Vlas surfaced. The difference between then and now was excruciating. What had I done? What was I doing now, entertaining this beautiful pleasure when Solomon and I...when this world...? Another kiss on my breast pulled my thoughts away.

Fighting back my rising panic, I stroked his hair as he pulled down the other strap, exposing my other breast and kissed it. Solomon's love for me came through my very skin, from the tender brush of his lips. With his hips against mine, I felt his male desire burgeoning, hard, pressing. We were so close, close to the very thing I'd been resisting. To have these moments of love and then watch Solomon leave to get married…

He stopped and unbuttoned his own shirt and pulled off his vest. Then his bare skin brushed against mine as he kissed my lips and neck again. His hand slipped under the skirt of my dress, stroking my thigh, feeling me over my underpants. His breath sounded heavily and quickly in my ear. I felt how close we were to joining and my terror mounted equal to my desire. There was the strangest, most intense fear of dying. All secrets would die. And I would die of the pain of love.

Solomon slipped his fingertips under the waist of my underpants. It was clear he meant to pull them down.

I stayed his hand firmly with my own. "Solomon, we must stop." My body was stiff. My heart pounded painfully.

He removed his hand and I pulled the skirt down quickly. "Why, Hannah?" He still breathed heavily and seemed stunned from the curt way I had ended our loving. "Did I hurt you?"

I sat up and fixed my brassiere. "No." I began to button up my dress with swift fingers.

"Then what is it? Please tell me!"

"I don't know. I mean…it's…"

"It's what?"

"Wrong!" I wriggled out from underneath him and swung my legs over the side of the bed. I sat on the edge, my fingers gripped at the mattress on either side of me. My body still felt the pulse of Solomon's breath and lips and hands.

Solomon gently grasped my shoulders from behind. He sighed. "I pushed you, didn't I? I'm sorry, Hannah. I couldn't help it. I've loved you for so long and you were finally here, in my arms."

I closed my eyes. My shoulders sagged under his hands. He squeezed them.

"What is it, Hannele?" he said when I did not answer.

"Why do you have to ask? Don't you already know?"

Solomon said nothing, and his silence angered me.

"How can you not answer, Solomon? You're going to be married!"

Solomon moved closer and embraced me. "I'm sorry." He nuzzled my hair and the side of my neck. "I have not been able to find an answer."

"An answer to what?"

Solomon kissed my shoulder and squeezed me gently against him. "An answer to the question of how we can stay...together."

A surge of anger welled up and I pulled away from him. "There is no answer. We both always knew the time would come when you will have to go away and leave me here!"

"I am not going to just leave you here! I would not! I cannot imagine my life without you."

I closed my eyes as his words coursed inside of me. "What will we do?"

Solomon reached out and caressed my hair. He swallowed hard and I saw his Adam's apple move. His hand trembled as he stroked my hair. "Keep faith with me, Hannele," he said softly.

My eyes flew open and I stared at him. "What?"

Solomon swallowed again. "I know I've no right to ask this of you. But I cannot be forced to make such a choice. I didn't ask to be betrothed to Chava. I love *you*."

His words spiraled through me. Especially that last confession. One emotion after the next poured through me. And then, the implications of what he was saying reached my conscious mind. "Do you mean…" I continued to stare at him.

Solomon bowed his head. "Yes, Hannah. I would not just…make love to you…without taking care of you. I love you."

My hand went to my mouth as I began to shake. "Solomon," I said quietly, "We can't…I mean, what are you thinking?" How could I possibly be his mistress? And live with the torment of knowing we could never really be together and watch him go home to his marriage bed time and again after we'd been together?

"Hannah, I just told you I love you. Don't tell me you don't feel the same way. I see how you look at me. Would you deny it?"

Again, I pulled away from him. Could this be possible, what he was suggesting? "Is that what you think of me?"

"Aren't you listening? I cherish you! This is the only way! I must keep my word to the Wolensker rebbe. If I didn't, I would be worth nothing to you as a man. You would be better off alone." He stopped, waiting for me to answer, but I felt only hysteria inside.

"Hannele, the rebbe is dying."

When he said that I clutched at my stomach which churned suddenly, cruelly. I shook my head. "No!"

He leaned forward and put his hands on my shoulders. "Don't you see? You and I, we've stayed in two different worlds, afraid to choose one or the other. Now life is forcing us to choose."

"No! That is not true!" I began to sob. "What crazy ideas you have, Solomon!" I sobbed hysterically, feeling I had lost all capacity for reason.

"I beg you, Hannah, stop talking this way. You are wounding my heart. What just happened now, between us, I've never done before. Any of it." His hands came out in a pleading gesture. "Don't you know I would cut off my own hand before I would knowingly do anything to hurt you?"

What he said was true and I felt a stab of shame, but my terror had possessed me and I had already gone too far. "You believe that now, Solomon. But that day will come! It always does! Besides, you *have* hurt me!" I said. "The rebbe, Chava, they have always been lurking in the background! You have always had this weapon to use against me!"

Solomon squeezed my shoulders and shook me slightly, forcing me to look at him. His golden eyes flashed and anger creased his brow. "How can you say such things, Hannah? What have I done to make you mistrust me? I have always told you the truth! Has anyone ever cared about you as much as I have? Where's your father now? Where's that *mamzer* with the violin who was waiting to devour you?"

I squirmed to release myself, but he held me fast. I had not realized Solomon was this strong. "Let me go, Solomon. My father loves me!"

"You're lying!"

"I am not!"

I continued to squirm and twist. "You're hurting me!"

At this, Solomon released me. He was breathing heavily and his eyes were dark and flashing. For several tortuous moments he said nothing, only watched me. "Maybe I should go," he said finally. The usual softness in his voice had disappeared and was low and flat.

I looked at him as if he had slapped my face. "Maybe you should!" I stood up and took a few steps toward the door of my room, but Solomon leaped from the bed, staying me with his hand on my shoulder.

"I don't want to go, Hannele," he said. "Stay with me. We will find a way. I am home when I'm with you."

I began to sob when he said that. How I wanted to beg him to stay here with me and turn and fall into his arms. But how could I? Especially now. I did not deserve him. And even if I did, I could not possibly share him with Chava. And even if, by some miracle, I could, he would certainly drop me the instant he found I wasn't a virgin. "I can't."

"Why?"

"I just can't."

Solomon did not answer and I avoided looking at him. I did not want to see how his face looked. His hand dropped from my shoulder. "Does this mean the end?"

"It has to!" I cried. Hadn't he known this all along?

I heard small, muffled sounds and realized he was buttoning his shirt. I covered my mouth with both hands, as if to stifle a scream, and stood with my shoulders hunched. I could not wait for him to leave, yet, felt I would die if he did.

"You've broken my heart," he said. "Can't you at least look at me?"

Slowly, I took my hands from my face and looked at him. He had put his yarmulke back on and was as neatly dressed as when he had first come in. I saw his hand grip the door knob, as if he would pull it off.

"Good-bye, Hannele," he said. "I mean, Hannah."

I winced when he corrected himself. I could not answer, although he paused, seeming to wait. Then he was gone.

I stood, listening. I heard the front door open and close. I removed my hands from my mouth and gasped. Then I sat down on my bed, staring at the floor, gripping bunches of my skirt in my fists. "I cannot share!" I said out loud. "I cannot! I cannot! I cannot! Who would?" Then I lay down, my words repeating in my mind. Maybe if I said them enough, I would know I had done the right thing.

PART TWO - WAITING FOR THE MESSIAH
Winter 1939-40

"Here is your tea, Solomon." I set down the glass of tea on a saucer with a sugar cube next to his open book.

"Thank you, Hannele," he says. "You take good care of me."

I squeeze his shoulder gently and start back to my work in the kitchen. But when I go to pass by, he takes hold of my arm and tugs me gently into his lap.

I laugh. "Solomon! What about your studies?"

"They can wait." He puts his arms around me. He begins to nuzzle my breasts and kiss them over my dress.

I stroke his hair as my eyes flutter closed. He makes me feel like the most beautiful woman in the world.

"Ha Shem forgive me," he mutters. Solomon always says that when he wants to interrupt his study of Scripture and carry me to the bedroom.

"My soup can wait too," I say as I slip off his lap. He rises and scoops me up. I laugh...

When I opened my eyes, the room was brightening into morning. I breathed heavily, waiting for the dream to pass, but the ghostly images clung to me, like wet clothing to my skin. The dreams always did. I sighed, wishing I could reach for Masha and stroke her to help me go back to sleep. I looked to the other bed, but it was empty. Empty. Empty. Empty. No Mashele. I hated how Mashele was never there anymore and never would be. So I closed my eyes and lay back. I felt no reason to get up anymore.

I opened my eyes when I heard Mama come to the doorway of my room.

She sighed at the sight of me, still huddled under the covers long after I should have been up. "Hannele," she said, "Are you going to stay in bed all day? We go through this every morning now."

I turned and stared at the empty spot on Devorah's bed, then at my bedside clock.

Mama came and sat down on the edge of my bed. "You could come to school with me and help in the classroom."

"I don't know how to teach."

"You taught Solomon to speak Polish, didn't you? What happened to your childhood dream of being a teacher?"

I sighed. "That was a long time ago."

Mama looked up at the ceiling. "Hannele, what will I do with you?"

I looked at her. "Just let me be, Mama. I don't want to go teach communism." I rolled over and looked at her. "What is the point? Can you tell me?"

Mama sighed again. "Would you rather Wolensk had ended up on Hitler's side of Poland? Did you like the things his Nazis did while they were in charge? They were only here two weeks and look what happened! The Soviets are different. They leave us alone for the most part, and many Jews are doing quite well."

"Mama, please!"

"No, Hannah, *you* please! You must get on with things now!" Mama paused and closed her eyes for a moment. When she opened them she looked over to my dressing mirror where I kept my photograph of me and Papa. "You yourself told me just to agree on the outside and you were right. You helped me see that I must teach to keep food on the table. It is something I thought I would never have to do, but here it is. Sometimes survival is what matters. Have you forgotten what you said that day?"

I couldn't deny I was being hypocritical. "All right. You could ask Uncle Leo to use me in the store more than just a few hours a week now that he has it back."

"Sylvia helps him now. There's not enough to go around."

"Well then…" I took on a sarcastic tone, "Maybe I will go work on one of those new collective farms."

Mama stood up and smoothed down her skirt. "I have heard enough from you." She started to walk away, but I threw my pillow down on the floor, and she stopped to stare at me. "All I wanted is a little sympathy! Don't you think it's hard getting along now without the people who were my best friends? You were not close with Reb Weiss like I was! Now all I have left of him is that scroll in my drawer!" I crossed my arms and leaned back against the wall, sniffling.

Mama sat back down. She reached out and brushed back my hair. "I am sorry, Hannele. I forget sometimes. I love you. It's hard for all of us."

I looked down at my hands, at the nails I had tried unsuccessfully so many times to stop biting. Now, they were shorter than ever. "It's all right," I said. "I love you, too."

Mama stroked my hair some more. "Why don't you dress and come have breakfast with me and Auntie Sylvia? Come sit at the table with us instead of standing and staring out the window while you eat."

"All right. I suppose I should, but it's been horrible to be around Auntie Sylvia lately. She looks like a ghost."

"She's worried sick about Yoav. God only knows where he is, but he's a survivor. That much I know." She shook her head. "Would that your own father worried as much about you as she does about her stepson."

"Mama!"

She put up her hand. "All right! All right! I won't start. Just please come to the kitchen."

"I will!"

Mama stood up and went to the door. "Hannele," she said.

"Yes?"

"You know, maybe Solomon's going on to his new life is best for you both."

I shrugged wearily and leaned over to retrieve my pillow from the floor. "I don't know. I don't know anything."

After Mama and Auntie Sylvia had left for work, I did the dishes. When I finished, I dried my hands and left the kitchen. I felt aimless and alone, my only companion the ticking of the grandfather clock by the front door. I wandered into my room and stood by the dressing mirror, staring at the photo of me and Papa I had stuck in the frame. He was kneeling next to me, his arm around my shoulder. I was smiling, happy that Mama was going to the spa and I had a whole week to be just with him. This was shortly after they had separated and he still lived in Warsaw. Even though he spent most of his time with Mr. Rosen and some other men they were friends with, he had taken me to see moving pictures and to the ice cream parlor for pineapple ice cream. That time with him had been like a precious gift.

I sighed and went to draw myself a bath. I love to soak in the tub each morning when no one else is home. Then Uncle Leo won't bother me about steaming up the mirror or using too much hot water. I just make certain to leave the bathroom looking as if it had not been used at all during the day, and then he doesn't say anything.

After my bath, I went into my room to dress. I'd just finished buttoning my blouse when I heard the front door open and slam shut. I stood still, listening, terror chilling me, praying it was just Uncle Leo coming back for something he'd forgotten. Only, Uncle Leo never forgets anything.

Silently I padded out of my room into the hall. "Hello?" I called. When no one answered, I began to shake violently. Maybe they had come to deport me for not being a productive Soviet citizen. In a matter of moments I would be on a train to Siberia to starve in one of their gulags! "Hello?" I called again, inching my way down the dark hall, past the bathroom, which still emitted warm moisture from my bath.

As I drew closer to the kitchen door, I could hear muffled sounds coming from within. The ice box slamming shut, cupboard doors opening and closing loudly, then the scrape of a chair as it was pulled away from the table.

I grabbed one of the candlesticks from the dining room table and stood by the kitchen door, preparing myself to find out who was in there. Apparently, they had not come looking for me. But there had been refugees pouring into Wolensk from the Nazi side of Poland as the weeks had passed, and I now feared one had broken into our house to steal food. Not that I wouldn't give it willingly. It just would have been better to be asked.

I took a giant breath and pushed open the kitchen door, letting out a gasp at the sight of the filthy, scraggly man seated at the kitchen table, devouring a piece of chicken. Food littered the entire surface of the table.

When he heard me, the man looked up, strings of chicken hanging from his mouth. He stared at me a moment, then went back to eating as if I weren't there.

I just stared back at him until I realized I knew him. "Yoav!" My shoulders slumped and I almost dropped the candlestick to the floor.

"Hello, Hannah," he answered through a mouthful of food.

I went slowly over to the table, incredulous that this shadow of a starving person was really my magnificent Yoav. I set the candlestick down. "You frightened me."

Yoav swallowed his giant mouthful of food. "I didn't know anyone was here." He seemed concerned only with filling his belly.

"Were you in the forest too?" I sat down, but he asked me for some water.

"Where wasn't I?"

I brought him the glass of water and sat back down. "Where's Ruthie?"

Yoav picked up the water and gulped it all down before answering. Then he simply shrugged. "I don't know. I had just left her house when it all started. I ran." He wiped his ragged sleeve across his mouth and sat back, apparently winded from his ravening. He belched and sat staring down at the scattered remains on the table. "What are you trying to say, Hannah? Should I have been a hero?"

I stared at him. "I...no...Yoav...I didn't mean anything."

"Yeah, sure. Everyone thinks they'll do the right thing in a situation." He reached out and pushed a mutilated loaf of my bread away from him. "Until you're there." With that, he stood up. "I'm going to shower. It'll be nice to be clean for a change."

"All right," I said, still shocked from how he had spoken to me. "I'll wash your clothes if you'd like."

"Yeah, thanks."

I watched him leave the kitchen then cleaned up the mess he'd left behind. When I finished, I ran to the store to tell Auntie Sylvia that Yoav was home, so she wouldn't worry anymore. It was the least I could do. She did her best, after all, to be good to me, even though she was married to Uncle Leo.

Of course, Auntie Sylvia was beside herself with joy when I told her about Yoav. She grasped my shoulders. "Hannah, is it true? What happened?" she cried, not caring about the dreary selection of customers who looked up at her when she did.

"He escaped Warsaw. Somehow he made it here. He was starving, but he ate and went to bathe."

Auntie Sylvia hugged me and ran to the back calling, "Leo! Leo!"

I heard their voices from the back and Auntie Sylvia's sobs of joy. She reminded me then of Reb Weiss the day Solomon came home from the army. Then she came rushing out of the back with her coat on. "Hannele, will you stay here for me? I must see him!"

I nodded and she grabbed me again and gave me a big kiss before running out. I took off my coat and put it in the back where Uncle Leo sat at his desk, wiping his eyes. Then I went out to take care of the cash register.

Working there now wasn't much different than before everything happened, aside from Russian soldiers coming in, gaping wide-eyed at how much there was to buy, and Uncle Leo not actually owning the store now. The Soviets had nationalized all commercial property and kept the profits, distributing to Uncle Leo his equal amount. Every night he grumbled about it. He wouldn't have had he been here when the Nazis came rather than in Bialystock where they hadn't gone. He would be grateful for what he did have and shut up about it.

I went about my work, catching myself looking out the window every few seconds. Finally I grew sick of it and berated myself inwardly. *Stop it, Hannah!* I thought. Those days were long ago over. The Wolensker Rebbe was too busy and too important to come in for the Yiddish newspaper now. And besides, he had always bought it for his father. And Reb Weiss wasn't here anymore either. Such was God's cruelty.

Contrary to the past when Yoav came home, I did not look forward to going back to the house now. Constant images of my handsome cousin, ragged and starving, stuffing food into his mouth after all he'd suffered assaulted my mind. Yet at the same time, I felt horrified that he had not gone back for his girlfriend. In spite of what he'd said about how people think they know what they'd do in any given situation as opposed to what they really do, I couldn't help but start comparing him to Solomon.

Even though Solomon too, had run off when the Germans came and disappeared into the forest, I couldn't compare him to Yoav if I was honest. Solomon really had been terrified that he would have led the Nazis to me and Mama and to the scroll and of what they would have done to us. And, when Solomon came back, he came immediately to see that I was all right. He had said how much he missed me. He had fallen to his knees and begged my forgiveness for something over which he had no control. I thought of Yoav's haggard face and the way the food had hung from his mouth, like from a wild beast, and the vacant expression in his eyes when he had looked up at me as if I weren't really there and his callous response about Ruthie. The two men had both suffered, yet had behaved so differently. It seemed that there was already something in a person's nature that caused them to respond to similar situations differently.

All this I felt walking home in the dark, frozen twilight. The air smelled of snow and the anticipation of Hanukah.

As I approached the house, I could see Yoav's washed clothing hanging from the line in back. I hadn't laundered them as I had promised, but since Auntie Sylvia had asked me to stay and work for her at the store, she had washed them.

Yoav was asleep when I went in. Auntie Sylvia came out and put her finger to her lips. I nodded and hung up my coat, staring upward toward his room. Before I had left to come home, I would have wanted to go up there and climb into the bed with him and have him snuggle me. Not that he would have, but I would have wanted it. But now, after all that I had thought about on the way home, I felt his presence in the house like some dark burden. It seemed suddenly quite unfair that he had survived and Reb Weiss was the one who passed away.

Mama, too, was napping on Devorah's bed when I went into my room. Thankfully, she wasn't snoring. Mama snores terribly, and I am always grateful that I never had to share a room with her. But now that Yoav was back, I would. I hoped I would survive it. I looked at her on Mashele's old resting place, then sighed and went into the kitchen to help Auntie Sylvia with supper.

~~~~~

"Hannele, I want to love you right now," Solomon whispers. His breath is warm and his soft beard tickles the skin of my cheek. He reaches up under my nightgown and gently squeezes my breast. He knows if he does this I'll open to him.

"But what about Papa?" I say. "He's right there." We listen to Reb Weiss who snores in the other small bed nearby.

"It'll be all right," Solomon answers before he drops soft tender kisses on my neck. He reaches down below and caresses me there, parting my legs with a gentle hand. I feel very self-conscious with Reb Weiss so nearby, but Solomon is always able to weaken me. While he kisses me I pull down the bottoms of his pajamas so that he can nestle between my thighs and fill me. He keeps his mouth over mine, using kisses to muffle my sounds of passion, so I won't cry out when there is that delicious explosion...

I opened my eyes and Solomon was gone. But the snoring was still there. I lay quietly, breathing heavily as if still in the dream. The snoring had been Mama's, and I had heard it the whole time.

I stared into the shadows for a few moments then picked up the little clock on my nightstand. It read 3:30. Suddenly, I was seized with the most fervent need to try and get into the apartment behind the synagogue. I rose from my bed and tiptoed into the front hall. I put my coat on over my nightgown and stepped into my boots. It was freezing outside, but I was sweating from my dream and didn't care.

Outside the night air helped to cool the heat which surrounded me like a fever. I looked down the street in both directions, but it was silent and cold. I began walking toward the synagogue, knowing only that I needed to be surrounded again, if only for a moment by what had once been Reb Weiss' world...and Solomon's. I felt angry and hurt, but still, he had been my friend.

It was so dangerous to be out here. There were always soldiers about, but I didn't care about that either, seized as I was by this sudden pounding desperation.

I went to the door of the apartment, which I had not dared go near since the Germans had come. I tugged on the boards, but they refused me. "Oh no! Oh no!" I cried out softly as I continued to tug at them. The utter futility of my tugging reached me. I stopped and stood, sobbing quietly, my forehead against the door.

Desperately, unexpectedly, I thought of the mezuzah on the doorpost above my head. Although I couldn't get inside, I could at least have that little bit of memory. Removing the mezuzah was probably a sin but I didn't care. I began to pry at it frantically with my bare hands. "Please! Please!" I cried softly, but it, like the door, refused me.

Suddenly the mezuzah was bathed in light. I gasped and lowered my hands, then stood, frozen, like a frightened, trapped animal.

"*Shto eta*?" I heard a male voice behind me say in Russian. "Turn around," he said, this time in Polish.

Slowly I obeyed. A light pierced my eyes and I squinted. Behind the light was the silhouette of a uniformed soldier.

The soldier lowered his flashlight and stepped toward me. I heard a clicking sound in his other hand. When he drew closer, I saw a rifle in his other hand.

I trembled and pressed my back against the door as he approached. He was about Solomon's height and wore one of those gray-brown uniforms. He looked at me in a way at once relieved and suspicious.

"*Dyevooshka*, what were you doing?"

"I...I'm sorry." My eyes went suddenly heavy with a rush of tears. "My father lived here. He died a few weeks ago and I miss him so terribly. I wanted to find a keepsake."

The soldier slung the rifle on his shoulder and I almost dropped to the ground with my relief. He went into his pocket. In the light I saw the flash of a knife blade. In a moment he had pried the mezuzah off the doorpost, examined it briefly, perhaps to determine whether it was worth anything, and handed it to me.

I took it in both hands, fighting back another spate of embarrassing tears. Both Reb Weiss and Solomon had touched this mezuzah everyday, every time they crossed this threshold. To me, the simple wooden carved piece with the scroll of words from the Torah hidden inside was a priceless treasure. To the communist soldier who stood before me, the mezuzah was a worthless relic, something to be discarded. "Thank you," I said. "Thank you so much."

The soldier shrugged. "Sure."

I put the mezuzah into the pocket of my coat. Then I turned and looked one last time at the door.

"What is your name, *dyevooshka?*"

"I....I'm Hannah." I looked at him as if he would decide to pull the rifle out again suddenly.

"Hannah, why does your husband allow you to go out like this?" His voice was flat and slightly nasal.

"He doesn't...I mean...I am not married." My answer caused me to wince inwardly. I always told these soldiers I was married if asked. I don't know why I told the truth now. I wished I had simply lied. "And I do not go out like this, usually."

He grinned. "You have boyfriend?"

I felt my face burn. "Thank you for your help," I said. "I must go."

"My name is Uri," he said, as if I had answered his question.

I nodded. "Thank you," I said again. I began to walk away. When I reached the street again, I glanced back, but did not see the soldier called Uri.

Back at the house I slipped inside, closing the door quietly. I leaned against it with my eyes closed, listening to the silence. Those moments just before dawn were so very quiet, the house invitingly still. I wished I could wake up each morning to enjoy this time of day, but it had been only my dream of Solomon that had awoken me.

I put my hand into my coat pocket, gently grasping the mezuzah. I shivered, one of those shivers that pass through a person when he has escaped, by mere fortune, a terrible situation. That soldier could just as easily have arrested me, but he was a young man, probably Solomon's age. And I was a girl.

I felt suddenly very sleepy, as if I had gone through an entire, grueling day in just that short time. I slipped off my boots and padded on tiptoe to my room. Mama was still snoring away, so I pulled my bedclothes and pillow off my bed and settled myself on the living room sofa to sleep. I crawled under the covers, scrunching them all around me like a cocoon, then closed my eyes, the mezuzah still clutched in my hand under my pillow.

~~~~~

Has Yoav always really been this obnoxious? Or is it just that I have been terribly blind with him? He never says please or thank you to me for anything I do for him, and I have been waiting on him practically like a serf. In fact, he barely has two words for me at any given time. He's even rude to Auntie Sylvia who dotes on him worse than I, and she never says anything to him about how he acts. It's like we're all supposed to ignore it.

Maybe Yoav figures that because he is now getting rich on the black market food smuggling he's been doing, he's invaluable to us. I'm sure that's why Uncle Leo lets Yoav speak to him however rude he pleases. He's afraid of Yoav and wants the money his son brings in, especially since he takes in much less from the store under the Soviets. What does Yoav think? That because of what he went through he can do whatever he likes? Mama and I, and everyone else here suffered too!

What's worse, though, is I disgust myself the way I still fawn over him with my nose stuck in his behind, as if I somehow believe that treating him well will change how he feels about me and transform him into a man more like...Solomon. If my motivation is to make my cousin into a better person who loves me, then I just need to stop because such a plan will *never* work. Not with Yoav anyway. So today when he comes home for lunch, I'm going to have already left for a long walk. If I'm not there, he'll have to get his own lunch. I don't even care that it is the dead of winter and that most everything is weighted down with mounds of snow. I'm going!

Late in the morning I put on several layers of clothing and stockings and went out. Outside was the kind of day I love, cold but with a bright blue sky, and the sun making everything glitter, including the air. As I walked down the road that led out of town, I cast off behind me the Soviet village with its Russian street names and placards of Joseph Stalin, the village that had once been Wolensk. I shivered and sped up my pace when I passed the turnoff that led to the compound of the Wolensker rebbe. I didn't even remember the last time I'd been down this way.

On the very edge of town, at a street sign, stood a group of Russian soldiers, standing casually, a cloud of cigarette smoke around them. They watched me as I drew near, but I passed quickly by, ignoring their remarks to me, none of which I understood anyway except for the word *dyevooshka* which I know means a girl or young woman. I suppose I really should learn some Russian. I mean, I am already fluent in Yiddish and Polish, and can get by in French and German. What's one more language to me?

A bit farther down, I came to the stone bridge that crosses the river and continues to flow toward Bialystock. This was where I turned, following the river bank, past the meadow which in summer blazes with poppies and daisies, the meadow where Masha lay buried. I just kept walking, not ever caring to stop or go back. But I did stop when I came to the old mill. In winter, no one ever comes here. Except for me and Solomon, of course. Last winter, we wandered in here. It was the only time we ever went out for a long walk together, except for when we buried Masha.

The sight of the old building pulled me. I went up onto the large mill stone, an old giant block someone had put there to serve as a stepping stone. I put my mittened hand against the rotting wood of the door. Strongly, like the headiness of my mother's French perfume or the sounds of fists on flesh in the marketplace the day of the Endecja, the memory of that day Solomon and I had explored its insides was there. Almost as if we had left a part of our spirits inside.

That day I had understood something, a moment unlike any other, surrounded by the rotting wood and the rush of the stream underneath. Solomon had come to stand in front of me, looking into my face. Golden shafts of sunlight were penetrating the weakened walls of the mill and I remember thinking how that color was the same color as Solomon's eyes. But I had looked back at him longer than I ever had, captured by some mysterious force, unable to turn away. Everything he felt for me moved from inside of him, through his eyes, into mine, and I knew only the utterly helpless feeling of slipping and sliding, falling, like on an icy pond. The terror of it was unlike anything else I'd felt. The weirdest part was that I didn't want to be anywhere else. I had my final resting place. But then my mind had spun with thoughts, horrible thoughts that I would be left helpless, at Solomon's mercy, unable to spend a single moment away from him without complete devastation. My soul would be joined with God and we would vanish.

So I had turned away, but not before Solomon said that we should not come here again.

Without thinking I had asked, "Why not?"

But he had only said, "Please, Hannele, don't make me explain."

"Hello, Hannah," a voice said behind me.

I caught my breath. I had not heard anyone come up behind me this whole time, and for one brief moment, I actually thought it was...

I turned quickly. First there was disappointment. A soldier stood before me. I stared at him. Then, a churning of fear began in my chest. Had he followed me?

"Hannah, have you forgotten me already? I was back there when you passed by." He stepped up onto the millstone.

Then I recognized him. Uri. It had been dark when I had met him, and I had been so frightened and hysterical. I had not seen then that his eyes were a smoky greenish color or that his cheeks were terribly pockmarked, the way they are when someone has had a horrible childhood illness. He had helped me that night, yet, the fear in my chest still pulsated.

"You are expecting someone else?"

I wanted to tell him yes, but it was so obviously a lie that I shook my head. "No. I just like to come here."

"But it is very cold, no? You don't freeze?"

"I don't mind the cold."

He did not answer. He reached into his coat pocket and pulled out a small flask, unscrewing the cap with a gloved hand, and taking a gulp. He closed his eyes as he swallowed, then held the flask out to me.

I shook my head. "No, thank you."

"Go ahead. It will warm you."

His insistence made me feel guilty, as if my refusal would slight him. I considered taking the flask. Maybe one sip wouldn't hurt. After all, he had rescued the mezuzah for me. I reached out and took the flask from him, and slowly brought it to my lips. The odor of vodka was acrid, invasive. I tried not to wrinkle my nose as I wondered how he could drink it. But I took a small sip. Oh God! How it burned! A trail of liquid fire slid from my throat all the way to my stomach. I coughed furiously, my hand clamped over my mouth. Uri took back the flask, and when I was finally able to look up at him, he was gulping from it and watching me.

He chuckled as he screwed the cap back on and replaced the flask in his coat. "It's good, the vodka, no?" A tiny crooked smile played about his lips.

This annoyed me as I shook my head. He chuckled again. The sound was so familiar, a mocking, derisive sound, which I had grown to dislike. Yoav chuckled like that.

Uri leaned his shoulder against the wall of the mill. Again, he went into his coat pocket, this time pulling out a cigarette, which he lit. Within seconds, a cloud of smoke surrounded us. It, too, smelled very bad and burned in my throat and nostrils, but the vodka was tingling in my head and skin and I did not mind as much.

"Are you from this town, Hannah?"

I looked at him and narrowed my eyes, partly in suspicion, and partly because my vision had become slightly blurred. "Yes." I sighed and blinked. My eyes, too, burned.

Uri regarded me with a slight squint as he puffed on his cigarette. "You seem afraid of me. Are you afraid?"

I leaned heavily against the wall and shrugged. "I don't know."

He chuckled again as he finished his cigarette, which he dropped onto the millstone and ground out with his boot. This made me cringe, and I thought, just fleetingly, that Solomon would never do something like that. Solomon had a reverence for all things and people.

"I do not bite," he said. Then he smiled. "I only look mean." He leaned back against the wall, the sleeve of his coat touching mine. He looked out at the forest and sighed. "This place reminds me of home."

I looked at him. "Are you far from your home?" I felt a twinge of sympathy for him, but did not know what else to say.

He shrugged. "Always I am far from home." He lit another cigarette. The smoke mingled with the vapors from our breath. Again he studied me through the cloud. "You spend much time alone, no?"

I pushed my mittened hands into my coat pockets. "Not usually. But my best friend just moved away."

Uri blew out a puff of smoke. "To get away from us?"

I looked down, realizing after a twinge of guilt that by *us* he referred to the Soviets and not me and Uri. "No. To get…married." Tears came, but I blinked them back hard.

"You can visit her, no?"

I shook my head. "No."

He sighed. "Well, you will make new friends." He made it sound so simple. This, too, was as annoying as his chuckle.

"It's not that simple."

He took a puff of his cigarette. I watched the orange glow as it burned up the paper and tobacco. The ashes fell indifferently onto my millstone. I wanted to tell him to stop. I screamed inside my head for him to stop.

"Of course it is, Hannah," he said. "Everybody is equal. You must be willing to make friends."

His words made me feel very sad and I looked away from him, outward. The gray of the sky was darkening. "I-I'm sorry. I must go home."

Uri mashed his cigarette under his boot. I winced again. The millstone now looked littered and dirty. He stepped closer. "You will come back here, Hannah?"

"I suppose," I said, feeling that flutter in my stomach.

"When? Tomorrow?"

He sounded so eager I felt I could not refuse. As before, I thought of my mezuzah. It was as if that morning he had showed me a kindness I could never repay. "I...uh...tomorrow. Yes." I knew I should be telling him no, but, I thought, at least I would not be wandering around by myself, lost only in thoughts of the past.

"I will meet you here tomorrow," he said.

I nodded.

Uri followed me along the edge of the forest and along the edge of the meadow, until the church came into view.

"See you tomorrow, Hannah." He stopped walking and watched me continue. I waved at him and went home.

~~~~~

"Hannah, will you come up here?" Yoav called down to me the next morning.

At first my heart pulsed. Yoav never had me in his room when he was there. I went up the steps and stood in the doorway. "What are you doing?"

Yoav had a satchel on his bed and a pile of laundry next to it, all new things he had procured for himself over the last few weeks, courtesy of his new occupation. "What does it look like? Come, help me fold these things."

I bristled at the way he ordered me, but said nothing. I never said anything to him. I went to the bed and picked up one of his shirts, a white button down dress shirt that needed careful folding. I set down and started doing up the buttons. "Where are you going?"

"First to Bialystock. I'm going to stay with Devorah and Isaac. And then, probably farther east." He stood on the other side of the bed, folding more of his new things.

"Deeper into Russia?" I asked. "Why?"

"Because you-know-who is going to come back, and I plan not to be here when they do."

"Do you mean the Germans?"

"Yes. These Russians are nothing against them, Hannah. I've seen what the Krauts can do."

"You're scaring me, Yoav," I said. "Hitler and Stalin have an agreement."

"They're both murderous bastards." Yoav stuffed the last of his things into the satchel and buckled it. "A pact means nothing to either of them. You can stay here if you want." He picked up his bag and started from the bedroom. "But I'm going."

I followed him down the stairs. "What about Auntie Sylvia? She'll miss you so much!"

"I offered to take her and my father, but they're too frightened."

"This is our home."

Yoav set down his satchel and went into the kitchen where he began rummaging for food to take with him. I did not help him. Let him get his own food.

"Hannah," Yoav said as he wrapped some bread and cheese into a piece of cheesecloth, "for your own good, you'd better redefine what *home* means to you." He passed me on his way out of the kitchen and gave me a peck on the cheek. "Don't worry, I'll stop and see Sylvia on my way."

I followed Yoav to the front door and opened it, pulling my sweater more tightly to me when the winter air came in.

"Just remember what I said, Hannah," Yoav said as he put on his coat.

I sighed. "Are you sure you have to do this?"

He wrapped his scarf around his neck. "If you'd seen Warsaw, you would understand and your bag would be packed right now." He picked up his satchel. "Take care of yourself."

I nodded. "You too." I stood there, with the freezing cold air coming in, watching Yoav the Magnificent, my beautiful cousin whom I'd worshiped for so long, just walk away. Somehow, I knew, without a doubt, that I would never see him again. And worse, I wasn't sure if I minded. When he turned the corner and was no longer in my sight, he suddenly slipped away from inside me, from my heart.

He was gone. Really gone. I didn't make him leave. I just couldn't make him stay because he didn't want to be there.

I closed the door behind me and went into the kitchen for a glass of tea. Afterward, it would be time to meet Uri. Oh well. When you can't go to the people who don't want you, you must go to those who do.

~~~~~

The only comfort I have now is with Uri. With him, I can always be in a world where it is possible to find pleasure, and it is never too cold, and everything always works out the way I would wish.

I don't know when I became the kind of girl who gives it away as I do. It wasn't what I had always intended, but it happened. And now that I have, I cannot stop. If I even think about not seeing Uri when we have planned to meet, my whole body begins to shake and panic grips my being. I feel I would die without this bit of pleasure. Why is that bad? I think of Uri most of the time when I am not with him. The thoughts, too, are intoxicating and I can be anywhere at any time and still have my private world.

Then, when we are together, he gropes at me with his lips and hands while I try to enjoy it and fend him off at the same time. I feel I am sinking more deeply every day into a grave with no bottom, yet am unable to stop. I need to accept that I am not a good girl and never was. Fathers don't leave good girls behind.

We don't talk much, Uri and I. His conformity to his nation's ideology is his survival and there is not much to say about that. I hate his beliefs. I would rather feel angry at God than believe He does not exist. Uri does not care about such things. I think he is amused by me. He often chuckles in that way of mocking amusement, especially when I shake my head at his outheld flask of vodka.

He didn't touch me the first few times we met. Then, the fourth time, he rapped on the door of the mill and asked me if I had ever been inside.

"Yes," I had answered, "A very long time ago."

"With your best friend?"

"Yes."

"Show me now."

I looked at him, feeling nervous, but did not refuse. He followed me inside. The river was still frozen, so inside the building was silent. "My friend told me that in spring and summer you can hear the water pass right underneath," I told him, pointing to the floor.

But he had not cared about such a thing as he stood in front of me and began his exploration of me under my coat and my skirt. He brought me to stand against the wall as he kissed me with lips and tongue sticky with stale cigarettes and vodka.

When I got home that day, I bathed and changed my dress, washing away the odors that lingered on my face and neck, in my hair and down below, where he had been inside of me. I scrubbed hard, with a wash rag drowned in hot soapy water, certain that anyone who came near me would smell him on me, even down there.

The weeks passed in unrelenting cold. I think I have grown quite fond of Uri. He seems to like me. I have grown to tolerate his blind faith in his godless world in favor of the momentary pulsing of my heart each time I near the old mill, the anticipation of being filled. Even the smell of his cigarettes and his vodka have taken on a magic I had not expected could be. They bring me to a place I only dare go for a little while, a place of winters darker, even, than the ones I know; of sadness and despair and forbidden things. Perhaps I have even pushed away the ghosts who are there, the ghosts of a young girl and boy, seated side by side, speaking of prayers and spiritual enlightenment, reeking of innocence.

Sometimes, however, I wish I were different, able to find contentment as a wife and mother, the way other women seem to, to be a normal woman with normal feelings. But I am not. I have enormous appetites which never seem filled. I am certainly not the Hannah whom Solomon knew. I wonder if he would even recognize me anymore. Would he recognize this girl who is heavier, with soft pouches of flesh filling out various parts of her body? A girl who cannot stop herself from sneaking into the kitchen late at night for extra slices of bread with butter, or for cookies, or some of what is left over from supper? A girl whose nails are bitten down and who needs larger dresses and skirts, who feels dead except in those few moments in the mill with the soldier called Uri?

"Do I look ugly to you?" I asked Uri one day. I had sensed from the first moment of our meeting that something was wrong. Perhaps it was my appearance.

Uri was resting from his exertion, puffing, in silence, one of his many cigarettes, after having buckled the trousers of his uniform. He did not look at me. He seemed wrapped in a private world in his own mind. He did not even chuckle. This made me think he would not answer. "Of course not," he said finally.

I waited for more. There was none.

He finished the cigarette and mashed it out under his boot. I no longer flinched when he did this.

"Look, Hannah," he said after a sip from his flask, "This is our last day."

I stared at him, wondering if I had heard correctly. After all, his Polish was sometimes not so good.

"Did you understand me?"

"I-I don't know."

"I'm leaving here. They are sending me away."

I swallowed hard and continued to stare at him.

He took another gulp from his flask. Then another. "I never stay in one place for long. Ever."

"Oh." I felt my eyes fill. He did not seem so upset. This made it worse. Couldn't he be just a little bit upset? I sniffled and roughly wiped my nose with the sleeve of my coat, then turned away.

"Come, Hannah," Uri said. "Don't tell me you thought that I, that we...? We both understood."

I shrugged. "I didn't think." I put my hands over my face, feeling his hatred of my tears. I wished he would just hold me, if even for a moment.

"Hannah, you mustn't cry. You mustn't be a baby."

His tone made me feel foolish, and I forced back my tears. I felt, once again, like that fourteen-year-old girl in Warsaw who watched her father leave for America. I must be utterly leavable. Even Solomon left me. I almost turned to Uri and spat my hatred on him, but I didn't. I was still paying for that first time. Instead, I turned slowly around and looked at him, forcing my lips into one of those fake smiles.

Uri took a step back and pushed his gloved hands into his pockets. "There. That's better." He leaned back against the wall, seeming relieved. "How will you get through life if you break down like a child at every little thing?" He then brought out his flask, sipped from it, then held it out to me. I accepted and took a tiny sip from it, hoping it would soften the moment. As usual, it burned.

"Is that how you see it?" I asked, a bit bolder now. "As a little thing?"

He looked down and shrugged. "I don't know."

I handed him back his flask. He took one more sip then put it away and shouldered his rifle. Then we left.

I walked in front of him the whole way back. When we reached the place where he usually stopped and let me go on alone, I did not turn around before continuing.

"Good bye, Hannah," I heard him say.

I turned and glared briefly at his face. When I saw it was tearless, I turned back around and walked away as fast as I could.

~~~~~

Spring 1940

My breaths came in short hard gasps. It was still cold enough, even in early spring to see the puffs in the air. I flattened myself against the side of the building, my sack of potatoes dropped, forgotten, at my feet. I didn't think he saw me, though I saw him and ducked away as quickly as I could. Chava was walking next to him. I'd never seen her before, but who else would it have been? Especially with her belly so swollen, as only it looked when a woman was pregnant.

I stood, stunned. Chava's face, delicate and pretty, with her pale cheeks flushed bright pink. She could just as easily have been mistaken for a Polish peasant girl. And Solomon looked so like a rebbe should in his gabardine, his earlocks grown back to their full length, his face both serene and troubled. They appeared to walk together, yet, at once, remained in separate worlds. They did not appear as newlyweds.

I squeezed my eyes shut as I fought to regain my breath, but gasped when I felt a tug on the sleeve of my coat. Turning, I looked down into a pair of brown eyes so huge, they could have been the eyes of an owl. I could not tell if the person staring up at me was a young woman or a boy. Then I saw the skirt hanging below the tattered coat. In the eyes I saw only fear.

"Do you know my cousin, Yankele? He was on his way here when…they came. He's all I have left."

Although the coldest days of winter were over, her lips were a strange purple color. She clearly was ill. Even so, I could see that she was very pretty, and delicate.

"Do you live here?"

The girl shivered with a passing wind. "I do not live anywhere now."

I then understood. She was one of many who had fled eastward when Hitler had bombed Poland, only to end up here, on what was now the Soviet side of the country, with nowhere to live. I felt a protectiveness rear up in me, such as I never had felt in my entire life. I wanted only in that moment to ease her suffering. "I am Hannah." I put my hand on her shoulder. She felt so thin I nearly shivered.

"I am Miriam." Then she smiled and I felt something in us lock together.

"Come with me." I picked up my sack of potatoes, shouldering it like a peasant, then offered her my other arm.

Slowly, for she was weak and leaned on me heavily, I led her home where Mama and I tended to her.

Miriam slept for several days. I had never seen a person sleep as much. I sat on the edge of my bed, watching her. She was so far away, deep in some other world. When she finally awakened and could sit up, I fed her soup and tea.

When she was stronger, several days later, she wanted to tell us what had happened. She had just eaten and I sat behind her, brushing her dark wavy hair. Mama sat nearby.

"You don't have to, Miriam, if it's too difficult," I said.

But she shook her head. "I must tell you. We lived outside of Warsaw, my parents and my brother and I. When the bombing began, we fled eastward, like so many, taking cover in the forest at night. In the day we hid in barns and begged for food. The planes strafed from overhead every day and night. We stayed the winter on the Russian side. My mother and brother died of fever. Papa wanted to go back over to the German side to find his sister, but the Soviets arrested him at the border. They took him somewhere, but I don't know where. As soon as winter was over, I came here looking for Yankel." Her voice dropped off and she looked at us, the same way she had looked at me that first day. "Do you know him?"

I put my hand on her arm. "No, Miriam. I am sorry."

"He was a follower of the Wolensker Rebbe," Miriam said. "It had always been his dream to go see him."

I caught my breath and felt my blood ice in my veins, but said nothing.

"Rest now, Miriam." Mama rose and picked up Miriam's empty plate.

"I hope I find him," Miriam said as she lay back in the bed.

"Let's see what happens." Mama smiled at her but I did not miss the knowing glance she gave me.

"Thank you both so much." Miriam hadn't noticed our tension at the mention of the Wolensker rebbe. "Ha Shem must have guided me to you."

Mama handed me the dish to wash and pulled the blanket up over Miriam. We watched her wrap herself deep within the covers, as if a warm bed were a miracle, a gift to be cherished.

Miriam's story was so horrible that Uncle Leo, to my amazement, was moved to pity and let her stay with us. I was very happy to share my room with her. She soon became my dear friend, the sister I had always hoped for but never had in Devorah. Only her nightmares frightened me. Her cries awakened me and I went to sit by her bedside where she would grasp my hand. I could feel the pulse beating hard in her thin arm while her brow was plastered with sweat.

"Almost every night they come, Hannah," she whispered. "I tell my mind before I go to sleep not to let them come, but they always do."

I squeezed her hand. "It's all right, Miriam. You're here with me."

Miriam leaned over and nuzzled my hand with her cheek. "Can I come and stay with you, Hannah?"

I stared at her a moment. Her fear and need were so great, so palpable, they frightened me. What if I could not make it better for her? But I could not refuse her. I already loved her. "Of course you can."

Miriam climbed into my small bed with me and curled up against me, her arm linked through mine the way she did when I had walked with her outside on the street to help her regain her strength.

"Hannah," she said when we had settled in, "I need to find Yankele. I pray that he is alive. I was so sad when he left. He is the only boy I have ever loved." Miriam pressed her face against my arm. Her hair brushed my chin. "We were going to be married. But he was not supposed to see me or touch me before the wedding. Then one day, in the barn, we hugged and kissed and he touched me here." She touched one of her breasts with her hand. "He told me we had sinned and that I had tempted him. It was then that he left."

I reached up and touched Miriam's shoulder. "I'm so sorry, Miriam."

"Do you think we sinned, Hannele?"

"No," I said. "How could it be a sin if you love each other?"

Miriam sighed. "I don't know. That's one of the things I want to ask the rebbe. I have so many questions. Questions I had never thought before to ask."

"I know the rebbe would tell you that what you did was not a sin." Only after the words were out did I freeze, realizing what I had just admitted.

Miriam propped herself up on an elbow. "Do you know him, Hannah? Really? Can you take me to see him?"

I chewed my lower lip, my mind coursing with fearful thoughts.

"Hannah, what is it? Please answer." She waited. "Hannele, you seem afraid. Whatever it is, you can tell me." She squeezed my arm. "You are the best friend I have ever had."

I knew I had to tell her about Solomon and me. I could not keep her from seeing him out of my own selfish fear, especially after all that she had been through. And hadn't I already sinned enough myself for the both of us? I sighed. "Yes, Miriam," I said finally. "I do know the rebbe."

"Oh!" Miriam breathed excitedly.

"But there are things I must tell you first so you will understand."

"Of course." Miriam settled back down next to me.

I did not begin right away, needing several moments to think of how I could possibly convey to her the story of a fourteen-year-old girl and the strange boy of mystical visions, the future Wolensker rebbe who had followed her around, about a friendship that had begun long before their actual lives had touched and had continued when he had saved her life. And about a friendship that had ended in horrible sadness.

I told Miriam almost everything. The only part I left out was how close we had come to making love and that the reason for our fight had been my refusal to be with him after he was married. At first I was so afraid that she would hate me for what I told her, but she only reached up and stroked my hair. "Hannele," she said, "I feel terrible for you."

Her touch was like a soothing balm and I almost began to cry. "It's all right, Miriam. Perhaps it's for the best."

Miriam shook her head and snuggled against me. "He loves you, Hannele. I am sure he still does. Just as I still love Yankel."

I did not answer, but lay, staring up into the darkness. Sadness mingled with the relief that Miriam knew and did not hate me. I felt now that she and I were not mere strangers brought together by war, but two girls who knew intimate details of each other's lives. I wondered if I would ever be able to tell her about the other things I had done.

I waited for her to ask me again about meeting Solomon, but she didn't and I could tell by her breathing that she had fallen asleep. I felt my eyelids grow heavy, glad that I would soon follow her.

Miriam did not mention Solomon again. Nor did she speak of Yankel. Days passed and I wanted very much to ask her the reason for her silence, but could not bring myself to.

"Hannele," she said one night as she finished brushing my hair and handed me the brush to do hers in our new bedtime ritual.

"Yes?"

"I have decided something."

"What, Miriam?" I began to run the brush through her hair, which was very soft, and dark, almost the color of mink.

"I cannot go and ask Rebbe Solomon about Yankele."

"What?" I stopped brushing her hair and grasped her shoulder. She turned and looked at me. Strangely a surge of righteous anger washed through me. Miriam was so pretty and delicate with her large, trusting brown eyes and heart-shaped face. How could that man have gone and left her, this sweet, beautiful girl who loved him so?

"I want to believe that Yankele is alive and happy somewhere. Maybe with a wife. Maybe he will have found the spiritual perfection he was so desperate for. I could not bear to know if he were dead. Not now." She turned back around, and I once again lifted the brush to her hair. "Or that he no longer loves me."

For a long while, I could not answer. I did not understand and felt only a growing contempt for this cruel cowardly Yankel whom I had never met and probably would never meet. I continued to brush Miriam's hair well after it had become completely smooth. Only after a long while was I able to answer her. "If you ever change your mind, Mirele, I will help you if I can."

Miriam turned and looked at me. Her soft hair fell against her cheek. "I know you will," she said softly. "No one has ever helped like you have."

~~~~

Summer 1941

"Come on, Miriam," I said, "Let's go just this one time. It will be fun!"

Miriam sat on her bed opposite me, her shoulders hunched. She really was terribly shy. "I can't, Hannah. I don't know how to dance."

"I'll show you. It's easy. Besides, you need to see that there will be men who will find you pretty."

"Oh, Hannah." Miriam shook her head. "There will be soldiers there. They make me nervous. I don't like how they look at us."

"They won't hurt you. They're just men, too. They have to be there. It's their job."

"Well…"

"We'll be together the whole time."

Miriam tilted her head, considering. "Do you promise?"

"Yes, I promise."

"Oh, all right."

I jumped up from my bed. "You'll see, Mirele, we'll have a wonderful time! The communists may have taken God away, but at least they give us dances."

"Hannele!" Miriam scolded. "What things you say!"

But I wasn't listening, already standing at my mirror, thinking of a beautiful summer evening in June, with strings of lights, and music blaring from a phonograph and people laughing and boys and girls dancing together. An image of some sort of normal life. A life we never had and could only grasp at for a few blessed moments.

~~~~~

Miriam and I tiptoed into the house. The scent of summer air mingled with perspiration from dancing so much with so many boys lingered on our skin, and our jaws were sore from laughing. We were so late, even the moon had gone to sleep and the sun was not long to rise. We padded into our room, our shoes dangling from their straps slung on our fingers, as we stifled our giggles.

Still in our dresses, we fell onto our beds, drunk with the fresh memories of the glorious time we'd just had. We lay quietly, not speaking, lest we burst into more giggles and wake everybody else.

I must have begun to doze because I was awakened when the bottles of perfume and hairbrush on the bureau began to rattle loudly. The ground shook and I looked out the window into the faint pink light. My heart crashed in my chest.

Suddenly Miriam was on the bed with me, clinging onto me. "Hannele, I'm frightened!"

I put my arms around her and we rocked each other. "Me too, Miriam."

We curled up on the bed as the rumbling grew louder and we could hear explosions in the distance. We squeezed each other as tightly as possible and waited…

PART THREE - KADDISH
Wolensk Ghetto, Winter, 1941-42

I would give anything to have the Soviets back. They were absolutely beneficent compared to these Nazi bastards. The Russians only killed or imprisoned you if you didn't agree with them. But the Nazis hate us and want us dead simply for who we are.

Yoav had been right about everything, but it was too late for *could-have-dones*. Besides, even had I known his predictions would prove correct, how can I know what I really would have done? I hated the way he left and what it did to Auntie Sylvia. She has never been the same since, and now especially that we are utterly trapped, and don't even know if Devorah and Ruchele are alive, I don't think my aunt cares if she lives or dies anymore, the way she just stares at you silently when you speak to her, and how she mindlessly does Uncle Leo's bidding, never complaining when he steals her rations. Or ours.

I dare think Mama might have felt the same if I had left. And if this were true, how was I going to turn around and do the same to her? And then there was Miriam. We wouldn't have found each other if I had run away. And maybe she might even have died from sickness and hunger had I not been standing in her path. And I, with the gaping hole in my life left by Solomon's absence, might have died of loneliness.

Sometimes I wondered if Papa didn't actually know all of this and not want to separate me from Mama, who would have been miserable beyond anything. Although, really, if he knew what it would be like for us at the hands of the Germans, I'm certain he would have tried harder to bring me to America. He wouldn't have wanted me to be so hungry all the time, would he? Oy! The way the pangs gnaw at me and give me such headaches! I'm so tired all the time and food occupies so much of my thoughts, that I barely remember there were ever flowers, meadows full of them, or times when we laughed, or when I closed my eyes as I listened to the men's voices in prayer, drifting beyond the wooden walls of the synagogue, blending with the aromas rising from the heavily laden Shabbos tables.

Really, I believe I could deal with this war much better if it weren't for the hunger which is just so very depressing and leaves me listless much of the time. I mean, how can they expect us to survive on a couple of kilos of potatoes and a few carrots and rutabagas per person? Yes, there are a few other things, tins of ersatz coffee, some sugar and a few dekagrams of bread and margarine. But the rations never last long and it is nearly impossible not to wolf them down all at once.

And as if it weren't bad enough, we have to hide most of it from Uncle Leo who steals from us when we're out working and, of course, roundly denies it. As if he needs our rations. He gets extra, connected as he is to J.L. Wolfberg, the Nazi-appointed head of the Jewish Community Council. And all Uncle Leo has to do is go around with a member of the Jewish police when they confiscate the personal belongings of the ghetto dwellers. He even let them take my and Mama's wristwatches, not so much as giving us the chance to sell them for a few precious zlotys to buy food or clothes. Thank God I was able at least to hide Mama's silver candle holders from him. Probably I will have to use them someday for money, because things could always get worse. But for now, they are under a floorboard in Mama's room. Not even Mama knows they are there. Miriam knows, though, because she accidentally saw me burying them. Of course, she promised never to breathe a word to anyone, not even Mama.

And Solomon's Torah scroll! Before the ground froze, Miriam and I sneaked out in the middle of the night to a small, bare patch of land as far as possible from anyone who could catch us and using empty cans and tins from our eaten rations, did our best to dig a large hole and bury the precious blanket-wrapped item so that no Nazi or Jewish Police member could ever find it and steal it.

True to my personality, I found my own way to get a few extra rations. Very shortly after they locked us into the ghetto in November, I learned that if I give it away to certain people, I can get a little more to eat. And now I am giving it away more than ever. Before Vlas, I hadn't ever thought I could be like Eva, who also sucks around the barracks of the Jewish Police like a stray cat. But I am.

I didn't go looking for it, though. At first I really thought that Jozef—who, by the way reminds me very much of Aaron—liked me and wanted me to be his girlfriend when he first approached me on the street. But then, after our first time together in his quarters, he pulled out a stack of extra ration cards from a tear in the mattress of his cot and handed one to me before I left, saying this would be my reward every time.

At first, my heart felt sliced through, but then I saw reality. In times like these, a girl can't afford to give herself to a man simply because she likes him. There has to be something in it for her, too. I mean, there is not one of us here, man woman or child, whose belly is ever full. Wouldn't anyone with any sort of bargaining power use it?

Miriam doesn't know how it really is. She thinks Jozef and I are really going together. And I let her believe it because I can't bear to tell her the truth. How sweet and innocent she is! Sometimes I ache to be that way once again. But my innocence is long gone and that's just the way it is. Anyway, Miriam would be horribly upset if she knew and would beg me to stay away from him. She would say all kinds of things about self-respect and dignity, and then she would invoke Solomon's name for the thousandth time and remind me once again of how much I really still love him and how I am betraying him.

And it's not like she'd be wrong. Solomon still haunts me, the fool that I am to have thought he would simply disappear. Since the day of the horrible fight, he is still there. From the last time we spoke, I could not sit at the kitchen table with a glass of tea without remembering all the times he had been there with me, trying to make me laugh. I stopped baking challah because I couldn't stand that he wouldn't be there to give it to. And Shabbos, well, right after our fight, it became too utterly excruciating to even light the Shabbos candles, so I stopped. Now, that all seems a different lifetime.

I try not to think about him if I can help it. He is there enough without my invoking him. As far as I know, he is not in this ghetto here where I am. You see, the commandant, a man named Haffmann who has since been replaced with a more *enthusiastic* officer, arranged for two ghettos in Wolensk, a larger one and a smaller one, to prevent crowding. I'm in the larger ghetto and can only pray that Solomon is in the other one and not lying dead somewhere in a ditch.

I do wonder if Solomon would really feel I am betraying him. After all, he did go off and get married. But, well, you have to look at it as survival. If you think about it, I am doing this for Miriam too. She is so small and hollowed out by thinness, and she has already lost so much, that I am desperate just to see her eat enough to stay alive. I'm always terrified that one day she'll just curl up on our mattress in the corner of the kitchen (Which is where we stay because Mama's snoring is so viciously loud we wouldn't get any rest if we shared her little room with her) and never get up again. She is my beautiful and sweet Mirele, and there is not a day that passes I don't curse Yankel, wishing he would rot in *Gehinnom* the way he abandoned her.

But at least I'm not like Uncle Leo. At least I'm not turning in my own people to the Gestapo! How can he possibly find it within his conscience to do that? Now I understand more than ever where Yoav inherited his slick, uncanny survival instincts.

Nor does my uncle feel inclined to use his position to protect me and Miriam from being snatched off the street for forced labor. By some grace, and not Uncle Leo's intervention, we have not been sent to labor camps where the rations are even worse and the work many times more strenuous. Miriam and I were fortunate enough to be picked off to clean the homes of Polish families living nearby the ghetto. Each day, we are escorted from the ghetto by Jewish police or Ukrainian guards. I wish I could work in the soup kitchen like Auntie Sylvia who has access to food all day long, which I know she slips to her husband. But housecleaning is the next best thing. I spend the days sweeping and dusting and doing laundry, as does Miriam. Mama is teaching in the elementary school in the ghetto. We'll see how long that lasts. She'll have a job as long as the children are alive, I suppose.

I know that I'm quite fortunate to have this job, for at least I'm inside where it's warm and I get a bit more meat in my diet which is missing from our rations. But really, it's quite degrading to be cleaning these peoples' toilet for a couple of Reichsmarks per week. The wife seems suspicious of me and I always find her staring at me and at the yellow

Star of David stitched on my clothing. The husband works all day, but the wife is home with their two little children, a boy and girl. They seem like sweet children, but I have to watch them eating all kinds of delicious food and smell it cooking all day. I suppose they don't have terribly much, either, but compared to us, it seems a feast. She does give me some food at the midday meal, some bread and s small piece of sausage and a glass of tea, but it is never enough for how much work I do. I've been tempted to steal from her pantry at times when I just feel I will go crazy from the pangs, but I don't dare because if she caught me, she could have me killed.

Today I was not feeling so well. My greatest chore was simply to rise from the mattress, and then, only with poor Miriam having to pull at me from outside, and the fear of missing that little bit of food that the wife gives me at noon on the inside.

The way Mrs. Woyinka was looking at me today, I became terrified she might withhold my meal. I know I am slower and clumsier than usual in my work, and almost broke a nice vase she has on her fireplace mantle when I went to dust it. Her glances are more pained and suspicious than usual, and all I can think is that my very existence displeases her.

In the upstairs bedroom, I looked at my face in her dressing mirror. Thankfully, my hair was brushed and neatly pinned up, except for wisps of it which escaped while I worked. And there were coal smudges on my cheeks from the kitchen stove. But for all the apparent neatness, my clothing had become tattered, and my face gaunt, and I felt a horrible shame to frighten her so.

I treated her as nicely as I knew to be, and made her tea in the afternoon, but when her husband came home, I heard them in the kitchen arguing about me.

"She makes me nervous," Mrs. Woyinka said. "And she doesn't clean well. She's clumsy and slow."

"She seems to be doing a good job to me," Mr. Woyinka answered.

"I think she steals food from us."

"Maybe she's hungry. She is very thin. Give her a little more to eat. We have enough."

"I give her plenty to eat! And that's just it! Why do you notice whether she's thin or not? I don't like the way she looks at you! As if she's some innocent angel. But their women are wolves inside! They have diseases. And she wants to steal you away from me!"

I clutched at the door frame in my horror. How could she say such things? And Mr. Woyinka did not defend me from the last charge. Why was this happening? I had never done more than smile at him in greeting when I saw him. All I wanted to do was my work and have something to eat. Every moment of every day we teetered on the edge of death, and to have a moment or two of safety, however fleeting, was a gift I no longer took for granted.

I receded in to the hallway and stood shivering, in spite of my coat.

Mr. Woyinka came out of the kitchen and approached me. He was slim and pale, with thinning dark hair brushed over his scalp. "I'm sorry, Fraulein," he said. "I cannot keep you here."

I nodded, but inside me there was just a burning humiliation. I wanted to scream out in my defense, but their power of life and death over me silenced me.

Mr. Woyinka let me out the front door so I wouldn't have to see his wife, and I, feeling small and freezing and nauseous, walked back to the ghetto. Everywhere were the Ukrainian guards, staring at me. At one corner there were two. One put out his rifle, like a bar against my chest, forcing me to stop. I looked at him in terror, for it was already darkening, and if he kept me out past the curfew, I would be shot. He asked to see my work pass which he examined at his leisure while I stood, shaking. Finally he snickered and handed it to me. Turning to the others, he said, "She is a nice girl. I'll walk her home." But the tone in which he spoke was sneering, and the others laughed.

The guard left me at the gate where the Jewish Police let me in. Instead of going home, I went straight to Jozef's quarters, but he was not there. Another policeman, Marek, told me he would not be back until later, then asked me why I looked so distressed and invited me to his room. Marek was strange and bulbous looking with oily brown eyes. He rarely ever had a woman even with the offer of extra rations. I said I had to go and would come back later to see Jozef. By now I felt sick and just wanted to lie down and have a little bit to eat.

Marek offered to see me back, but I refused him politely and walked slowly to the tiny bungalow I shared with Miriam, Mama, and my aunt and uncle. My body felt a heavy ponderous thing in spite of the weight I'd lost and everything passed by me as gray shadows. I longed to see Miriam's face and hear her voice and thought that maybe God had given her to me after all, as he had once given me Solomon, whom I had done no better than spit on. Maybe I was just a blind, stupid girl. Maybe there was a chance I didn't really know everything.

No one was in the bungalow when I got there. I looked at the small, dingy outer room. The Poles who had lived here had been poor, but at least we had a real roof. Uncle Leo had arranged for that. I thought of the last few potatoes Miriam and I had hidden away from Uncle Leo and knew I should peel and cook them. But by now I felt the weakest I ever had and the mere thought of standing a moment longer exhausted me.

I lay down on Miriam's and my mattress and closed my eyes, waiting for Miriam to come back so I could tell her what happened and feel her comforting embrace.

When I opened my eyes next, gray light poured through the small windows on either side of the front door. I felt Miriam stir gently beside me and went to sit up, but couldn't. Heat radiated from my body and my stomach churned viciously. Then I realized I had not gone back the night before to see Jozef. "Oh no!" I struggled to sit up. My stomach surged when I did this and I lay still again, afraid to empty its contents into our mattress.

This woke Miriam and she sat up quickly and grasped my shoulders. "Hannele, what is it?" She looked at me and put her hand to my forehead. "Oh my God, Hannele. You have a fever!"

"Shh! Don't say it so loud! If my uncle knew…" No doubt Uncle Leo would report my condition to the proper authorities. We all knew the true fate of sick people who supposedly went to the "infirmary."

"No one else is here," she whispered. She jumped up to soak a cool cloth and put it to my forehead.

I started sobbing. "Jozef! Jozef! I didn't go to see him! He'll hate me!"

Miriam stroked my hair. "No he won't," she crooned. "He'll understand when you tell him what happened. You must get well."

"No, he won't! He won't! He'll find someone else!"

Miriam put her arms around me and rocked me gently. "It's all right, Hannele. When you get better you'll go see him." Miriam continued to comfort me and stroke my hair, and I calmed down. But if I hadn't felt so run down, I probably would have jumped up and run to the Jewish Police barracks just to see Jozef and have him reassure me. I couldn't bear the thought of him replacing me. He was handsome like Yoav and could have any girl he wanted.

"Let me go with you today, Mirele. I want to get rations too."

"You should rest." Her voice trembled and I knew she was as frightened as I.

"No!" I hissed. "We can't let on that I'm sick. You know what'll happen. You know what happens to sick people."

Miriam didn't answer but sat quietly behind me on our mattress while she brushed my hair. I could hear her trying to stifle sobs but had only the strength to surrender to the feel of the brush. She is much gentler than I with the brush, which is good because my hair has grown quite long, now reaching past the middle of my back. Miriam starts at the top, up by my forehead, and brushes straight back and down, all the way to the ends. Over and over she does this, like the most careful, loving sister. With each stroke of the brush, my eyelids fluttered and I leaned my head back.

"I love your hair," Miriam said.

"Yours is beautiful, too."

"Not like yours, Hannele."

"Mine is probably so filthy. What I wouldn't give for a long soak in a tubful of hot water, with a cake of soap and a washrag! To feel the water permeate my skin, right through to my bones!"

Miriam giggled softly. "Oh, please don't tell me!" She sighed. "A long time ago, Mama used to yell at me for taking so long in the tub. I loved to play with the bubbles."

"Me too."

"I never thought about it then. Not being able to have a nice hot bath." She finished brushing and set the brush down.

"I'll do yours."

"Not today, Hannele." She wet the rag again and gently wiped my neck and back and arms.

When she'd finished, we sliced the last of our bread to have with some watery grain coffee. Then Miriam and I put on our coats and went to wait on the ration line. We shivered in the bitter air, pulling our coats tightly around us as small frozen flecks of snow dropped and stuck on our faces and clothes. The line moved slowly, and I found it more difficult to stand and leaned more heavily on Miriam.

"Hannele, do you feel all right?" Miriam's voice was heavy with concern.

"Yes, yes, I'm fine. Just tired." I turned my thoughts to our rations and was soon completely taken with the idea of food. My stomach would never be full, but my mouth began to water just the same.

"You, fraulein!" a voice barked in my ear. I jumped and turned.

Noah Wasserman, the head of the Jewish Police pushed his gray, nasty face into mine. I wanted to tell him to speak Yiddish like the rest of us, but didn't dare. I felt Miriam grasp my arm and huddle against me.

"There is a day's work for you at the garrison," he said. His voice was as cold as the air around us.

"What kind of work?"

"Can you handle a broom?"

"Of course."

"Then come now. It is not a request."

"Hannah!" Miriam's eyes on me were full of fear. She looked even smaller than she was when so frightened.

"Just get our rations," I said to her gently. "I will see you tonight."

Miriam nodded but still clung to my arm. Wasserman yanked me from her. She cried out but I was already being steered briskly away. The others in line ahead of us and behind us had remained quiet the whole time, lest they, too, be recruited to go God knows where. I did not dare turn to look back.

Wasserman brought me out of the ghetto. Farther on we went, up Polaski Street, crossing over to the same neighborhood in which I had worked before. Several of the beautiful homes on Karavel, across from the town square had been taken over to house Gestapo and Nazi officers. Wasserman pushed me in front of him through the front door of one of them. It was said that the family whose house this had been could trace their lineage to Polish nobility for centuries. That is, until the Soviets came. After that, they disappeared, like many, I've heard said, to gulags deep in the frozen darkest reaches of Siberia.

I had never been in this home before, but imagined it not unchanged from its prewar glory. A majestic banister, tapestries and Oriental rugs and some wooden antique furniture remained, no doubt retained as the property of whoever was the occupational force. The wood floor had been highly polished, and served to reflect the background echoes of telephones ringing, typewriters and voices speaking German.

By my arm Wasserman pulled me through the front hall toward the kitchen where the glorious aromas of cooking food curled and taunted. A heavy Polish woman with a frightened face stood by a steaming pot on the stove, silently watching Wasserman drag me to a door while in my mind I cursed him to rot like a dead fish. He opened the door to reveal a small broom closet. "Do every room," he said. He handed me a piece of paper with my work order, then clicked his heels and turned on them. I shivered at how gleefully he had taken to his new employers.

I picked up a broom and went slowly out of the kitchen, feeling the eyes of the Polish woman on my back. My heart beat fiercely and I even wanted to run after Wasserman and beg him to let me go back to Miriam.

I went to the first office. Two men in dark crisp uniforms and shiny boots were standing by a desk, speaking together. Through the haze of my fear and fever, I could see the giant splash of red flag with Nazi symbol in black and white draped on the wall behind them. They looked up when I appeared in the doorway, then back to each other without a word. I began to sweep, moving the dust into one pile which I swept out the door into the hall. I did the same in each office, and in each office, the officers looked up then away.

I went back to the broom closet for the dustpan and swept up my pile. I had begun to sweat horribly in my heavy coat, but dared not remove it lest it get stolen or taken from me in an anti-Semitic taunt.

By what force I don't know, I made it up the stairs to the second floor whose once luxurious bedrooms of Polish nobility now served as living quarters for the officers. I sighed. Hunger made all this movement difficult. The floor seemed to stretch ahead of me in endless, highly-polished plateaus. But I forced myself to work as if nothing was wrong. I couldn't depend on anyone to protect me from the typhoid hospital with its harsh disinfection, a mere waiting room of death by disease or deportation to God knows where. But at least all the rooms in which I worked were empty.

Finally I reached the last room at the end of the hall. It, too, was empty. Thank God, I soon would be finished and hopefully, they would let me leave. I just wanted to go back to Miriam and to a bowl of soup. I was about to sweep the pile to the larger one in the hall when I heard bootsteps echoing from the stairway. Male voices were laughing. Their sounds were harsh. Momentarily I froze, but when they drew close, I began to sweep again in quick strokes. The voices stopped in the doorway, leaving an eerie silence, like still hot air before a thunderstorm.

"Fraulein," one of them said, his voice emanating from the deadly silence.

I stopped sweeping and stood, my hands gripping the broom handle.

"Let me see your face."

Slowly, I obeyed, my movement bringing me face to face with him, a young officer. I had to look up to see him. Cat-like blue eyes regarded me with a condescending amusement. Dark hair peeked out from under his cap. "Ah! They have sent us a beautiful one this time!"

His two companions murmured in what sounded like agreement. I dug my nails into the wood of the broom handle as he took a step closer to me. I went to move back but the wall was behind me, trapping me. He reached out and took a lock of my hair, rolling it between his fingertips. His enjoyment of my fear was hideously obvious.

"You needn't be afraid," he said. "I have a soft spot for Jewesses, especially beautiful ones."

He then released my hair and touched my cheek. My skin, too, seemed to meet with his approval. What would he have done if he had thought me ugly?

The other two were quiet except for occasional snickers as he continued to touch me, moving down my neck and over my collarbone. He pushed aside my sweater and squeezed my breast. "Did you know, Fraulein, that there are places where women take their clothes off for men who pay to see their naked bodies?"

The others laughed as I shook my head, unable to stop the tears that welled in my eyes. He continued to feel my breast, then turned to the men behind him and said something I did not understand. One of them went and closed the door to the room. They all three stared at me.

"What is it, Fraulein?" he said, "You look at me as if you see a monster before you rather than a man!"

I shook my head again, my hair rubbing against the wall.

"We will pay you. One extra pound of flour from downstairs." He ran the palm of his gloved hand down my front. "Think of how much you will have to eat, you and your family. You are hungry, are you not?"

"Yes," I answered, my voice in a whisper. For the first time since they had come into the room, my hunger was stronger than my fear, having been roused by the mention of extra rations.

The Nazi officer lifted his hands away and took a few steps backward, his eyebrows raised expectantly.

Now, I am sure there are women who would have refused, who would have screamed for help or tried to run out. Miriam certainly would have. But not I. I stood still and began to unbutton the front of my dress. I seemed not to have the ability to refuse a man anything. I had refused only one man. And he had loved me.

When all my clothing was on the floor around my ankles, stockings and all, I stood and waited. In my mind I was lying in bed next to Miriam. She had reached out and stroked my hair once when I had awoken from a dream, and she was doing it now.

"Now, lie down on the bed," he said.

I stepped from the pile of clothes and moved toward the bed. I had once seen an old Polish peasant woman walking along the side of the road. She moved laboriously, each step a world of work. It was more work than that for me now, but I did it.

I watched, seeing another face above mine, feeling another one of them over me and inside of me. That was the second officer. Then the third one was there. The only thing that changed was the color of his hair. There was the same strange curl of the lip, the same strange hunger in the eyes, the same distinct pleasure from being watched. When the third soldier moaned and shook in his climax, I felt all possibility of tears recede, down from my eyes, somewhere into an invisible depth, where sorrow goes and is swallowed. And I knew they could have me, whenever they pleased, one extra pound of flour or not.

When he stood up and buttoned the trousers of his uniform, neither he nor the other two seemed to take any more notice of me. I rose and went to pick up my clothes. I dressed quietly in the corner, took up the broom and went toward the door, my eyes averted from them.

"When you come back tomorrow, fraulein," the first one said. "You will have your ration then."

I looked at him then quickly down. "I…I would be grateful," I whispered. Then they let me leave. I swept up the pile of dust into the pan and went down the stairs, leaning heavily on the banister.

Back in the kitchen, I replaced the broom and pan and closed the door behind me. The Polish woman was still there, watching me. I looked back at her, as if desperate for some kindness. Her eyes regarded me fearfully yet she pointed a fat hand. On the table was a small hunk of bread shining with margarine. I nodded at her and picked it up, stuffing it into my coat pocket as I left to find a guard to escort me back to the ghetto.

Miriam threw herself on me when I walked in. Mama was home, too. She hurried over and put her arms around me. I was too tired and hungry and dead inside to speak to them. Miriam brought a small bowl of soup and a piece of bread. I took some spoonfuls of soup but showed her the bread I had been given. "Keep the other for yourself," I told her. She nodded reluctantly and sat quietly with me as I ate.

The food and Miriam's quiet company were soothing, and I soon had enough energy to speak. "I will have an extra pound of flour tomorrow," I told her. "In addition to whatever the Jewish Council will pay me for this work."

"I don't care, Hannele," Miriam answered. "I just want you to be here with me."

I smiled although I avoided her innocent gaze as I lay back down. "Thank you, Mirele."

Miriam took away the bowl and spoon then came back and got into the bed next to me. The room was dark and cold, but together we were warm. Miriam stroked my hair, and I could tell that she sensed something had happened to me, but she said nothing, knowing how tired I was. "I love you, Hannele."

"I love you, too, Miriam." I said, feeling my exhaustion overtake me under her soothing touch…

The next thing I hear is the rippling sounds of water and the rising heat of steam. "Is the water hot enough?" I ask.

Solomon smiles at me from the other end of the tub. "It is just right." He is sitting back against the tub. Droplets of water glisten in his beard. The hairs of his chest are darkened from the water and lay flat against his skin.

I love watching him.

Our toes are touching under the water and I sink lower into the tub as the steam rises in front of my face.

"Why do you hide under the water?" he asks gently. "I hope you are not ashamed."

I feel my cheeks burn and an embarrassed giggle escapes me. Solomon has seen me naked many times by now, but I always feel this way.

"May I see you, Hannah?"

I smile. I love him and would not refuse him. He has earned my complete faith and trust. I rise onto my knees in the tub and the water recedes downward, just below my belly button. The heat from the nearby stove warms my exposed skin.

Solomon's eyes fill with appreciation. "Baruch Ha Shem," he says quietly. "He has blessed me a thousand times."

His words and the way he says them take away my embarrassment and I want only to please him. He leans forward and picks up my hand, kissing it gently. I reach out and touch his beard, brushing my fingertips against its softness.

Solomon rises up and puts his arms around me.

I, too, reach out to embrace him…

But then there was no water. Only darkness. And the tight sound of my breaths. I could then feel my clothes, how they clung to my damp skin.

Miriam stirred beside me. "Hannele?" I felt her small hand on my shoulder.

"I'm all right," I whispered as I turned onto my back.

"Were you dreaming of Solomon?"

I sighed. "Yes."

Miriam propped herself up on one elbow. She leaned over me and gently touched her lips to my forehead. "You're still warm."

I didn't answer, but closed my eyes at her soothing touch. "The water was hot."

"What water?"

"The water in the tub."

"You were in a tub?"

"Yes. We were."

Miriam caught her breath. "You? And Solomon? You were both in the tub?"

"Yes."

"Oh my." Miriam giggled under her breath, stifling the sound with her fingertips. But then she stopped and I felt her grow serious. "Hannele, why don't you try to find him? There must be a way."

I looked at Miriam even though it was too dark to see her face. "How could I? After what happened? He must hate me. Besides, I don't know where he is."

"Yes, you do, Hannah," Miriam answered. "And I'm sure he doesn't hate you." She touched my arm again. "Don't you miss him?"

I closed my eyes. Solomon's face was in my mind. I could clearly see his payos, his soft beard, his eyes of melting honey. The remembrance of his gentle ways reached to me, beyond the horrible feeling of what I had done in the garrison with those soldiers. The anger I had carried toward him all this time seemed to have been pummeled out of me. "Yes," I whispered.

Miriam reached out and gently stroked my hair.

When next I opened my eyes, two faces were staring into mine. Angels. Angels floating in the air above me, behind them light as bright and as hot as the sun. I closed my eyes again in a wave of ecstatic relief! So this was what it was like, that sweet welcome release from the hell of this life!

But then, I felt a gentle pressure on my forehead. I still had my body. I began to cry.

"She is burning hot, Mrs. Herzel," Miriam's voice said. The pressure on my forehead lifted, then pressed down again.

"Hannele," Mama said, "You're ill!"

I cried some more. Oh God! I felt so very tired and awful. How could the Master of the Universe be so cruel? Then I remembered. The promised extra ration! Even in my fever I felt the drive of hunger, and if I didn't show up, they'd come for me. God only knew my fate then!

I grasped Mama's wrist, pulling her hand from my forehead. "I am fine. I have work today." I sat up quickly, forcing Mama and Miriam to step back. I was still in my dress from the day before. "My work order is in my coat pocket. I must go."

"Hannah, you have a fever!" Mama said. "You must rest!"

I looked at her. Hysteria was rising in me at the thought that they would keep me from getting the extra ration. "I have fever because we are hungry. They promised me extra rations."

"Who promised you extra rations?" Miriam asked.

I stood up quickly, too quickly, for I teetered weakly on my feet. Miriam reached out and grasped my arm. "The Nazis. Who else?"

"No!" Miriam cried. "You cannot go there! Mrs. Herzel!" Miriam turned to Mama, who looked very afraid. "Tell Mr. Goldman! He will stop this!"

I pulled away from Miriam and moved toward the door of the bedroom, my blood churning with terror. What would they do to me if I did not show up to work? And how could we live without the extra ration?

Miriam grasped my shoulder. "Then I will go with you, Hannah."

I turned and put my hands on her shoulders. She was so thin that I cringed. If she came with me, they'd do it to her, too. She was too good and sweet for such a fate. "I am going, Miriam. And you're not. There is no choice. Don't speak to my uncle."

Miriam's cheeks were wet with tears. "Why not?"

I glanced at Mama, at the fear in her eyes. The fear. Fear! Fear! Fear! The disgusting, cowardly fear! The same fear that emanated from Uncle Leo's eyes. I remembered Solomon's words. But Miriam's eyes. God, Miriam's eyes were so beautiful! I would come back to her just to take the worry and anguish from them. I leaned down and kissed her forehead. "Because," I said, "you cannot rely on cowards for protection."

"Hannah!" Mama whispered as if to scold me, but she knew it too. She could not fight with me today as she had in the past. It was a lesson she, too, had learned. You could not ask a coward for help.

I turned and walked out.

At the entrance to the ghetto, I showed my work order to one of the Ukrainian guards who were posted there, and he walked me to the garrison.

"Walk faster," he told me when I began to lag behind him.

My heart quickened and I stepped up my pace. "I…I am sorry."

The guard looked at me. He was young, but older than I, with high cheekbones and almond shaped eyes. He did not answer, but his demeanor softened a bit, and his pace slowed noticeably. Could this possibly have been an act of kindness?

We stopped at the gate to the courtyard of the house turned garrison. The guard looked at me, then in the direction of the front door. "Go in," he said.

I turned obediently and went slowly up the walkway to the front steps.

"Dyevooshka," I heard him say in Russian behind me. I turned.

"Be careful."

I stared at him. For a moment, something moved in me, a flutter in my chest. I was right. He was kind. A small warning like he had just given, a slowing of his pace to accommodate my fever seemed great acts of love, worthy of my surrender. If he had thrown a crust of bread to me on the ground I would have retrieved it like a dog, on the ground, with my teeth if he had asked it of me!

I looked at him a moment longer, then nodded. When I turned, he would be gone, gone along with his kindness. Such kindness was as rare as a full stomach, and I wanted to grasp it desperately. I turned and went in.

The sack of flour that had been promised to me sat on a chest of drawers by the officer's bed. All signs of yesterday's sex show had been erased, the covers on the bed pulled so tight that one surely could have bounced a coin on them. But next to the flour was something else, something small, wrapped in a piece of paper. Slowly, quietly, I picked it up and undid the folds of paper. I caught my breath. What angel was smiling on me today? There, in my hand, was a small piece of sausage, like the ones I had seen hanging in the window of the Polish butcher shop on Polaski Street. Cold though the meat was, it glistened with oil. I thought of the Polish woman in the kitchen downstairs. It must have been she who left this extra little gift for me.

The smell of it drove me to a sense of madness and I stuffed it into my mouth, whole, barely chewing it before swallowing it almost whole. The ferocity with which I devoured the morsel of sausage made me pant. Now that it was gone, I thought immediately of Miriam. How selfish I had just been, not saving any for her! God forgive me!

Then I heard the now familiar bootsteps and froze midway in wiping the back of my hand across my mouth.

"Fraulein!" he said behind me, his voice smooth and menacing, satisfied that he could control me by my hunger. I cringed at the sound then went numb. I heard him cross the room, stopping right behind me. He grasped my shoulders, his breath heavy in my ear. "There are many kinds of hunger, fraulein," he said as he reached around me and squeezed my breasts. I bit down on my lower lip and closed my eyes tightly. *Miriam. Think of Miriam*, I thought. I would make up my transgression to her later.

"Bend over," he said.

I obeyed, of course, placing my elbows on the bureau, my fingers gripping the edges, as he lifted my skirt and yanked down my stockings. I kept my eyes squeezed shut against the pain. His hands alternately stroked and pulled roughly on my hips. *Miriam, hold me. Please!*

I felt him collapse on me, breathing heavily. Still I did not open my eyes. Punishment. Punishment. For having felt and said the worst things. For the hatred inside of me. Had I expiated my sin?

He stood up. The clink of his belt buckles behind me. I remained bent over, leaning on the chest of drawers. If I moved he might kill me. My underpants and stockings clung to my thighs.

"You Jewesses are all whores," he said. "Now finish your work and get out."

I pulled up my underpants and stockings and went to retrieve the broom. But then he grabbed my shoulder and yanked me around to face him. Time was lost to me in this instant by the shock of this roughness, rougher even than the previous moments, blurred by the most horrible intense fear.

I saw his hand rise in the air, then pain on my cheekbone. The blow was so hard I cried out and fell over onto the polished wood floor. Another blow in my ribs and I collapsed. But this time I screamed. He was kicking me! I screamed and screamed, utterly surrendering to my impulse for survival. Let him shoot me this time! I didn't care. I curled up in a ball, a screaming ball, against the toe of his boot in my ribs and back and buttocks.

Then the kicking stopped, and there were hands, strong hands lifting me up, off the floor, onto my feet. In my screaming I had not heard the officer who came and yelled at him to stop, reprimanding him in German. Through a haze I could see him. Tall. Gray hair. Firmly he pulled me from the room. Down the hallway we went. He was half pulling me, half holding me up as I fought back more screams and tears. He's going to take me outside and shoot me in the mouth or the side of the head. Or maybe he will walk me to the center of Polaski Street and force me to undress in the freezing air at gunpoint and then shoot me. A bullet between my breasts. Maybe Solomon will be there to see me die.

He retrieved my coat and led me outside where the freezing air cleared my vision. The officer called to a nearby guard to escort me back to the ghetto. "Go home, fraulein," he said, giving me a small push toward the guard. "Have someone see to you. I am certain you have a broken rib."

I blinked and stared at him.

"I know you Jews have many doctors among you," he said.

The guard grasped me by my upper arm, near the armband which distinguished me as a Jew, and led me back to the ghetto.

Miriam was peeling a potato when I came back, but when she saw me, she threw it down and rushed over to me. "Hannah! Oh my God! Your face!"

I started to cry and fell to my knees before her.

She knelt down and put her arms around me. "Hannele!" she cried.

"I ate your food, Mirele," I sobbed. "I am so selfish! So very selfish!" I felt naked now. As my body had been naked in the sight of those officers, so was my heart naked now, to her.

Miriam stroked my hair, rocking me, crying into my coat.

"There was...a piece...of food!" I choked out. "Not from him...from her!...but...I didn't...save...you any!"

"Hannele, I don't care! I would rather starve!"

It was then that I realized the flour! I had left it there! After all that! "The flour!" I cried. "I left it!" I sobbed in horrified mourning for the bread we would not be eating.

"I don't care, Hannele! I don't care! I forbid you to go there ever again!"

I slumped against her. "I am so tired, Mirele," I sobbed. "But I love you so!"

"I love you too, Hannele."

Miriam held me, stroking my hair until I began to grow calmer, and then tried to lift me. But a horrible pain stabbed my side. Slowly, with my arm across her shoulders, she was able to get me onto the mattress, coat and all.

Miriam removed my shoes, then stood up. "I must go for Dr. Shulman."

"Mirele, don't leave me!"

Miriam came to me and smoothed back my hair. Her tired face was stained with tears. "You're burning up.

"Please hurry, Mirele, please." I was so desperate, crying and begging her like a child, as if she could protect me from more bootkicks in my side or on my soul.

"I will hurry." She leaned over and kissed my forehead.

Her small, thin body rushing out was the last thing I saw as a great wave of exhaustion took me. I closed my eyes, the lids pressing together, burning with fever. The whole room felt on fire, with flames as I imagined there were in gehinnom itself.

Through the flames came voices. I heard Miriam's voice, sobbing, begging. "Dr. Shulman, she was beaten!" she cried. I felt my coat opening, then my blouse, then a gentle hand on my ribs and on my cheek. Hands were lifting me up and something was being wrapped around my middle. How gentle those hands were, loving me, comforting me, healing me.

I opened my eyes to see my healer. Through the undulating, shimmering heat was Solomon's face, his soft golden eyes and dark beard. His beautiful lips smiling at me. I smiled back. I could not stop smiling. My Solomon! "Solomon!" I called to him. "Solomon!"

I could feel my body being lowered down again and something wet and cool on my forehead. When I closed my eyes I could still see Solomon, always with me, never leaving me. Oh, how I had hurt him! The flames crackled around me, loud, deafening. But Solomon was still there. In the midst of gehinnom, he was still there. "Solomon!" I cried. "Forgive me! Solomon! I love you! I love you! I love you!"

"Sha, Hannele, sha!" I heard Miriam crying. Her voice outside of the flames sounded desperate.

But I could not stop pouring my heart to my beloved Solomon, who now flew down to me on a cloud of feathers. I gave myself to him without reserve, without fear while he held me and kissed away my wounds. He loved me in a soft warm bed and we laughed and held each other.

Miriam's cries grew more and more faint. Even as I lay in Solomon's arms, I could hear her, begging Mr. Goldman not to take me to the typhoid hospital, begging him to spare me the disinfection. "She'll die there!" I heard her crying.

So I turned instead to Solomon who spoke to me of God and life and death, and who told me he loved me a thousand times. Let me die here, I said to him. I want to die here with you. Solomon didn't answer, but stroked my hair, loving me with the sweet honey of his eyes.

When I woke, Miriam was sitting on the bed, looking down at me. A rag covered her nose and mouth, but I knew it was her with those large, soft, doe eyes. "Baruch Ha Shem," she was whispering, the rag moving with her lips. Tears made dark spots on the rag. "We're going now, Hannele," she whispered, taking my arm and putting it across her shoulders to hoist me out of the bed. Around us were the moans of others in the throes of the fever. The room, once a small schoolhouse, smelled of death. "Walk, Hannele, walk!" She pulled and dragged me out of the makeshift hospital.

It was dark outside, and still so cold. Though still terribly weak, I struggled to walk without putting my weight on Miriam. I thought she was taking me home, but then I saw the wet cobblestones of the marketplace as we skirted the edge of it, staying in the shadows. A large dark building loomed in front of us. The warehouse and large woodshop.

Miriam rapped lightly on the door to the woodshop. When it opened, she dragged me inside, across the large room to the corner. I felt another pair of hands on me, gently lowering me down onto some blankets. What a soft bed it was! Then she fell to her knees beside me and pulled the rag off her face. I heard her sobbing, but I was still so exhausted and couldn't even open my eyes. Poor Miriam, I thought. She must really be an angel. What had I done to deserve such loyalty?

"Who's here?" I whispered.

"Mr. Pearlman," Miriam answered. "You must stay here and not make a sound. Do you hear me?"

I nodded, feeling her small delicate hand on my hair. "How did you get me out of there?"

"Hannele," Miriam said, "I had to trade the candlesticks to take your name off the list. That and my ration card."

"Mirele!" I began to cry.

But Miriam's hand clamped down over my mouth. "Sha!" When I'd calmed, she removed her hand. "Sleep now. Sleep and stay absolutely still. Mr. Pearlman will check on you in the morning."

I heard Mr. Pearlman kneel down beside Miriam. He reached out and patted my cheek. He'd always been so kind.

The last thing I felt was a shower of something soft, covering my face and body, the sweet aroma of the forest, of shaven wood.

"Can you see her?" I heard Miriam say.

"No," I heard Mr. Pearlman answer. "She'll be safe here."

"Hannele, don't move. Don't make a sound."

I heard their footsteps receding in the darkness and the door closing. Then all around me was darkness, stillness and the smell of the forest. Breathing in the majesty of the trees, I fell asleep on a bed of needles on the forest floor. Solomon was there next to me.

For several weeks I lived under those shavings, alternately sleeping and listening to the sounds of the woodshop. Several times, I could have sworn I heard Solomon's voice. After all, it was possible he could be there, as talented as he was with making things. At night, Miriam would come to me with a bit of soup and feed me and clean me because I would soil myself during the day. Thankfully, the wood shavings piled on top of me absorbed the odors so no one would guess I was under there. God bless her and Mr. Pearlman forever.

Finally, I was strong enough to get up and walk home, with my saviors on either side of me, holding my arms. And once again I slept on my mattress next to Miriam with renewed health and the excruciating knowledge that Uncle Leo must really have wanted me dead to have let them take me to the typhoid hospital. Most people paid every last groschen they had to keep a loved one out of there. For that matter, Papa must have wanted me dead not to have struggled to bring me over to America all those years when he had the chance. He hated me, too. Was I really so horrible and repulsive? I must have been, especially now that I'd given myself to just about any man who'd wanted my body. What did Solomon see in me? What does Miriam see that she risked her life to get me out of that hospital?

The next day, I slept the entire morning. When I woke, Miriam had left for work, but Mama was there, having come home when school let out. She had saved her bread for me, which I devoured. She stroked my hair and watched me with reddened eyes. She did not look well and I had to force myself to return her gaze. She thought I'd been in the hospital all this time. I thanked her for the bread and then got up, telling her I had to register for employment. I had no money to buy rations and needed to get a new card for Miriam who would starve to death now because of me.

Fortunately, after several hours in the employment office, work in a nearby factory was found for me, making belts and other items for the German army. I would start the next day.

I left the employment office and went straight to the Jewish Police barracks. It was about this time that Jozef usually went off duty.

Of course, Jozef was there with some girl I didn't recognize. There were plenty of us girls willing to trade our favors for a little help with survival. Jozef and she were on the way to his room when I walked in. He greeted me with a simple, "Hello, Hannah. I thought you'd forgotten about me."

I began to shake. "Forgotten you? No, Jozef!" I cried. "I've been deathly ill for weeks. But I'm better now." Even in saying it, what had I thought, that he would simply send this girl away and take me to his room instead?

Jozef sighed and threw his hand up, that is, the one that wasn't around the girl's waist. "I'm sorry, Hannah. Things are different now." Then he tweaked my chin gently. "You're so pretty, though." Then he went off with his new girl.

I just stood with my back against the wall, my eyes closed, still very weak. When would I learn? Had I been stronger, I probably would have run away, which is what I've always done in upsetting situations. But I was forced to stay there with my degradation and misery.

"Hannah?" someone said. It was Marek's voice. I sighed. He had probably heard the whole thing. He had witnessed my humiliation. I wondered when he did his job since he seemed always to be haunting these barracks, a bottle in his hand. He reminded me a bit of Uri with his flask.

"Hello, Marek."

"Hannah, I'm sorry about what happened."

I nodded. "It's not your fault."

"You look tired." Stepping closer, he reached out and touched my hair. "You're too good for us, Hannah," Marek said. "We're scum, you know, we Jewish Police." He looked like a pained little boy in his ill-fitting blue uniform and cap.

Fighting back tears, I averted my gaze from his. "Don't be ridiculous." I could never have said that to Jozef. "I'm no better."

Marek didn't answer. He just stared at me and continued touching my hair. His face was close to me and his breath reeked of cigarettes. "I'll take you home," he said softly. "But will you just spend a little while with me?"

When he asked me that, I began to cry for real. I felt an ache as Solomon's face flew suddenly into my mind. I wanted to see him, to have him hold me and love me, expecting nothing from me in return. But now, I felt beholden to Marek for his kindness. As if my body had a will of its own, I nodded.

Marek picked up my hand and gently tugged at me. Weakly, I stood away from the wall and let him lead me to his cot.

Being with Marek was horrible. When he lay down on top of me and lifted my skirt, I was back there, in the garrison. It was all I could do not to start crying while he was doing it to me. I think I made him feel awful just the same, the way I lay there like a stiff doll, staring upward, barely breathing, my injured ribcage still paining me. They were all there with me, Vlas, Uri, Jozef, and the three beasts. *All you Jewesses are whores.* I don't know about all of us. Miriam certainly isn't one. But I am one, beyond any reach of decency at this point. I wished then and there, with Marek on top of me, trying to have his pleasure, that Miriam had just left me there in the typhoid hospital to die.

But Marek let me rest for a while and did give me a ration card for Miriam. He then walked me back as he'd said he would, letting me lean heavily on his arm. Around us, the snow was dying, leaving muddy wet filth on the cobblestones beneath our shoes. The stench of garbage and human waste from the rotting overused plumbing was now ripening with the coming of warmer weather.

When we reached the door of my bungalow, Marek picked up my hand. "Why do I feel you won't see me again, Hannah?"

I looked at him. Though it was dark and I could not see his face so well, his voice sounded hurt. I always hurt those who were nicest to me. "I'm sorry, Marek." I started to cry again. "I'm still sick. Very sick."

Marek reached in the pocket of his uniform and pulled out a small sack, which he put in my hand. "It's not much," he said. "Some sugar and candles for Shabbos. "You seem like a religious girl, really."

I thought of Mama's candlesticks which I had hidden away from the likes of him and Uncle Leo who mercilessly confiscated such things regularly. The candlesticks Miriam had traded for my life. "Shabbos candles?"

"Yes."

"Thank you, Marek. Thank you," I whispered. "I will light them. I miss Shabbos."

Marek nodded. "I better go. Maybe when you're better."

I nodded, but we both knew I wouldn't be back.

"Good bye, Hannah."

The bungalow was quiet and dark. I set down my coat, hiding my package under it and slipped off my shoes. I lay down beside Miriam, and for the first time, reached for her on my own, snuggling up tightly to her small body. I pressed my face into her hair.

Miriam started, lifting her head. "Hannele?" she said sleepily. With my arms around her, I felt her surprise. She grasped my hand and held it to her. She did not ask me where I had been. I think she knew.

"I love you, Miriam," I said, softly crying into her hair. "You've been so good to me. You're an angel."

Miriam kissed my hand. "I love you too, Hannele," she whispered. Then she turned over, her face to me, and wiped my tears with her fingertips.

"Mirele, how is it you've stayed so sweet and good when you've lost so much?"

She stroked my hair. "I don't know. I've never thought of myself as good."

"But you never do anything bad."

"Yes I do. I think sinful thoughts about men sometimes."

"You, Mirele?"

Miriam giggled softly. "Yes. I used to think about Yankele all the time that way. It made me drop things and break them. Papa used to yell at me."

"But that's not so bad."

"Well, when I was younger, I stole some groschen from Mama's purse to buy candy from a peddler."

"You did?"

"Yes. We were poor, and I was never allowed to buy anything. I just wanted to feel what it was like to buy something. Not to pass the cart empty-handed one more time. Just once."

"Mirele," I said, "I wish I'd done only the things you've done."

Miriam lifted her face and kissed my forehead. "Maybe Ha Shem has forgiven both of us."

I sighed. "Maybe you. But—"

"Don't speak such a way, Hannele." She turned over again and we lay together like nesting spoons.

"Do you think Solomon has forgiven me?"

"Yes. I do."

I sighed again and rested my cheek against her hair. "I pray he has."

Miriam nuzzled my hand to her cheek. "Sleep now, Hannele. You're still not well. Please, get well."

~~~~~

It is a gray morning when I leave the bungalow. I always loved spring mornings like this, everything covered with soft mist.

I don't know where I'm going when I turn and move down the wet cobblestones. Up ahead, there's a wheelbarrow full of rotting planks. Nearby, a young man is repairing a wall. The blows of his hammer ring in my ears. When I get closer, I can see the side of my synagogue. They must have moved the synagogue into the ghetto.

The young man has dark hair. He's wearing nothing but baggy trousers and a white undershirt. But I can see his earlocks swinging with the movements of his body. I stop behind him, but he doesn't seem to know I'm there. My face is burning and my heart feels choked. "Solomon?"

He stops hammering and turns. There are flames burning in his eyes. But he smiles when he sees me. It is as if no time has passed. "Good Shabbos, Hannele."

Good Shabbos? That's all? Doesn't he realize how long we've been apart? I haven't seen him in forever and he's acting like nothing's wrong?

"You're coming to tell me my breakfast is ready, aren't you?" he says. "You make the best challah."

"Solomon, I don't understand."

He laughs. "What's to understand? I'll be right in." He leans over and kisses my cheek.

I shake my head and turn to go to our apartment, but I can't find it. There's only a wall and no door. I can smell the bread baking inside. I pound on the wall but nothing happens. When I turn around to look for Solomon, Marek is standing there, smiling at me. In his out held hands is a box of white candles...

I sat up, gasping. It was still dark. As usual, I woke Miriam, who wrapped her arms around me. I started to cry. "I can't tell anymore, Miriam."

"Sha, sha," she whispered, stroking my hair.

"Mirele, I have candles now. For Shabbos. We'll light them, okay?"

"Yes, yes, Hannele. Tonight."

Once at Mr. Pearlman's, I had seen him carve out a raw potato to use as a candleholder. I did the same with our potatoes and took out two of the candles Marek had given me and put them in the holders, which we set on Mama's chest of drawers. Mama had a precious book of matches in her purse and Miriam went out and returned with a cup of water and a slice of bread to make the blessings.

"*Baruch atah adonoi, eloheinu melech ha olam…*" I chanted softly, drawing my hands above the flames of the Shabbos candles before covering my eyes. Miriam and Mama did the same. "*Asher kidishanu b'mitzvosav vitzivanu l'hadlik nair shel Shabbos.*"

We then made the blessing over the challah and then the wine, holding our cups of water. I closed my eyes as I sipped the water, drinking in the sweet timelessness of the Shabbos blessings.

The three of us sat on Mama's bed, watching the candles burn. I gave myself over to the comfort they brought me. For just a moment, I could feel Reb Weiss's presence in the room. And Solomon's too.

A little while later, we heard the front door scrape open and I rushed to extinguish the candles and stuff them under the floorboard where the silver candleholders had once hid. Then we stood very still, listening to Uncle Leo and Auntie Sylvia's voices. They sounded like they were arguing about something. Auntie Sylvia was crying.

Miriam and I looked at each other as if we expected Uncle Leo to come charging through the door, demanding to know what we were doing. But he didn't. He and Auntie Sylvia went into their tiny room, closing the door behind them, at which, all three of us took a deep breath at the same time.

"Should we light them again, Hannele?" Miriam asked.

I shook my head. "I don't want to take the chance." I sat back down on Mama's bed, staring at the floorboard under which the Shabbos candles were hidden. Miriam sat next to me and leaned her head on my shoulder. Mama, too, sat quietly, her hands pressed together, doing that digging thing with her nails. "It doesn't matter," I whispered, although I longed to relight them. "At least we have Shabbos back again." I closed my eyes, remembering the flames, how I had looked between those flames at Solomon's face across from me at the Shabbos table. What a terrible ache I had, remembering such a thing! But now, as I had never felt before, the pain of feeling closer to Solomon in my memories was better than the cold, barren wasteland of life without them. After all, what little of God I had in my life, Solomon had brought. The very least I could do was put aside my fear for just a moment and honor that. Some things were more important. Solomon had once said that to me.

'Please, God,' I prayed silently, 'Let me live to make him more important! Don't let me live in such fear!' I closed my eyes, pressing them tightly shut. 'Solomon, Solomon!' I cried silently. 'I love you!'

~~~~~

Early Spring 1942

"When this war is over I am going to bake strudel every single day!"

I looked up from the belt I had been working on, across the table at Mrs. Pearlman. Between us was a mountain of belts needing holes punched. Edith Pearlman was a pretty woman, a little younger than Mama. A strand of her dark hair had fallen across her forehead. In the dingy light, the dark circles under her eyes looked ghastly deep. She smiled at me. "And I'm going to eat every bite myself!"

I couldn't help smiling back. Food took up a great deal of our conversations during the long days in this factory, and just the mention of strudel sent imaginary vapors of warm cinnamon and eggs and sugar curling up into my nostrils. My mouth began to water. "Will you save me some?"

"Of course I will, Hannele."

In silence we continued to punch holes in the belts, but my pace had slowed because of the pain of my freezing, chafed hands. I glanced up at Miriam who was farther down the bench. She must have sensed my gaze for she looked up. Her brow crinkled when she saw my hands unmoving. "Don't slow down, Hannah!" she whispered, then looked down quickly as one of the Ukrainian guards who patrolled the factory passed our table. We bent our heads over our work until he was well on the other end of the room.

"What are you going to do, Hannele, when we are once again free?" Mrs. Pearlman asked.

At the mention of the word *free* I felt a pang. I did not know the meaning of the word. I had never felt free. But I considered her question. "That's easy. I am going to soak in a long hot bath every day!"

Mrs. Pearlman closed her eyes. "Oh, the thought of that!" Then she opened her eyes and looked at me. "*Um Gottes willen*, Hannele, yes?"

I nodded and looked back down at the belt in my hand. Solomon had been the last person I had heard say these words. I fit the hole punch on the strap of leather where I had marked it and bore down. "Ouch!" I cried softly each time. The guard passed behind me and I pressed my eyes shut, praying he had not heard. He might tell Herr Beckman, the Volkdeutsch who ran the factory. But more time passed and Herr Beckman did not come by. Although compared to the Nazi beasts, Herr Beckman could almost be considered kind. He even allowed an hour each day in which all the women who worked in the factory had a turn to go to the toilet. I looked very forward to my turn each day, the only time I had a few moments alone, even though Herr Beckman kept a guard posted by the door of the lavatory, monitoring our comings and goings. If you were in there too long, the guard would bang on the door. This had horrified me at first, but it was common knowledge in this factory that some months ago a woman had tried to kill herself during her turn.

When it was my turn, I set down my work and went to the lavatory, all the while rubbing my hands, which were red and beginning to blister.

The Ukrainian guard who had passed by our tables earlier was now standing by the lavatory door. "Perhaps you need to rest your hands," he said.

I caught my breath and looked up. His voice sounded familiar, an echo of one I had heard in the past. I looked at him. His head was shaved, but the regrowth, which was just beginning to sprout around his cap was golden red. The memory grew. I stared at his high cheekbones slanting downward to a pointed chin and full lips, at his eyes shaped like almonds. Yet still I could not think. The fever I had suffered seemed to have slowed me.

"My hands are cold. That's all." I looked away, bracing myself to be castigated. "I will work faster."

"I was not checking on you."

I did not answer, nor did I look at him as his presence filled the small space around me.

"What is your name?" he asked.

I thought of the soldier, Uri, and the way he had spoken to me, his tone almost always mocking, amused. But this guard did not sound that way.

I hesitated a moment before answering. "Hannah."

"I am Peter."

I nodded, although a chill passed through me. I had heard his voice before.

"Give me your hands," he said.

I obeyed although my blood felt cold. I imagined him grabbing my hands and dragging me off somewhere, telling me about the men who pay women to take off their clothes and lie down for them. Or maybe he would throw me down and trample me to death with his boots. I have come to expect anything. But he gently took my hands between his own, covered with tattered gloves, and rubbed them. The coldness began to leave and they felt less sore. I realized that my hands had not been warm in a very long time.

He released my hands. "Is that better?"

"Yes. Thank you.

"You're welcome." He put his thumb under the strap of his rifle. "Go ahead." He gestured toward the lavatory.

I turned and went into the dingy little room. Thankfully I had remembered to bring a rag with me. I sat down on the toilet and slumped over, my elbows on my knees. I stared at the door, breathing relief in my moment's solitude. Then I remembered the guard called Peter. *Walk faster*, he had said. Then he had slowed down. He had told me to be careful that day, the day I was raped in the garrison. And now, he had not informed on me to Herr Beckman of my too-small pile of finished belts. I felt once again like the dog who would retrieve a crust from the dirty ground. I felt desperate and almost began to cry.

I sat up quickly when I realized how long I was taking. I flushed the toilet to indicate I would be out momentarily. God help a woman who had to do more than just urinate.

When I went out of the lavatory I looked at him. Faintly I smiled.

"I remember you, Hannah."

I nodded and looked away, embarrassed as if he knew what had happened that day in the garrison. "I remember you too."

He leaned toward me slightly. "May I see you?"

I looked down, surprised at the polite, almost pleading way he asked, as if he were courting me. I felt an ache then, an ache that had been haunting me for a long time. Then I nodded. "I'm in the large ghetto."

"I know. I remember. I will wait for you behind the ration quarters. I will make certain you do not get caught."

"All right."

Peter looked away, back in the demeanor of a guard at work. "Go now," he said, though not unkindly.

I turned and went back to my seat. I looked over at Miriam. She was watching me, her eyes questioning and scared because it seemed I had been gone too long. I smiled at her to reassure her and then went back to my work. I sighed. My stomach growled painfully, but for a moment I did not care. I had not agreed to meet Peter in the hopes of earning extra rations. For the first time I did not care so much about food. My heart was aching.

~~~~~

"Where are you going?" Miriam whispered when I began to push the blanket off me and rise from the bed.

I put my finger to my lips and leaned over, my face close to her ear. "I must go out for a while. I will be back soon."

But Miriam grasped my arm in the darkness. "Must you go, Hannah?"

I felt the desperation in her grip and guilt stabbed me. I was always the bad one. Gently, I pulled my arm away. "I'll be back, Miriam. I promise."

"You're going to see him, that guard. Aren't you?"

I sighed. "Yes."

Miriam turned over and lay still.

I knelt by the bed and touched her shoulder. "I will be back soon. I promise."

But she did not answer. I sighed again and tiptoed out. Miriam had never been with a man, I told myself. She would not understand.

Peter was waiting for me. When I approached him, he took me by the arm and led me behind the building where there was a doorway, like a storefront, under shelter. He pressed me gently against the door. We would not be seen here. "I'm sorry I do not have a nice room to take you to, Hannah," Peter said. "A place that is warm and peaceful."

I did not answer. I stood, waiting for him to lift up my dress and do his business. But instead, he touched my face delicately with his thumb, tracing my cheekbone and my lips. He ran his fingertips down the curve of my neck, along my collarbone. I shivered slightly. "You're a pretty girl, Hannah." His voice sounded very sad.

"Thank you," I answered, although after what had happened with Miriam, I felt ugly. I stood quietly, listening to him breathe, shivering as he explored me, touching me as if he could not believe I was real and might vanish from under his hands at any moment.

"Will you put your arms around me, Hannah? Please?"

Hesitantly I reached up and embraced him. When I did, he uttered a small gasping breath and returned my embrace, pressing himself against me. I stood quietly, feeling his body tremble in my arms, his face pressed into my neck. I felt moisture sticking his cheek to my skin. My arms softened and I stroked his hair.

I caressed the soft stubble of his hair until I felt his lips on my neck. I stiffened, expecting him to pull down my underpants, but he didn't. He kissed my cheeks, then my lips, which I parted slightly, guardedly. I did not understand what he was doing, why he was not yet inside me, rocking himself away into that carnal oblivion men go to. That is, after all, why he was here with me, I thought. But he continued to hold me and kiss me, still as if he could not believe I was really there. "Hannah," he whispered. "Hannah."

He brought me into his coat with him, shielding me from the cold as he finally went inside of me, moving gently with me, kissing my lips and cheeks, whispering my name.

My body relaxed, although always there was a tightness inside me. The movement in my womb was gentle and somewhat pleasurable. I appreciated his gentleness and that he did not disappear into his own pleasure, leaving me alone with the knowledge that that was all I was there for.

When he had finished, Peter rested against me, breathing heavily. I waited quietly, my arms still around him, for him to pull away from me and send me away with my payment. But he did not.

A cold rain began pouring down. Peter kissed me as he did up his trousers and pulled up my underpants. He smoothed down my dress. "Hannah, stay until the rain finishes."

"All right."

He then lit a cigarette and puffed it silently as he watched the rain. He put his other arm around me. "I am from a small village in the Ukraine," he said. "Lutsk. Near the border. Or, what was the border." He sighed as he flicked ashes off of his cigarette. "They took me prisoner a year ago. I have been a guard ever since."

"You seem too gentle to be a guard," I told him. I felt suddenly sorry that he had been ripped away from his home as I had been from mine.

"I wasn't. Not at first. I was frightened and angry and felt as if I had power over your people." He dug the toe of his boot into the ground. "Huh," he said, making a strange choked sound. "Some power it is, beating on a man who is starving and already half dead with typhoid. And why do you beat him? For working too slowly." He shook his head. "It takes much greater strength to be kind. Much greater strength."

He fell quiet and we listened to the rain, which had already begun to lessen. When it had stopped, Peter turned to me. He reached into his coat pocket and took out a small package wrapped in a cloth. He pressed it into my hands. "This is not a payment," he whispered. "It is a gift."

I looked at him. He was kind, it seemed. "Thank you, Peter."

"Will you see me again?"

"Yes."

"We will meet here in three days. The same time." He leaned down and kissed my cheek. "Go now."

I left him and quietly went back to my house. I slid into the bed next to Miriam and opened the package Peter had given me. There were two small pieces of sausage and a small pair of gloves. The gloves were ragged and full of holes, but they were gloves. I set them on the floor next to the bed and took a bite of sausage, chewing it very slowly, making it last as long as I could.

After a few minutes, Miriam turned over. "Hannele."

I looked at her. "You're awake."

"I was waiting for you."

I turned over and smoothed back her hair. I felt like crying with relief. "I thought you hated me."

"I don't hate you. I don't want you to be hurt anymore. I don't want to lose you."

I was still holding the sausage I had begun to eat. I held it out to Miriam. "Eat this. You must keep up your strength. I don't want to lose you, either."

Miriam slowly took the bit of food. "Thank you, Hannele." She took a bite and closed her eyes with the pleasure of the taste. I listened to her chewing and put away the other one for the next day.

"It's not how you think."

"Nothing is how I think."

Then we lay quietly, snuggled against each other. I felt Miriam take my hand, lacing her fingers with mine. I turned my head and kissed her cheek.

The next time I saw Peter, he seemed especially sad. As before, he smoothed down my dress after he had finished and then put his arm around me, quietly smoking a cigarette. When he had thrown the stub to the ground and mashed it with his boot, he turned his face to me and pressed it close into my hair. I stiffened, certain that he would be repulsed by the smell of my unwashed hair and push me away from him, but he did not seem to mind.

"Your hair is so soft," he said. He reached up and stroked it gently. "It reminds me of Lilya's hair."

I looked down at my shoes. "Who is Lilya?"

"She was my girlfriend. I knew her my entire life. We were going to be married. She was beautiful, like you, with long soft hair." He was quiet for a moment, then picked up my hand and squeezed it. I could feel him remembering. "When they came," he continued, "they took Lilya from me. I was visiting her in her home. They grabbed her from my side and…" He stopped.

I squeezed his hand.

"They raped her in front of me. They forced me to watch while they raped her. Then they shot her." Peter was silent then.

"I'm sorry, Peter." Horrible images were in my mind. Sounds of screaming. Peter watching, helpless. I looked at him, his face partly illumined by the moonlight.

"Thank you," he answered. "What about you, Hannah? Was there someone?"

I looked down. "Well, sort of. We had a fight. I haven't seen him in a long time."

"He must have been a fool not to try to get you back and marry you and be with you every day of his life."

I was silent. I bit down on my lip as I realized the beauty of what Peter has said to me. I was a human being to him. I reached up and covered my eyes with my other hand. "It was not like that. I was the one who ran from him. I was cruel. I said cruel things."

Peter reached out and tenderly smoothed back my hair. "I cannot imagine you saying cruel things. There must have been a reason. What did he do to make you act that way?"

I shook my head. I avoided looking into Peter's eyes. "He loved me," I said quietly. "He loved me and wanted to be with me. Nothing else."

"And what about you?"

I sighed. I was so tired. Tired and cold. "I was too afraid," I said. Then I shivered.

Peter put his arm around me. "It's all right, Hannah," he said after a few quiet moments. "We are all afraid of dying."

~~~~~

Late Spring 1942

The weather was giving over to greater warmth and we no longer had to wear our coats and heavy stockings. Peter has taken to unbuttoning my blouse and his shirt, and resting against me, our bare skin pressed together when he has spent himself. In those moments, I breathe in the scent of him, a masculine perspiration. I had smelled it once before, on Solomon that one time, and even though Peter was not Solomon, it made me feel safe, protected, if just for a few moments. I felt desperate for that joining of man and woman, to feel a certain completeness, that small blissful explosion that made loneliness and hunger and the stench all disappear. Those things always came back, preying, prowling, like a graveyard full of dybbuks. But at least, for a moment, they were gone.

"I will be sorry when I cannot see you anymore," Peter said once. It was the end of May, and wafts of sweet air carried on the breeze, intermittent with the usual stench of overworked plumbing.

I felt a panic. "Why do you say that?" What would I do without these few moments each week?

Peter sighed and nuzzled my forehead with his lips. "There is a transport of guards and workers going to a place called Treblinka. It's not very far from here. The Germans are building a new camp there. I must be prepared to go with them."

I leaned my head back against the building, saying nothing. What had I been imagining anyway?

"Do you promise you'll remember me, Hannah?"

I looked at him. I sighed. He had been very kind to me. "Yes. I promise."

The next time I went to see him, he was not there. But in his place, on an overturned crate, were two small sacks of flour. I covered my mouth and gasped several times, pushing back the panic that rose.

I picked up the sacks of flour and hugged them to me as I walked quickly home.

Back in the bungalow, I took off my sweater and wrapped the flour in it, setting it aside until morning. Then I slid onto the mattress.

Miriam turned over. "You're back so soon," she whispered.

"He was not there. He's gone."

She did not answer. But I felt her small body trembling beside me.

"What is it, Miriam? What's wrong?"

Miriam lifted her face and sniffled. She was sobbing. "This means you won't leave me at night anymore. Baruch Ha Shem."

Anger and shame burned in me when she said this. I crossed my arms over my chest, refusing to look at her. "Why are you so relieved? Your belly has been a bit more full since I've been seeing him. And now you guilt me for it."

Then I felt her delicate hand on my arm. "Please, please don't be angry at me, Hannele. I beg you. Don't you see? You're all I have in the world! I can't lose you!" She pressed her forehead to my arm and continued to sob.

I sighed. What kind of monster had I become? With a monstrous face and monstrous hands? A monstrous heart? My shame deepened. Yet, in her cries, her pleading, I heard my own voice. How many times had I done the same, pleading with her to eat more, begging her to stay alive? Wasn't it only because I needed her as much she needed me? Was she not only saying what I felt too, but was too proud to voice?

My arms softened and I turned to her. I put my hand on her shoulder and she came to me, putting her arm around me. We lay there together in the quiet darkness. I stared into it, sighing with every few breaths. I squeezed Miriam closer to me, wanting to make up to her all my absences, wanting to shield her from the fear she had felt as I climbed from the bed in the middle of the night. All I could think as I grew sleepier was how unfortunate Miriam was to have only me in all the world.

~~~~~

Summer, 1942

Miriam slipped her hand into mine, as she did each morning that we trudged behind Mama and Auntie Sylvia down the filthy street which led to the entrance of the ghetto. The two of us were never out of each other's sight for more than a few moments at a time. How else could we ensure that we weren't taken from each other? My time in the typhoid hospital was closer than either of us could take, and so if we went, it would be together.

At the gate, however, we were lost in a press of people. It took only a moment to see that they were being herded into the ghetto by Ukrainian guards on the outside and Jewish police on the inside. None of the four of us had the strength to fight our way through and stood, holding onto each other, letting them pass, a seemingly endless stream of people with bundles, crying children, and miserably unhappy faces.

We heard the gate to the ghetto clang shut and lock. Miriam and I looked at each other. We had missed our chance to go to the factory and would probably lose our jobs, although soon, it probably wouldn't matter, as there had been talk of the factory being shut down and moved.

I asked a man passing by where these people were from, learning, with a pang, that they had been forced out of the other ghetto into this one. Auntie Sylvia, Mama, Miriam and I had no choice but to go back to our bungalow. Later, Uncle Leo would probably have explanations as to what was happening.

Once inside, Miriam turned to me and grasped my arm. "Do you know what this means?" Her eyes were shining and her face radiated joy.

I stared down at her as if I did not understand, but really it was because I felt dizzy.

"Solomon!" she whispered.

"I know."

Miriam frowned. "What is it? What's wrong?"

I sighed. "You weren't there. You didn't see how horrible I acted. You'd understand otherwise."

Miriam squeezed my arms and shook her head. "I beg you, Hannele. Don't be foolish. We have already suffered so much." I didn't answer and finally Miriam released my arm. "Hannele, don't be like me, a coward. Have faith that Solomon is alive and that he's here. And that he still cares. He's not Yankele. Yankele was afraid of everything."

"But you still didn't want to know."

Miriam looked at me with those huge owl eyes, and I thought even in that moment that I'd never seen a girl so pretty. Even Eva. "It would have been better to know," she said softly. She reached out and squeezed my arm.

I watched her then go to our mattress and lie down where she curled up into a ball. Mama and Auntie Sylvia had already disappeared into their rooms as exhaustion had overtaken all of us. I went and lay down beside Miriam and cuddled up to her, resting my cheek against her hair. I thought about Solomon with an ache in my chest. Miriam was right. I did want to know if he was alive. I wanted to see that he had enough to eat. I did care.

~~~~~

Tonight was Shabbos eve. The ghetto would be quiet, everyone pulling off of the streets to observe the holiest day. And I knew where Solomon would be if he was alive. For the first time in so very long I felt some hope burn in me, some reason to go on, especially because I knew where to find him.

After Mama, Miriam and I had lit the candles, I went to look for Solomon, but not before Miriam had hugged me and told me how proud she was of my courage.

I stepped out of our bungalow. A light rain had begun to fall, cooling the heat of the summer air. I pulled my sweater closed as I walked down the muddy cobblestones. Never before had I been so grateful for the pair of sturdy shoes I wore. Some families in the ghetto had only one pair of wooden shoes between them.

In spite of the sudden swelling of people in the ghetto, the streets were reverently quiet and almost empty, but for those unfortunates here and there without shelter, huddled under the eaves of bungalows.

Soon I found Abram Mender's house, the Hasid who, by some connections, worked in the ghetto bakery. A good man, he had used his position to make extra *matzos* on Passover and give them out secretly to everyone he could. It was his house that was used as the Hasidic prayer house. Lights glowed from the window and up close, the men's voices were audible in prayer. I closed my eyes and listened. How long it had been since I'd done that! I stood quietly as the sounds filled me, and within a few moments, I clearly heard Solomon's voice among them. Never before had a sound been so sweet and beautiful and my heart set to pounding painfully in my chest.

Cautiously I peeked into the window. Inside, a sheet hung on a string, dividing the tiny room. The men were on the side I couldn't see, and on the window side, were several women and one young girl of about ten, huddled together, quietly listening. The room was hauntingly empty of young children. One of the women looked up and caught my eye with hers. I let out a small gasp and ducked down. I thought about running away, but couldn't bear to leave now that I was possibly once again near Solomon. So I sank to the ground, huddled up under the eaves, my arms around my knees, and rested in the feeling of safety that came over me.

When the prayers were over, I listened to the murmuring voices, wishing each other Good Shabbos. There were people sobbing and crying out their joy that they were once again with their rebbe. I caught my breath. He *was* here! Emotion trembled through me. My whole body quaked. Suddenly, I began to cry, knowing I was an intruder. Solomon probably hated me, and I didn't want to know. But I couldn't leave, either. So I just sat, my face buried in my arms, and sobbed.

"Hannah?" a voice said. "Is that you?"

Immediately I looked up. In the light from the window, I saw him. Solomon! He was thin and pale. Gone were his earlocks and beard, and his hair, like all the men, had been shorn almost to the skull. He looked very old and strange. "Solomon!" I cried softly.

Solomon knelt down and put his hands on my shoulders. We looked at each other. There were dark circles under his eyes, yet he was looking at me with tenderness, the way he always had. This was the last thing I had expected him to feel. "Hannele!" he whispered. "You're alive! Baruch Ha Shem!" He pulled me into an embrace, and squeezed me, rocking me gently. "Baruch Ha Shem!" he said over and over.

I let myself embrace him, burying my face into his shirt. I felt his hand cradling the back of my head as we huddled together under the eave. Close to my ear, I could hear his sobs.

I don't even know how much time had passed when Solomon pulled back to look at me again, smoothing my hair back from my face with a gentle hand. At his tenderness, I felt horribly ashamed and guilt. "How can you bear to look on me?" I whispered.

"Hannele, I can no longer bear not to."

His words, like the sweetest balm both comforted and distressed me. The memory of how I'd treated him that day haunted the joy of this reunion. "Don't you hate me?"

Solomon touched my cheek and smiled at me. "No, Hannele. I tried to hate you at first. But my heart, it wouldn't harden. I missed you so much."

"But I was so cruel!"

"*Sha, sha.* You weren't cruel. The truth is you were frightened, and so was I. Blame is useless. The only thing that matters is that the Master of the Universe has let us find each other again. And if you hadn't been here tonight, I would have come looking for you."

"Oh, Solomon! I'm so sorry! I love you!"

Solomon leaned over and kissed my forehead. "I love you, Hannele," he whispered in my ear.

"Solly?" a woman's voice said.

We both looked up. Slowly he stood up and helped me rise. "Chava," Solomon said, "this is Hannah."

Chava looked at me, her pale face was pretty as I'd remembered it, but she looked hauntingly sad. "The girl who took care of your papa?"

I glanced at Solomon. So he had spoken of me to her. I wouldn't have thought it. I'd always assumed I was a great, shameful secret.

Solomon nodded. "Yes."

"Hello, Hannah," Chava said. "It was you I saw in the window. Baruch Ha Shem, you're alive."

"Hello," I murmured. I tried not to stare at her. She was almost as petite as Miriam, yet seemed even sadder and more frightened. I felt a mixture of jealousy and sympathy for her all at once. I'd never known it was possible to feel that way.

"I would like Hannah to have Shabbos with us," Solomon told his wife, who nodded obediently.

"Oh!" I cried softly.

"What is it, Hannele?" Solomon asked.

"I left Mama and Miriam! They'll be worried."

"They are welcome, too." Solomon turned to Chava. "Make room for them with the women," he told her. "I'll be back soon."

"Yes, Solomon," she said and went back in.

Solomon took my arm gently. "Come. Show me where you live."

We began to walk, but once we'd turned the corner, Solomon stopped and embraced me again, swaying back and forth as if he were praying with me in his arms. "Hannele," he whispered. "I can't believe it. How many times I've dreaded I'd never see you again."

I closed my eyes, my cheek resting against him. "I felt the same way."

When I said that, Solomon took my shoulders and held me from him, his gaze boring into mine. "Do you really mean that, Hannele?"

"Yes." At that I began to cry again. "I do."

Solomon lifted my hand to his lips and kissed it. "Shabbos will always be ours, Hannele."

As we stood there, the soft rain, which had stopped for a while, began again. It felt cool and soothing, mixing with my tears. How was it that in such a place, with such horrors around us, that I could have felt such joy?

Solomon urged me gently and we resumed walking the short distance to the bungalow where Miriam and Mama waited. Silently we walked, our arms linked together, while the quiet rain washed everything else away.

When we reached the bungalow, I opened the door and drew Solomon inside by the sleeve of his coat. When I turned I saw that Miriam was staring at him, her eyes full of reverence. I felt immediately ashamed. I had just grabbed the sleeve of the Wolensker rebbe as if he were an ordinary person. How familiarly I had treated him! I felt my shoulders sag as I thought how familiarly I had always treated him.

"Solomon, this is Miriam."

Miriam took a few shy steps toward him. Her entire face was shining, including her eyes. "Rebbe Solomon," she said, her voice a reverent whisper.

"Hello, Miriam."

Suddenly Miriam began to cry. Solomon reached out and took one of her hands, pressing it between his own. "It's all right, little one," he said.

Miriam smiled and brushed at her tears with her other hand. "Please forgive me."

"There is nothing to forgive. I am honored."

"Hannah has told me so much about you." She looked down. "You are as beautiful as she said."

Solomon bowed his head. "Thank you." He then looked at Mama. She, too, was sobbing quietly, her hands covering her face.

Solomon gently released Miriam's hand and went over to Mama. Gently he put his hands on her shoulders.

Mama looked up with her reddened wet face. "I'm so sorry!" she cried suddenly. "I am so sorry, Solomon!"

"Sha," Solomon told her softly, as if speaking to a small child. "It's all right, Mrs. Herzel. It's all right." He put his arms around her and held her as she cried.

Miriam and I looked at each other. Miriam's eyes were still glistening.

When Mama had calmed, Solomon released her. He then touched her cheeks with his fingertips. She looked into his eyes and I saw her become peaceful.

I then told Mama and Miriam about Shabbos and the three of us gathered up the meager meal we'd prepared for ourselves and offered to share what we had.

Chava, Mrs. Mendel and the other women accepted us graciously. I was surprised to see that they had all waited for us before eating, as hungry as we all were. Within minutes, we felt as if we'd all known each other our whole lives, and we sat, crowded around the tiny table, all sharing chairs and plates.

The room glowed with warmth and Solomon was right nearby, on the other side of the sheet, his voice as he chanted the blessings over the bread and the wine, filling the small bungalow. The other men were in tears, praising the Master of the Universe for allowing them to be with their rebbe. And then the air resounded with the chanting of Hasidic melodies.

Solomon walked us back to our bungalow and bid Mama and Miriam good night. Then, together we stood under the dripping eaves. Before the two ghettos had been made one, we would not have been able to do this. But now, we were sealed in by barbed wires and the former curfew lifted. After all, where would we go now? In spite of this new "freedom," most people were indoors and the night air was quiet except for the gentle pattering of water hitting the cobblestones.

In the darkness I felt Solomon's gaze on me. "Everyday I prayed that I would someday see you again," Solomon whispered. "That you would be restored to me." He reached up and touched my cheeks with both hands.

The softness of his touch broke something in me and tears once again filled my eyes. There seemed to be no words that could possibly express how I felt. "I was so certain you'd hate me," was all I could say. At least it was true.

Solomon's whole body sagged, but his hands remained on my cheeks. "Did I ever make you think I could hate you, Hannele?"

I looked down. "I only mean because —"

"I know what you mean. But please, I beg you, forget all that. We have only now. Ha Shem knows how much time we have. None of it seems the least important anymore."

I nodded slowly. For the first time since we had fought, I felt some of the shame of it lift.

Solomon then told me of his life after he had left. He and Chava had wedded shortly before the rebbe's death and Chava had become pregnant almost immediately. He spoke of the death of his son, Abraham, of hunger and fever. Bitterly I cursed the same God who had brought us back together.

I told him of my own recovery from the typhoid and how Miriam had saved me from the hospital and how Mr. Pearlman had hidden me under the shavings in the woodworking shop. I felt a wave of shame. In telling him of my life until now, I had not told him of how I had been giving away my body. Now that Solomon and I were friends again, I felt terror of driving him away again.

At this, Solomon pulled me into an embrace. He held me for what seemed a long time, but however long it was, when he pulled away, seemed sorrowfully short. "I would stay longer but I must go back. I've…Chava…"

I nodded, still looking away. "Solomon, is this the last time?"

Solomon squeezed my shoulders. "I pray it isn't, Hannele. I would hope you'll be at my Shabbos table for as long a time as we have."

I started to cry and Solomon put his arms around me again. "Hannele, you must be strong now," he murmured close to my ear. "You must keep me with you whether we're together or not. Do you understand?"

I nodded and he embraced me again. I pressed my face into his coat. He had grown painfully thin, yet to me he felt strong. I had always relied on him to be strong for me and had fallen apart when he left. I was terrified to fall apart again.

"I swear I will come to see you whenever I can," he said. "You have my word." He held me a few moments longer, then gently urged me toward the door. "Please go in and rest. I couldn't bear if you fell ill again."

I looked up at him. "Solomon, I —"

"Sha." He stroked my cheek. "You must have faith that the Master of the Universe is a just and compassionate god. That he has not left us without love."

I grasped his hand and held it to the cheek he'd been touching. Whether this was a final good bye or not, I felt as if it were. "Solomon, I'm so sorry."

"Stop," he said. "Please go in and rest." Gently he kissed the palm of my hand and released it, watching me until I had gone in and closed the door.

~~~~~

Early Autumn 1942

Who would have thought that in the middle of the Wolensk Ghetto, I would become a gardener? For this whole past summer, it was my great fortune—after only five hours on line at the Employment Bureau—to be placed in the Jewish Council's agricultural plot which was created to supplement our meager rations and thus ease hunger a bit. We'd see if it worked.

I was given instruction on planting and tending to the seedling crops as they matured, but fortunately, I already knew a lot of this from helping Auntie Sylvia in her kitchen garden years back.

What I did not expect about this work was that I'd actually enjoy it so much. As weak and tired as I felt most of the time, I could actually forget about it while sitting on an overturned bucket, rolling the small seeds between my fingertips, and pushing them into the moist dark soil, the sun on my back, arms and face. The only thing that would have made this time perfect would have been having Solomon and Miriam here with me.

Solomon, who, thank God has managed to avoid being rounded up for forced labor, was employed in the wood shop, the very place where Miriam and Mr. Pearlman hid me. With all the skills Solomon has, proven himself very useful within the confines of the ghetto, repairing and maintaining the buildings, tools and machines. Since the beginning of our incarceration, Elder Wolfberg has billed men like Solomon as "essential to the efficient upkeep of facilities—a crucial component of providing a productive labor force for the German war effort." These were his exact words from one of his rousing motivational speeches. I say, whatever bullshit keeps Solomon here with me, please use it! Wolfberg even gone so far as to call this work "ghetto restoration," to improve our morale or something like that. How Wolfberg passed his proposals through the German authorities is beyond me.

Unfortunately, though Miriam is gainfully employed, she has the distasteful and more strenuous task of keeping hallways and facilities sanitized to prevent the spread of disease. That is, she pushes a mop and bucket all day long, receiving a bowl of thin soup and a slice of bread dotted with margarine for her trouble.

Believe me, my terror of losing Miriam to hunger and illness has tempted me to go to Marek again for the tiny bit of extra food he is in a position to give me. His tour of duty in the ghetto included the agricultural plot where I now spent my days, and he always made a point of speaking to me. But then, if one evening Solomon came by to see me and I wasn't there, I would miss him—each time together is always possible our last—and have to live, or go to my death, knowing the truth of my absence. Also, neither Solomon nor Miriam gets extra rations, especially not in an unseemly way, so why should I? It is a constant battle going on inside me between my nagging hunger and my desire to be good and do the right thing, an impulse which Solomon's presence seems to inspire in me.

God, I wish I could see him more! We both work dawn to dusk on almost nothing to eat. Then there is my constant worry that one of the Jewish Police will come and snatch him off the street to a labor camp, something he risks anyway by being a religious leader.

So far, I see him only on Shabbos Eves, and the time waiting in between is torture! I wait all week for those few minutes we spend under the eaves by my front door when he walks us back after prayers and our Shabbos meal, such as it is. He touches my hair and cheeks and tells me how much he loves me. Something in my soul falls open when he says it and I know now that it's because he was the first person in my whole life who's ever said those words to me that I believe.

I, too, reach up and touch his bare cheek, so starkly white without his beautiful beard and payos. I tell him I love him back, and mean it with my whole heart, though the words move back through me with a thunderous strength. I've always been a holding back kind of person and expressing my heart feels almost the most frightening thing.

We only have a few minutes each time because for one, it's not safe to be out walking too long after dark, and two, because Solomon does not want Chava to worry about him. "I have not been such a good husband, Hannele," he says sadly, almost every time.

"I can't imagine that, Solomon," I answer. "That seems impossible." But I don't say anything else because I'm not certain I want to know what he means. "You're a good man."

Solomon presses his forehead to mine. "Your faith in me is a great gift," he whispers.

Then that dreaded moment comes when Solomon gently pushes away from me. "I'm sorry, Hannele."

I don't say anything, but my answer is in the way I grip the sleeves of his jacket. I look up into his face, shadowed by the brim of his cap. Through the worlds that separate us, he allows us one kiss. In it, I feel everything that's right and wrong, beautiful and ugly. I hold onto him as long as I can, trying not to cry because it would make him feel worse than he already does.

Solomon always waits until I'm safely inside, although once I've closed the door, I crack it open again, my ear pressed to the outside so that I can listen to the quiet *tap tap* of his shoes as he walks away.

~~~~~

Late Autumn 1942

For several weeks this past autumn, I was certain I would lose Miriam. Her work and being so hungry had worn her down very badly and she looked so sad most of the time. I stayed home with her every evening and held her every single night as we fell to sleep, but there was not much else I could do. I had no extra rations and it was a horrible struggle just to keep up my own strength.

There were a couple of times she was even too tired to go to Shabbos at the Mendel's with Solomon, and insisted I go without her. The first time Solomon saw she wasn't there, he made sure I got back earlier to be with her and went in to see her. Then, each time, he came in and sat with her a while, even taking her hand and squeezing it gently.

At first, this made me sickeningly jealous. After all, Miriam is one of the sweetest and prettiest girls there are. What would stop Solomon from falling in love with her? She's already quite taken with him. Thank God nothing like that happened, and I had to be glad for her time with him because she always looked happier and better after he'd been there.

After several weeks, thank God, Miriam was much stronger and not quite so tired, and when she came with me and Mama to Shabbos, I almost started crying in my relief.

Miriam's recovery was a miracle, but in spite of it, I really don't know how much longer we can go on with almost *bupkiss* to eat every day. At this point, I believe it is Solomon's being here so close by and the moments of joy we have in his presence and that I have in his arms. Somehow, this keeps me from giving up. That's what it must be, because our bodies just seem to keep going on somehow, no matter what. Mama's too. Though she pisses and moans and cries from feeling so hungry and frightened, she, too, goes on and on.

One evening in the middle of the week, Solomon appeared at the door. Mama and Miriam and I were sitting on Mama's bed, resting from the day and Auntie Sylvia was asleep in her room, as usual, and Uncle Leo had not yet returned from the Council offices.

The three of us crowded around Solomon as if the Messiah himself had just showed up on our doorstep to lead us out of the ghetto, and he accepted our greeting graciously, though I sensed he was uncomfortable with being fawned over and admired, as if he didn't deserve it.

He visited with us a few minutes though there wasn't really anything to offer him but a crust of bread I filched from Uncle Leo's rations. He doesn't think I know where he keeps them. But then, Solomon asked Mama her permission to speak with me alone. Mama nodded and pointed to her small room. Solomon followed me in and I closed the door behind us.

For a moment we stood, quietly looking at each other. My heart began to pound heavily. This is it, I thought, he's going to tell me he's leaving or dying or something horrible like that!

"Don't look so afraid, Hannele," Solomon said. "What are you thinking?"

"That…that you're going to tell me some horrible news of some sort."

Solomon shook his head and reached up to pull off his cap. "I'm sorry if I made you think that. I just wanted to be alone with you, if only for a little while."

My whole body sagged with relief, and I rubbed at my eyes which began to show tears.

Solomon gently grasped my arm. "Is it okay if we sit down? I'm quite tired." When I nodded, he sank down on the edge of Mama's bed and I next to him. He sat hunched over, shrinking wearily into his tattered coat. His dark hair had been shorn to a stubble, and he rubbed one large hand over his scalp.

After a few moments, he sat up and looked at me. "I do have news, actually, but not bad news."

"What is it?"

He sighed. "A miracle has happened. I was able to get Chava out of here."

"Really?" I couldn't imagine something like that at this point. Our people seemed to be in a downward funnel, the opening getting smaller and smaller as we slipped toward death. "How?"

"Some Volkdeutch family she worked for as a nanny was able to take her. The husband has connections and he had been working on false papers for her. I think they were heading to France." His shoulders sagged. "The least I could do for her was to let her go. Perhaps she'll have a chance." He bowed his head. "I'm sorry I couldn't do the same for you, Hannele." He scrubbed his hand over his shaved head. "I would give anything to know you will live."

I stared at him. Understanding flooded in. He had come to be alone with me because now he could. For a few moments, we had the time together we'd craved. For me, this bit of time together was worth more than years apart. I had known such time apart from Solomon, and my life had been no real life. "I know, Solomon. You have nothing to be sorry for where I'm concerned. I'm happy when I'm with you."

"What had you wanted for your life, Hannele?" His voice was thick with sadness, he seemed so absorbed in his guilt he hadn't heard my declaration.

I felt a stab of pain. "It doesn't matter what I wanted. I would never have gotten it."

Solomon reached out for my hand. "You have always been prone to self-pity, Hannele. This is no good. It will always lead you to darkness."

I felt indignant. "But if I don't pity me, who will? My uncle who would wish me dead?"

"I've felt for you since before we ever spoke. Since that first time I saw you with Mashele. You know that. And what about Miriam? She is your devoted friend." He squeezed my hand. "Do you still see the world only one way?"

I hung my head. "No, I don't. You're right."

Solomon watched me quietly for a moment. "So?" he asked gently. "What is this life you would have wanted and could never have?"

At first, I couldn't answer and avoided his gaze. "I…I've always wished I could just be with…you…and Reb Weiss in your little house behind the synagogue. Nothing else. Just the three of us." When I finally looked up at him, I expected to be chided for my silliness. But he was only watching me, his golden eyes full of sadness.

"I wanted that too." He set his cap down beside him and reached up to touch my cheek. "Do you think I'm a bad man, Hannele?"

I caught his hand and pressed it to my cheek. "Solomon, no! Never!"

"Thank you. You don't know what it means to me to hear you to say that."

"Why do you think you're not good?"

Solomon didn't answer. Instead he leaned in and kissed me, a soft, sweet kiss that made me start to cry.

My tears made him pull back. "Should I stop?"

I shook my head. "No!" I grasped the collar of his coat in my fists, feeling a soft, sweet pain gushing through my chest, flooding, cleansing. "Solomon, Solomon! What have I done? What have I done?" I rocked back and forth. I must have looked mad.

Solomon put his arms around me. "I love you, Hannele." He stroked my hair as I sobbed against him.

He held me for what seemed a long time until I looked up at him again, and he began kissing me as before.

I surrendered to those beautiful kisses, wanting so much to be as close to him as two people could be, wishing with such pain in my heart that I had never done it before. I trembled a bit as I always did when I felt his fingers on the buttons of my dress, but I didn't stay his hands like I had that awful day, the only man I shouldn't have stopped.

Solomon laid me down on the bed beneath him. "Hannele, I've always loved you," he murmured between kisses.

"I know, Solomon." Tears continued to pour from my eyes, and he kissed them as they fell.

Solomon enveloped me in his arms and kissed me. I felt his hardness press against me, and I opened, instinctively, gratefully. He bared my breasts and covered them with kisses while I pulled down my underclothes and he undid his trousers.

He lifted away from our kisses and stared down into my eyes. The urgency of time spurred our joining.

"I love you, Hannele," he said again as we finally became part of each other. He moved slowly over me at first, then faster. In spite of our tiredness and hunger, we felt pleasure, and joy, and a moment of blissful forgetting when all that existed was physical ecstasy, the manifestation of love.

When it was over, we lay in each other's arms, until our breathing calmed and we dressed. Even then, we didn't want to leave each other, and lay snuggled close together, our cheeks pressed, eyes closed.

So enveloped were we in each other that the sound of voices outside the door gave no cause for alarm until there came a sharp insistent pounding on the door to the small room.

It was then, in Solomon's pulling away that I heard Mama's and Miriam's cries and Uncle Leo's angry shouts which were accompanying his fists on the door.

We both sat up as the door slammed open. Solomon shielded me from my uncle's view as I rapidly did up the buttons of my dress.

Uncle Leo stood before us in his rumpled gray suit, his fists clenching and unclenching. He reminded me of Papa the day I'd screamed at him and clung desperately to him at the same time. I'd hated and resented Uncle Leo in the past, but never before had feared him as I did now. Hunger and unendurable stress had driven him to a frightening madness. Behind him, crowded in the doorway, were the three other women of my family, staring after him in their failed attempt to keep him out of the room.

"What's going on under my roof?" he demanded, breathing wildly like a hunted animal.

Solomon stood up and I behind him, grasping the sleeve of his coat. At his full height, he was a head taller than Uncle Leo who cowed momentarily, but stood his ground.

"What do you mean by this?" Uncle Leo's eyes flashed at Solomon. "What kind of Hasidic rebbe are you?"

I flinched but Solomon remained calm. "Hannah is my dearest friend," he said in a quiet, dignified voice. "She has seen me through some of the most difficult times of my life, and I'm here for her now."

Uncle Leo let out a strange sound, somewhere between a laugh and a snort. He gestured toward the two of us. "So this is how you do it?"

"Leo," Auntie Sylvia called out to him softly, but he waved her off.

"You were a good son, a faithful son," Uncle Leo went on. "Stayed with your Papa until the end. So now you can do what you want?"

I stared at Uncle Leo. A light went on in my mind. His anger was really about Yoav. He was jealous and resentful that Yoav had not been dutiful like Solomon. The realization was like thunder when it cracked so close to the ground, and I almost laughed. But Uncle Leo, though more pathetic now than frightening, was still on the Jewish Council and still wielded some power over our fate. So I stayed quiet.

"I adore Hannah," Solomon answered. "More than anyone else in my life. I've never meant any offense."

Uncle Leo started slightly, as if he had expected Solomon to fight with him instead of speaking the way he had. But Solomon was not willingly giving my uncle any reasons to have him arrested or deported. As he stared into Solomon's face, his lower lip began to tremble and he looked like he wanted to scream or act threatening again. But he really looked no more than a pile of rags. "Get out," he said finally, his voice a croak of a whisper.

"No!" I cried. I flew out from behind Solomon and fell to my knees at Uncle Leo's shoes, my arms around his legs. "I beg you, Uncle Leo! Please! Don't make him leave!" I began to sob, and Uncle Leo tried to squirm out of my grip but I only squeezed tighter. "Please! He's my friend! My Solomon! Please!" Then I collapsed against Uncle Leo, who continued to try pulling away from me. In the next moment, I felt Solomon's hands on me, gently pulling me up, and I let him.

Once free of me, Uncle Leo turned and stumbled from the room, pushing past Mama and Miriam. Auntie Sylvia rushed to him and put her arm about his shoulders, and they disappeared into the other small bedroom. Uncle Leo's sobs and hysterical babbling carried to us through the thin walls.

"I had better leave," Solomon told me quietly. "I don't want to make more trouble."

But I threw my arms around him. "No! Don't go! It's not you. He's upset about his own son."

Solomon gently pulled away from me. "I understood that. But we mustn't also be fools."

Of course, Solomon was right, and I let him lead me to the front door.

Both Miriam and Mama followed us, their faces wet and red from crying, begging Solomon's forgiveness for not having been able to stop my uncle. Solomon assured them that they would have more easily stopped a freight train run off its tracks. Then he bid them good night and drew me out the door with him.

Solomon leaned heavily against the wall, and I could see that in spite of the composure he had shown in the face of my uncle's wrath, he was shaken.

"I'm sorry, Solomon," I said, now terrified that he had been driven away and would no longer love me.

But Solomon drew me to him. "No, Hannele. It is I who am sorry for all you've suffered at the hands of men." He put his arms around me, and I snuggled against him in the gathering darkness.

We stood quietly, Solomon stroking my hair while I listened to his heart beating through his coat. I began to wonder if we would ever have the chance to love each other that way again.

"Thank you for that blessed gift," he murmured. "I never expected us to have that special time. I would not have had you here against the wall like a pair of rutting beasts." At these last words his voice became steely and angry. "They have taken enough from us."

I said nothing, ashamed as I felt. For the times I had rutted, standing against a wall.

Solomon stood back, his hands on my shoulders. "Keep me with you all the time, Hannele," he whispered.

I began to cry again. "How?"

"It's not something I can tell you. But you're different now." He sighed. "I don't want to know what has ripped you open. Not now. I can't bear thinking of you suffering. But you're…different."

I threw myself against him and squeezed him.

He kissed my hair and rubbed his hands over my back. "Hannele, remember what I used to tell you about the transmigrations of souls?"

"Yes." I stared up into his face in the darkness. Solomon had always insisted that he and I had traveled over many lifetimes within the same cluster of souls, trying to be together because we loved each other so much. At first, I had thought it bizarre and farfetched, but now, standing here, I knew it to be as true and sacred as anything in the Scriptures.

"Good. Remember it always. No matter what happens in this life, hold fast to what you know. Promise."

"I promise, Solomon, with my entire soul."

He sighed, a distinct sound of relief. "I promise too, Hannele." He kissed my hair again.

We stood quietly for a short time, just holding each other. The possibility of what awaited us in the future was terrifying. My promise to him was the only thing that brought relief. And strength.

Finally, he looked down into my face, saying nothing. He leaned in and kissed me, a sweet tender kiss like before, then told me to go inside.

At first, I wouldn't listen. I couldn't bear his leaving. But then he told me again in a sharper voice to go in so I obeyed.

Once inside, Mama and Miriam came to me and embraced me, and the three of us sat together on Mama's bed until we were too exhausted to stay up. Normally we were already in bed at this time, but tonight, our hunger and tiredness had been forgotten for a little while. And now we remembered again.

On our mattress, Miriam held me close to her, stroking and kissing my hair, and I held on to her, letting her comfort me. "Thank you, Mirele," I whispered. My body had been trembling but began to calm in her arms. I began to fall asleep, my head against her breast like a small child. I felt her lips on my forehead, but then I was gone...

I press a gentle kiss into Miriam's hair as I hold her to me. Our bodies are damp with the perspiration borne of loving. Behind me, Solomon is holding us both.

I feel his soft beard against my skin and listen to his quiet breathing, and I rest contentedly in the languid warmth. I had thought I would be so jealous. I had been terrified that when Solomon saw Miriam's beauty, that when he kissed her and touched her, he would not want me anymore. And Miriam, when she had experienced the great gift of being in Solomon's arms, of being made love to by him, that she would want nothing else.

But I had been wrong. I had seen love as something transferable, as easily lost, and when I went past my fears I saw that I love them both so much and they love me so much, that nothing could have been more sweet and more beautiful. And now I rest. I have never felt more complete, more peaceful, more full of love. *Mother and father, sister and brother, friend and lover, are all joined inside of me and around me. And I rest in the sweetness of surrender...*

Pounding on the front door woke us. Male voices were yelling through the door for us to pack our belongings and assemble outside. I sat up quickly, blinking in my disorientation and rush of sudden fear. Miriam was looking at me in the pale dawn. We were both in our clothes, which we slept in during the freezing weather. Of course, Solomon was not there.

"Hannele," Miriam cried softly.

I looked at her, into her big, gentle, frightened eyes. We both knew. I reached for her and she for me. There was no thought, no wrong or right, only what we felt. We kissed, our lips pressed together. How soft and beautiful she was, my sweet little Miriam. The moment of pulling away was a great agony.

I packed a small satchel with nothing more than my remaining two dresses, a pair of stockings, the prayer book Solomon had given me for my nineteenth birthday, and the mezuzah. I moved quickly yet smoothly, as if I had known all along what was to be and had planned ahead in my mind just what I would take. My thoughts flew briefly to the Torah scroll, buried somewhere underneath the makeshift bungalows that now covered the patch of land that had been bare before the consolidation of the ghettos. Solomon was never able to retrieve it from its resting place. Now, the scroll would have to remain there where, I prayed, no one but a Jew would ever find it.

The sound of Mama's sobs came from her small room. I went in and found her sitting on her bed, her face in her hands. Her few belongings were strewn on the bed. Her satchel was on the floor by her feet.

"Mama, come now," I said firmly. I snatched up the things on her bed and stuffed them into the satchel. I reached out and pulled one of her hands from her face, forcing her to look at me, my strength emanating from a source I did not know I had. "They'll come in and shoot us or drag us out. Is that what you want?"

Like a little girl, Mama shook her head and took the satchel I handed her. She rose from the bed and pulled on her coat, following me out.

Uncle Leo and Auntie Sylvia were already packed and gone, and the horrifying thought passed through my mind that they had known ahead of time of this action against us.

Miriam, Mama, and I stayed close together as we stumbled outside into the confusion of cries and herds of slowly moving people and their belongings. We moved along with them. There were so many people around us, and there were members of the Jewish Police with clubs and Ukrainian guards with rifles herding us along. I looked for Solomon, but in the chaos he was nowhere to be seen. However I knew he was there, somewhere, because I could feel him.

Ahead of us the barbed wire gate to the ghetto had been opened, and we moved through it, a muddy, slow moving river of people against the background of screams and rifle shots as those who tried to escape through the barbed wires were silenced. From a mysterious source within me, the Mourner's Kaddish rose in my mind and repeated as we neared the barbed wire gate that had been opened. I had not said Kaddish since Reb Weiss's funeral, but now it resounded within me. *Yisgadal, v'yiskadash, sh'mei raba…* The prayer for the living, for those who are left behind, that they may know God has not left them.

Outside the ghetto enclosure was a line of wagons, so many that I could not see the beginning or the end of them. The guards prodded us in both directions. I clung to Miriam, desperate not to lose her in the confusion. Mama gripped the sleeve of my coat as we went. Some of the wagons were already full of people. We passed them on our way to the empty ones. *B'alma divra chirusei, v'yamlich malchusei…*

"Hannah! Hannah!" a voice called from above my head.

I looked up and saw him. There he was, my dear friend, my love, looking over the side of a horribly overcrowded wagon, pressed against the sideboards, watching me. Everything rose up in me at the sight of him.

"Solomon!" My voice flew to him over the din of cries. All I wanted in the world then was to reach up to him, to feel our hands touch, one last time, but the arm which held my satchel was pressed hard against me by the crowd of people, and Miriam clung to my other. It was impossible to do anything but move forward. "Solomon!" I screamed again. His gaze did not leave my face, his beautiful eyes, watching me as I was moved, helplessly along, away from him. "Sol…" I began to cry.

Solomon pressed the fingertips of one hand to his lips, then reached out toward me, over the side of the wagon. He never took his eyes off me. I, too, watched him until I had to look forward or fall and be trampled to death by the other frightened people.

Y'hei shmei raba m'vorach. L'olam ul'almei almaya…

A guard stopped us in front of an empty wagon. With the butt of his rifle he began herding us onto it. Mama, Miriam, and I were pressed tightly against each other. I heard Mama sobbing close by me, but I was staring over the back of the wagon, in the direction from which we had come, staring that way because now I knew Solomon was over there, quite close by. His presence made me feel stronger. The memory of the kiss he had sent to me through the air and his eyes on me were the only thoughts in my mind, even though fear pulsated through my body.

The sky pressed down, cold and gray. The passage of time was marked only by the changes of light behind the ceiling of clouds. We waited a long time without moving, waiting for thousands of people to be loaded onto the endless line of wagons, while the air echoed with their anguished and terrified cries. I continued to stare in the direction of the wagon in which Solomon, too, waited. Finally, the wagons began to move, bumping roughly on the old cobblestones, jolting our bodies helplessly against each other.

U vizman kariv. V'imru: Amen...

Along the side of the road some shabby peasants stood, watching us pass by, staring at our faces and at the yellow badges on the sleeves of our coats. Some watched with no expression at all. Were they relieved? Were they frightened? Some had tears. Maybe we were human to them after all. One man, old enough to be my father, a farmer in baggy trousers and a dirty smock and cap, fell to his knees, his big soiled hands over his eyes. Something happened in me at the sight of him, and I fell back into my body in furious explosions. "Papa!" I screamed to him. "Please help me! Papa!" I screamed and screamed, struggling to reach him through the slats of the cart. But he didn't not look up.

I felt arms around me, grasping me tightly. Mama and Miriam were crying as they held me. I felt how they wanted to protect me and I stopped screaming.

We leaned heavily against each other, bracing against the harsh sway of the wagon. I squeezed Miriam to me, Miriam, so small and frightened, yet with a core of great strength and faith. I could only hope to be as good as she was. I leaned down and kissed the top of her head as a strange warmth flooded me from deep, unknown sources.

Then I heard Mama, still sobbing, her hand clutching my sleeve. "Mama," I said.

Mama looked at me, her face red and swollen. Her eyes were glassy from fear. But as we looked at each other, her tears stopped and she grew quiet. In that moment, I forgave her for everything.

For what seemed a long time, we rode silently, though around us, people were sobbing and sniffling and the murmurs of prayers filled the sir around us. Once again, the Kaddish rose and repeated and I began to recite it in a whisper.

Miriam lifted her face to me and we looked at each other. "I love you," she whispered.

"I love you too."

A chilling wind passed through us, biting at our faces, pulling my scarf from my hair. How I wanted to reach up and put it back in place, for the wind seared my skin and my ears, but I couldn't move my arms, we were all pressed together so tightly in the wagon. Horrible waves of fear and dread began to crash through me. I didn't feel ready to leave! I started to feel my breath tighten in my chest, and I wanted once again to claw my way through the people and try to jump out of the wagon. The desire was overwhelming, blinding. I started gasping for air, and Miriam cried my name, terrified, for I was all she had in the world.

Again, that mysterious sensation arose, the one of deep strength and calm. My consciousness grew, becoming larger than my body and encompassing everyone and everything. I now watched Hannah riding in the wagon, the frightened, hungry people around her, pale faces with dark, terrified eyes, a clump of dark woolen coats and scarves.

So long ago, in what now felt like another lifetime, Solomon had told me of his mystical experiences and how they'd given him certainty that even in this physical world, there was more than our senses could perceive. He'd said that no matter how terrible he might feel or how much he might suffer, that his understanding never left him and gave him the strength to face pain with compassion. When I'd asked him how such a thing could be possible, he said he didn't know, only that it was. 'You are part of that light too, Hannele,' he'd said, more than once. When I scoffed, he reminded me not to be arrogant, that believing I know how things really are was exactly was keeping me from understanding.

The events of these last two years had finally caused me to realize I didn't know, that I don't understand. I'd always believed myself to be bad because of the things I've done and yet, I managed to care, to share my food when I was starving, to care for others above myself when to do so made me go with less. If I were evil, then perhaps I would understand what is happening now, but I don't. I don't understand how human beings could be doing to fellow human beings what the Nazis are doing to us. All I can hope for is to hang on to my own humanity, always, and never let them strip that from me...

I looked up at the sky where the early winter sun had burned away some of the clouds. I had always loved the sunsets, the colors which blazed in the sky against the meadows. Like a vast pool of melting honey. This was where we were now. In this pool. Drowning in it forever. The bliss of comfort was greater than I could ever have hoped for, even for that girl who had told her Papa she hated him for leaving her and who had cried for him ever since. For that girl who had lain down for so many men, who had sold her body for a crust of bread.

Ba'agalah u'vizman kariv...

Pools of melting honey. I had never allowed myself to look into them for long because I would lose my heart. Now, I stared. I would stare forever if I could. For it had been in pools of melting honey that I had first seen God. It was there, in those eyes that I had first known God loved me.

...V'imru: Amen. To be continued...

About the Author

Sedonia Jacobs wanted to be an author from the moment she ever read a book. From the earliest age, she sat up all night reading and began penning her first story at age nine. For years she has written romance under the pen name Sedonia Guillone. Years ago, her partner had told her about a former life of theirs together and suggested she tell that story. The first book, I Was Hannah took shape and has lain in a drawer untouched until she could no longer ignore the calling to publish this book and continue the series. Sedonia lives quietly in south Florida with the man she loves and her cat Molly.

Tell Us What You Think

We appreciate hearing reader opinions about our books. You can email us at Sedonia.guillone@gmail.com.

Kokoro Press

Whether you prefer e-books or paperbacks, be sure to visit Kokoro Press on the web at www.kokoropress.com for high quality fiction and non-fiction titles.

www.kokoropress.com

www.ingramcontent.com/pod-product-compliance
Lightning Source LLC
Chambersburg PA
CBHW061129200626
46817CB00016B/493